THE FORGOTTEN HOUSE ON THE MOOR

JANE LOVERING

Boldwood

First published in Great Britain in 2022 by Boldwood Books Ltd.

Copyright © Jane Lovering, 2022

Cover Design by Debbie Clement Design

Cover Photography: Shutterstock

A CIP catalogue record for this book is available from the British Library.

Paperback ISBN 978-1-80415-234-8

Large Print ISBN 978-1-80415-230-0

Hardback ISBN 978-1-80415-229-4

Ebook ISBN 978-1-80415-227-0

Kindle ISBN 978-1-80415-228-7

Audio CD ISBN 978-1-80415-235-5

MP3 CD ISBN 978-1-80415-232-4

Digital audio download ISBN 978-1-80415-226-3

Boldwood Books Ltd
23 Bowerdean Street
London SW6 3TN
www.boldwoodbooks.com

This book is dedicated to The Fortean Forum, and all the people thereon – at least, I think they are people, they certainly do a good impression – as the forum is where I got the main idea for this story. It sprang from the Fortean Times, and I've been a member for about ten years now. It's full of the weird and wonderful and if you have any interest in the supernatural or the paranormal from any angle, from the purely sceptical to the devout believer, why not pop over and join us?
We don't just talk about odd happenings either. There's plenty of complaining, general whingeing, and discussions about why washing machines have so many settings.
So, this one's for you, guys, I am proud to call you my friends. Yes, even the ones in Cromer.

1

I defy *anyone* to be happy to see the police on their doorstep at 4 a.m. I mean, even in the case of a returned lost puppy or the finding of your previously stolen car, at four o'clock in the morning, practically everybody is going to be a bit tetchy, aren't they? Especially since I hadn't lost a puppy, my car was still sitting on the road outside my window and hadn't been the victim of any crime, so the two police officers knocking at my front door were mere unwelcome interruptions to a dream about Ben Whishaw and a trumpet.

At first, it was just a knock. Loud, peremptory and clearly not allowing any turning over and ignoring. In lieu of traipsing all the way downstairs in the dark of a chilly June morning, I opened my bedroom window and stuck my head out. 'Hello?'

'Mrs Donaldson?' The two uniformed officers had to take a step back to look up at me beyond the burgeoning ivy growth that was crawling up the front wall like something out of a horror film. I was still too half-asleep to wonder at their presence.

I made one of those early-morning noises that might be agreement or clearing my throat.

'Mrs *Alice* Donaldson?' The younger of the two tilted her head up now.

'No, there's fourteen of us in here,' I snapped and then felt instantly guilty. They were only doing their job, and they probably weren't any happier about it being the early hours than I was. 'Yes. Yes, that's me.'

'Sergeant Anthony Williams and Constable Carley Evans. May we come in?'

I stood for a moment, looking down. The street lights were competing with the vague light of early dawn, nasty sodium shadows bleached by the tentative sneaky grey daylight in the empty road. Even the bins, crowded on the pavement for the morning collection, looked suspicious. I felt a presentiment of something nasty tingle down my spine. 'Why?'

'We'd rather come inside, if you don't mind.'

They'd taken their hats off. That meant bad news, didn't it? I rattled down the stairs to open the front door, heart pumping, desperately trying to think of anyone I knew who might have died, but I couldn't think of one single person whose removal from the world would have caused me a 4 a.m. disturbance. My parents were both long gone, there was my brother, but his wife would be the one to inform me of his passing – probably accompanied by complaints about him leaving the lawn unmown and a DIY project half-finished. The remaining aunts and uncles all had the cousins to fall back on in the event of their demise. It gave me a sudden realisation of how alone I was in the world. But then, I rationalised during my gallop along the hallway, doesn't everyone feel like that at 4 a.m.?

Cautiously wrapping my dressing gown tightly around me, as a fleecy defensive shield between the police and my very unglamorous pyjamas, I opened the front door to find the police officers had bunched up into my tiny half-roofed porch, like a pair of vampires eager to avoid the dawn. 'Come through.' I ushered them, uniforms brushing the hallway walls, down to the living room, still littered with the detritus of a single woman's evening at home, unplumped cushions and a plate of toast crumbs and biscuit wrappers. 'Sorry it's a bit untidy.'

'Sit down, Mrs Donaldson,' suggested Sergeant Williams, the tall male one. 'Please,' he added when I picked up the plate and a couple of old mugs and stacked them on a side table. 'I'm afraid we have bad news for you.'

'Calling me Mrs Donaldson is bad enough,' I said, trying to lift the atmosphere of gloom and realising that I'd left last night's socks draped over the arm of the sofa.

'But you *are* Mrs Donaldson? Married to Grant Donaldson?' The other officer looked around the room as though she expected to see stolen silverware heaped to the ceiling, and Lord Lucan grooming Shergar over by the sideboard. 'And this *is* 22 Cringle Moor Road, Pickering?'

'Well, yes. I just meant...'

But I was spoken over. 'Mrs Donaldson, I'm very sorry to have to inform you that your husband has been killed.' Both police officers acquired sombre expressions. 'Is there anyone we can call? Anyone you'd like to have with you?'

What? *What?* I'd heard the words, but it was as though my brain couldn't make sense of them; as though the policeman had been talking Polish or Martian or making random noises. Grant. Killed. Those were the salient words, but even those wouldn't penetrate the fog of confusion to gel into an image.

'I'll get you a glass of water,' the policewoman said, and there were noises of someone walking over the sticky, unwashed vinyl of the kitchen floor and rummaging around on the draining board for a clean glass. The pipes gurgled for a moment and then dispatched their usual reluctant trickle. I could only sit.

'I take it this has come out of the blue?' The policeman sat down and crossed his legs. A magazine slithered from the arm of the chair he was sitting in, to lie like a cast-off snakeskin in the pool of light from the overhead lamp. 'When did you last see your husband?'

Grant. Killed. The words didn't mean much more now that I'd given them a chance to permeate the layers of emotion and they settled in the sediment of 'things that have happened' at the back of my mind. 'About six years ago,' I said.

'Six *years?*'

'Well, he left me, you see. Said he didn't want to be married any more, packed a suitcase and went off. I heard he'd moved to York but...' I shook my head. 'We never bothered to get a divorce and I've been tearing up any post that came for him.' With less and less ferocity as the years passed, it must be said. 'So, yes. About six years.' I took a deep breath. 'How did it happen? Surely it wasn't murder?' I had to struggle to imagine Grant generating sufficient emotion in anyone to justify a killing; apart from the savage hatred I'd felt at being left with the bills and unfulfilled social obligations, even his leaving hadn't made me feel murderous. Grant now existed in my memory as a streak of opinionless grey and a stammered range of 'I'm not sure, whatever you like, I don't mind, whatever you want to do.'

The female officer came back in, walking carefully as though afraid that she might spill water, although what harm she thought it could cause to my 1960s furniture and ancient holey carpet, I didn't know. It had taken her such a long time to bring the water through from a kitchen only a matter of steps away that I presumed she'd been scanning the walls and reading my reminder board, searching for any clues that I might have detonated my ex-husband.

'It was a gas explosion.'

She handed me the glass and I sipped water, as though it were expected of me.

'A gas explosion? Where? I mean, do I have to identify him? And what about a funeral? Who sorts that out, is that me, or...?'

Time must have been passing because I heard my neighbour's front door slam and his footsteps on the brick path as he took their dog for its early walk, but in here, there seemed to be a stasis field holding me in that moment of *Grant killed*. There was no grief, it was like hearing that a distant acquaintance had died suddenly, a sadness that wrapped itself around the memories of happier early days of laughter and faint affection, but then was spiked and punctured by remembering the years of our marriage.

The police officers exchanged another look and pulled those 'this is going to be tricky' type faces. 'Er,' said one.

'The explosion was in a deserted house high up on the moors?' Why she made it a question, I didn't know. Was she expecting me to say, 'No, it wasn't'? 'We don't know the exact circumstances, we were hoping you could help us with that.'

'Six *years*,' I said, suddenly testy. 'I couldn't even tell you what haircut he had, let alone – a house on the moors? What the hell was he doing up there?'

'It was the old Fortune House.'

As though that explained anything. I'd never heard of the old Fortune House and didn't know whether it was a noun or a name. Was it like the Oak Island Money Pit? It would have been just like Grant to go looking for buried treasure; trying to get along whilst putting in the least amount of effort seemed to be his life's goal.

'It was supposedly haunted,' the policeman finished. 'Empty for the last year or so, since old Miss Fortune died, someone's been using it to do ghost hunts, what d'you call 'em...?'

'Vigils,' put in his sidekick. 'This professor type from the university has a group, they go up there and sit around in the dark, trying to talk to ghosts.'

My brain did the shutting-down thing again. Grant and ghost

hunting were about as far removed from one another as Sydney Harbour Bridge and my front porch. I could not think of one single reason why Grant would have been in 'the Fortune House'.

'Anyway, the place had propane heating and we think a cylinder got damaged or something, your husband went up there for a solo... vigil...' the policeman threw a glance at his companion, who nodded, 'and maybe lit a cigarette or set off a spark or something and... well. Because the place is so isolated, it burned for three days before anyone noticed anything was wrong. A pair of walkers eventually called it in.'

'A woman,' I said suddenly.

'No, it was two men.'

'*What?*'

'Er,' the policeman said again. 'What do *you* mean?'

'There had to be a woman. He was meeting a woman up there. It's literally the only reason Grant would be that far from a takeaway.'

Oh dear. I was clearly doing 'cheated-on wife' from the expressions on their faces. 'We've not found any... traces of anyone else,' said the woman, carefully.

'Traces,' I repeated. I couldn't, for any money, have told you how I felt then. There might have been a tiny bit of schadenfreude, if I'd been honest. Grant had refused to grow up, refused to accept that a life of mundanity and responsibility and bill-paying was his future, and he'd died in a flaming house in the middle of nowhere. Possibly the best 'I told you so' moment in history. But a man I'd loved enough to marry, even if only briefly, had died. How was I *supposed* to feel? There were no templates for this situation.

'We found your husband's wallet.'

'And his belt buckle.'

'And a tooth.'

I stood up in case they were going to go through a more extensive list, but they seemed to have stopped. The water from the glass I'd been holding slopped onto the floor, but I didn't bother to do anything about it. 'So.' I began pacing. 'You're telling me that my husband, my *ex*-husband, who I've not heard a word from in six years, has been incinerated in an explosion in a deserted house, miles from anywhere?'

They both made 'that's about the size of it' faces.

'And all that was left of him was his wallet, a belt buckle and a *tooth*?'

'Propane gas.' The male of the pair was also very young, I realised. He looked nervous, as though he was afraid I was about to start cackling like a movie villain, and I thought this might well be his first time breaking the news to a relative. He seemed to be simultaneously worried and slightly proud. 'It's very unpredictable. The, er, *items* were damaged, but appear to have been jettisoned during the explosive phase. Like I said, the fire burned for several days. The remains of the house fell into the basement, which sort of banked the fire. Your husband—'

He stopped so suddenly that I wondered if the policewoman had kicked his ankle.

'We will clear the debris, of course, and try to find any... further remains,' she said, delicately. 'There will be an inquest. But the intensity of the heat and the weight of the falling masonry... I'm sorry, Mrs... *Alice*, but we may not recover sufficient remains for a funeral.' She looked at my face. 'You can, of course, have a memorial service,' she added hastily. 'That's what they did for my uncle, when he was lost at sea.'

There didn't seem much more to say after that. They quizzed me lightly, presumably to make sure that Grant and I really *had* been separated with no knowledge of one another's movements, although the lack of any photographs of him and the fact that I had to go and hunt one out to give them in case they needed it seemed to reassure them of that fact. Then they went, leaving me with numbers to call should I need to, still holding a tumbler full of room-temperature water, most of it now over my pyjama-clad legs.

And Grant still dead.

* * *

Personal testimony, received second-hand from the daughter of the couple involved.

In October or November 1966, my mum and dad were members of a walking group who regularly walked several routes across the North York Moors. My mum told me this story on several occasions and the details never varied.

They, and a group of six or seven, had set out from a spot near the Whitby road, to walk across towards Levisham Moor, and they were passing near the Fortune House when a fog came down suddenly. Mum had been walking near the back of the group, and she found herself cut off from the others and lost. She stopped walking and called out, she was a bit scared and the path up there was known to be boggy and difficult and she didn't want to end up in one of the marshy areas.

The fog was really thick and she couldn't see more than a couple of yards. She couldn't hear anything, apart from some sheep and water dripping. She knew she was reasonably close to the Fortune House, and she thought she ought to find her way up there to wait for the rest of the group to come and look for her. So she started up the hill towards where she thought the house was.

She said that she thought she must have walked around in circles, because there was no sign of the house or any building and it was starting to get dark. She was really frightened by this time, because she couldn't see any of her group or anyone about, and she was cold and wet and lost, so she sat down on her pack and started to cry.

A few minutes later, she saw Dad and another man coming towards her through the fog. She didn't recognise the other man, but she said he was young, wearing a cap and tweeds like all the farmers did back then, and she assumed he must have heard her crying and told the rest of the walking group where she was.

Dad got her up and made sure she was all right, while the other man just stood in the background. She couldn't really see him because of the dark and the fog, but she said he was there, watching as if to make sure she didn't need any help, and then it got so dark that she couldn't see him any more. Dad started leading Mum off towards the rest of the group, who were waiting close by. They'd decided not to go on any further because of the fog and they were going to set up camp while they waited. Mum said that she wanted to thank the young man for coming with him to help her, but Dad said there wasn't anybody else. He'd noticed she was missing, and the group had been looking for her for about half an hour.

He said nobody had come with him and he hadn't seen the young man in the cap who'd been standing next to him when he found Mum.

2

It took me a week to sort the jumbled assortment of thoughts in my head into cohesive action. An inquest was opened and adjourned, apparently absolutely normally, I wasn't required to attend but did anyway, and the police kept me up to date with slightly diffident phone calls. I managed to ascertain the rough location of the Fortune House and get compassionate leave from my job – although Sheila, the office manager, did remark that 'compassionate leave' was being rather stretched as a term – but we had policies for spousal bereavement, which I insisted on keeping to, even though 'spousal' was even *more* stretched as a term.

I couldn't explain, not to her, nor Malcolm, nor any of the others at Welsh's Windows why I felt this need to see where Grant died. Maybe it was a kind of morbid curiosity, or maybe I was searching for a definite closure to our marriage, but whatever it was, I wanted to go there and find out what was so special about that bit of moorland that it had drawn my resolutely urban-dwelling husband out of town.

It was a week to the day after I'd been so abruptly woken that I found myself, rucksacked and booted, following a tiny trail on an enormous map, to try to find the Fortune House. The map had to be large in order to have the scale necessary to even locate the track, and it flapped and bent in the wind like a sail. I kept losing my place and having to sit on small clumps of damp heather to try to find myself again, tracing my route with a fingernail whilst fighting off disturbing memories of a long-ago Duke of Edinburgh expedition across similar terrain. I hadn't liked the wide, stretched skies or the featureless curves of moorland any more twenty years ago than I did now. The knee-high growth concealed random holes and boggy patches, and I bucked and plunged my way along with my map-sheet flapping, like a schooner breasting the waves of the Atlantic.

I didn't do walking. I didn't go in for the waterproofed gallivanting around mountains and hills with names like Black Ghyll and other medieval barons. My hobbies tended toward the sedentary – TV, magazines, avoiding housework, things like that – not this relentless striding across featureless landscapes occasionally interrupted by faceplanting into thorny bushes or sudden knee-deep squelches into hidden bogs.

'I am not an outdoor person,' I breathed heavily to myself, adjusting the straps of the rucksack borrowed from Malcolm, who was our entire accounts department. 'My natural habitat comes courtesy of Sofaworld, and the only wildlife I want to see has David Attenborough attached. Oh, bugger.' I caught my foot in yet another snarl of skeletal growth and unseen pothole and dropped to my knees yet again. 'But, more to the point, what the hell was *Grant* doing out here? And now I'm talking to myself, well, this is it now. I might as well go home and buy seventeen cats and resign myself to being a woman who mutters to herself in supermarkets.'

I pulled myself up to standing and found I was being watched. Up until now, my relentless hours of moorland walk had only been observed by inscrutable sheep or birds that I hadn't paid any attention to because of the lack of wildlife narration accompanying them. But it seemed that my most recent lurch had brought me into someone's eyeline and from this lower level I could see a man, hand up to shade his eyes from the light, watching me from behind a narrow clump of windswept trees halfway between me and infinite distance.

He was an outline, a sketch against the somewhat uneven horizon of burgeoning heather and gorse bushes, rocks and sky. I couldn't make out much detail, other than dark clothing, dark hair blowing in the wind and the raised arm, which indicated he was facing my way and probably laughing himself into a hernia from watching my progress across the terrain. I felt myself blush, a sickening creep of heat from my shins to my cheeks, and I stood up again, trying to look as though I'd just dropped to my knees to examine a particularly interesting example of foliage. Maybe he was a walker, a picnicker off the beaten track, or one of the subset of ramblers that seemed to enjoy this social deprivation and sensory overload. Anyway, he wasn't my problem.

But he didn't move and, following my fingernail-traced line, I began to close on him. It became evident that the lip of hill where he was standing concealed my destination and I tried to work on an insouciant expression and jaunty stride so that I would look like a habitual walker by the time I reached him. There had been something about that slender dark outline against the heather that made me not want to look like someone who only went outside to fetch the milk in when I reached him.

Everything conspired against me. Roots caught at my ankles, small splashes of junior bogland soaked my socks and I was hot and sweaty and red-faced, realising that the stone and a half that I'd gradually put on almost unnoticed over the last couple of years – that stone and a half that had tipped me over the edge from 'well rounded' to 'definitely plump' – wasn't conducive to several miles of off-road walking. Plus, the last bit of the walk was up a steep slope and the weight of my rucksack kept dragging me backwards, so I made it to the lip of the gulley where the man stood whilst giving the impression of one who was tied to an invisible companion by bungee cord. To make things worse, from the looks of it, the man had watched me every inch of my approach, because he was casually leaning against one of the gnarly stunted trees as I breasted the final rise and came face to face with him.

He wasn't alone. There was a woman there too, sitting on a rug on a patch of grass with her knees drawn up under her chin. Sunlight, dappled to pointillism by the trees and the frequent clouds, illuminated her and made it clear that she was crying. It looked as though I had walked all those miles over the landscape only to drop in on a Wuthering Heights remake.

'Hello.' I tried to smile and pass on by, although where I would have passed on *to*, given that this site was drawn all over in highlight pen on my map, I wasn't sure.

The man moved away from the trees and towards the crying woman, putting a protective arm around her shoulders as though I was about to go for her. 'It's all right,' I heard him say softly. 'Jen, please don't cry again.'

It looked like a stage set or a magazine shoot; slivers of sunlight falling on the tartan picnic rug and the blonde-haired woman in her cute dungarees, and highlighting the dark-haired man who bent over her in such a concerned way. Only a slight haze in the air and a faint smell reminiscent of kilns spoiled the illusion of emotional turmoil in nature. The woman dropped her head further onto her knees and sobbed harder.

The man straightened away, with a squeeze of her shoulder, and came over to me. He was dark and slender and had a pleasing arrangement of features, stubble and cheekbones that made me feel even bigger and pinker and plainer. 'Are you lost?'

'I'm looking for the Fortune House.' I waved my map as though to indicate my inability to become mislaid.

The man raised his eyebrows. 'You've found it.' He pointed to somewhere slightly further up the dip. 'Well, what's left of it. There was a fire a couple of weeks ago so there's not much to see now.' He looked me up and down. 'Professional interest?'

What an odd phrase. Or maybe he thought I was a fire investigator? I assumed anyone trying to look into the explosion and fire would have at least had an iPad. All I had was a Ford Fiesta parked on the road three miles away, borrowed gear and a lot of sweat.

'No. My... someone I knew died in the fire. I came to...' To what? Pay my respects to a man who'd dumped me, leaving me with a house we were supposed to be renovating and a diminished sense of self-esteem? Why had I come? Really? 'To see where he died,' I finished, rather lamely.

The man waved a hand again. 'It's this way.'

The woman had looked up, finally. Her face was tracked with tears, and she looked genuinely distraught. 'You knew Grant?' she asked.

'Yes. He was... I mean, we were married. But a long time ago.'

The woman got to her feet. Despite the dungarees' best attempts, I could see she was slim, as fine-boned and attractive as the dark man still hovering around beneath the trees. 'You're Alice? Grant talked a lot about you. My name's Jenna Allbright.'

She didn't clarify her relationship with Grant, but she didn't need to. Her tears and the fact that she was exactly his type, blonde and girlish and long-legged, told me everything I needed to know. I looked at the man and my look must have held a question.

'I'm Max Allbright. I'm Jenna's brother. This was my site.'

'Your...?'

'This place has a reputation for being haunted and I've been conducting research into the psychology of ghost hunting here.' He looked behind him, as though the ghosts might be hiding some-where among the rocks and trees. 'It's a fascinating place.'

I couldn't see anything fascinating about it. Boulders, tufts of sprouting bracken uncurling like cautious snails from their shells, those finger-like trees.

'This is the place that I really feel could prove something.' He didn't seem to be talking to me any more, it was as if he was muttering to himself. 'I've been trying to get evidence – I'm writing a book. Grant was getting interested too, and he'd started to come along. Sometimes.'

I felt myself gaping and forced myself to close my mouth. 'Grant actually went on *ghost hunts*? With you? Out *here*?'

I couldn't do it. I couldn't square the memory of my husband, whose entire view of the supernatural could have been contained in the phrase 'never really thought about it, but Buffy was hot', sitting out here in this forsaken wilderness waiting for spectral activity. It just didn't compute, like trying to imagine Marie Kondo in a chip shop.

'Yes.' A pause. 'You wanted to see the house?'

Wanted was a strong word for the emotion I had. But I hadn't trudged three miles off road out of mild curiosity, something had driven me out here, even if it was a feeling I still didn't really want to analyse. Loss? The absolute ending of something? But that some-thing had ended six years ago, when Grant had given me the 'I need to explore, find myself, do other things.' I had retorted that he was so beige he could find himself perfectly well using a magnolia paint chart and how had I ever stopped him doing anything he'd wanted to, when all he seemingly wanted to do was sit and watch TV, eat whatever meal I put in front of him and have no opinion on anything, ever?

It hadn't occurred to me then, and it had only struck me later, that what he'd really meant was that he'd met someone else, someone who'd found his vacillations and his lack of definition as charming as I had before I'd been married to it. And when the pain of rejection and the fear of having to manage on one income had faded, I had silently wished her well, whoever she was. It wouldn't have been this leggy blonde, who was still crying; tears making her skin shimmer and bringing her into even sharper contrast with my ruddy cheeks and damp hair. Even my eyebrows were sweating. Six years ago, she would have been, by the looks of it, still at school.

'I came...' I tailed off. 'I'm not sure why,' I finished, honesty winning out under the man's gaze. 'It all sounds so unlike Grant – so unlike the Grant I knew,' I corrected myself. After all, people change. But could Grant really have changed *that* much?

Neither of them answered me. We all stood, a tableau of confused misery, with the breeze drying the sweat on my face and down my back and whipping Jenna's hair behind her in a stream of gold. My hair, of course, was blowing into my face and getting stuck to my damp forehead, making it look as though I was under attack from my own head.

'I'll show you the site.' The man, Max, finally broke our increasingly embarrassed deadlock with a sweep of his arm in the direction of the head of the tiny valley. 'Leave your rucksack here, it's a bit of a scramble.'

I hesitated again. The rucksack was concealing the sweaty streak that my T-shirt had become, and its overloaded heftiness at least gave me an excuse for my inelegant perambulations thus far. But Max was holding a hand out in a way that indicated he might forcibly strip it from my back if I didn't take it off, and so I reluctantly shrugged my way clear of the straps to let it fall heavily onto the grass.

'Were you going to camp?' Jenna asked curiously, as the bag failed to crumple but stood upright like a scarecrow's torso, teetering on the rutted edge of the gulley.

'No, I just brought a few things I thought I might need,' I answered in as dignified way as I could, following her brother as he began to lead the way along the side of the hill. I definitely wasn't going to admit to being so ill-prepared for this jaunt into the wilderness that I'd brought a large wool duffel coat, an umbrella and a thick jumper, all of which were currently giving my rucksack its paunch. I *hadn't* thought to pack any food, or water, and my body was letting me know how foolish this particular oversight had been with little stomach gurgles and an incipient headache.

Max had vanished around a bend, hidden by a clump of weedy-looking trees with thin trunks scraping and waving against the pale sky. Their roots looked horribly veiny and gristly, clinging on to the thin soil and winding around the grey rocks that broke the ground as though the earth were bringing its bones to the surface. I stumbled, scraped my knee on shattered stone and had to use my arms to balance myself as, following the distant shape, I scrambled and slid down and around, until I stopped, horrified.

It wasn't a house any more. In fact, it was hard to tell it had *ever* been a house, it looked more like a demolition site after a run in with a hurricane; bricks littered the ground in a huge circle around a confused mass of crater, ash, dust, the odd skeletal piece of wooden beam reaching out to the sky, and shattered tiles. There was still a vague feeling of heat, but that could have been me after the exertion of clambering around the ghyll.

Shadows gathered around the base of the ruins, ebbing and flowing with the light as clouds scudded across the sun. The little scoop of valley felt a million miles from any town or civilisation, and I found myself shivering a bit, despite the warmth.

'Oh.' It was all I could say. 'Oh.'

Grant had died here. Blown to smithereens with the walls, roof and furniture. Anything left of him was buried under the remnants of the house, although it was hard to tell what had *actually* been the house and what had been thrown by the force of the explosion. But this narrow little pleat in the hillside, these anaemic trees and their accompanying whippy branches and forelimb protuberances grasping at the ground would have been the last things he saw.

For one over-imaginative moment, the place felt haunted.

I tried again to imagine Grant here. Small, unremarkable man, nondescript hair, clothes that always just *were*, nothing trendy but nothing old-fashioned, as though he were a time traveller that absolutely must not be noticed. Eyes a vague colour somewhere between brown and green, hair neither blond nor dark. A man with, I'd always believed, no thoughts, no original ideas. Here. In this maelstrom of life, with the wind flattening the ground cover and random examples of wildlife peeping and fluttering all over. A sky that stretched like a bucket of spilled milk over the top, white and featureless and serving only to trap the weather underneath it. *Grant. Here?*

'Are you all right?' The unasked-for concern in Max's voice made my eyes prickle.

'Yes. Yes, of course.' I kept my gaze on the gently smoking ruins so that the tears that threatened to surprise me didn't fall. 'I can't imagine why the hell Grant would be out here, of all places. I mean,' I started to gabble, to justify my frozen face, 'I know people change but it's only six years, not six decades, can anyone change that much in such a short space of time? Without, like, masses of therapy and introspection and self-analysis and Grant didn't *do* introspection. He didn't do extrospection either, come to that. Is that a word? Extrospection? Well, he didn't do it, whatever it was. Life happened to Grant, he didn't *do* anything.'

I ran out of breath and stopped on a gasp with that wrecked, tumbled building burning itself onto my retinas.

There was a light touch on my shoulder. 'It's still a shock.' The voice was soft now. 'You cared, once. That doesn't just go away.'

I sighed and turned around. Without the weight of the rucksack, to which I had become accustomed, and with the gradient of the little valley, I spun faster and more clumsily than I'd intended and almost whipped myself into Max's arms. I had to grab at his wrist to stop myself stumbling against him and precipitating the pair of us over the brick-strewn ground. He braced us both.

'There's a flask of tea back with Jenna,' he said, without commenting on my gracelessness. 'Would you like some? You probably need to sit down after seeing this.' He nodded behind him. 'And I think Jenna might like to talk to you about your husband.' His tone was kind, and I felt my eyes prickle again.

I didn't want to talk about Grant. I didn't even want to *think* about Grant. I was pink with embarrassment at my clumsiness, sweaty and moist, and comparing myself unfavourably with the blonde slenderness of Jenna and her sardonic, good-looking brother. I wanted to go home, have a hot bath and forget this place of ear-splitting silence and smouldering ruin.

But instead, I followed the dark, assured Max back along the vertiginous gulley to the picnic rug and a lot of questions.

3

Jenna had, at least, stopped crying, although her past tears had dried to shiny trails along her cheeks. She'd laid out some food too, the kind of picnic I'd always imagined posh undergraduates at Cambridge enjoyed amidst their upper-class studies; nibbles of filo pastry, olives, little fishy slabs. My stomach gurgled again over its early-morning cup of tea and nothing else.

'Come and sit down.' Max waved at the rug. 'Jenna, I've asked… Alice to have some tea. Seeing this place has been a bit of a shock for her.'

As if my ego hadn't been reduced enough in the face of this pair's organised appearance, it managed to shrink a little further at his words. He'd forgotten my name. But why wouldn't he? I'd bowled up into the midst of a gathering of the family Composed, looking like a jelly that's been left out of the fridge too long on a hot summer's day. Of course he'd have to grope for my name. Of course he would.

And secretly I was hoping that the cup of tea would extend to a share of the picnic nibbles. I was beginning to realise how hungry I was and how far it was to tramp back to the car through the heather and bracken.

Jenna immediately went into 'hostess' mode. 'That's a good idea. We could all do with some liquid, or we'll get awful dehydration headaches, and we probably need to get our blood sugars up a bit too.'

Max sighed. It was the first really human sound he'd made, and I smiled inwardly. He wasn't a total robot then. 'Have you been at those nutrition books again, Jen?' A half-amused, half-despairing tone told me how fond he was of his sister, how tolerant and how forgiving of her foibles. 'My sister,' he said, turning towards me as he sat down, elegantly, of course, on the mat, 'does tend towards being slightly obsessional about her interests in life.'

'Shut up.' Jenna shoved a plate in his direction in a less-than-elegant way and I started to warm to her a little. 'Judgey-pants. I want to talk to Alice.' A pale, fine-boned face turned up to me. 'Sorry, Alice. This is as awkward as hell, I know. I don't want to make you feel put on the spot or anything. But Grant...' As though the name brought too many emotions, she stopped speaking and began piling tiny delicacies onto a patterned plate. 'Sit down and have some food first, though.'

She kept gathering her hair behind her head and letting it fall, either because the nape of her neck was hot or she was nervous. The likelihood was it was nerves, as she was hunched and drawn in on herself, despite her words of welcome. I sat down, stiff after the long walk and much slipping and sliding, but pretending to a degree of elegance in the face of these two immaculate people. 'What do you want to know?' I asked, trying not to grab at the food. Max handed me a plate and I was slightly relieved to find that it was melamine. These two looked the type to have brought china to an outdoor meal, miles from anywhere.

'I don't... I'm not sure.' Jenna shook her head slowly and then did the 'gathering up and dropping' of her hair again. 'Grant and I had been together for three... yes, three years. We were starting to talk about marriage and settling down and all that sort of thing.' She threw me a sideways glance. 'He was going to ask for a divorce first, of course.'

'He never did.' I ate a piece of the filo pastry. It was stuffed with anchovies, and tasted home-made and delicious. Max passed me a cup and indicated the flask of tea and small jug of milk in the middle of the blanket, so I poured myself some to give me thinking time. 'He hadn't been in contact at all since he left. Nothing, other than signing a few papers to take his name off the house insurance and a couple of other bits, and I sent all that via his mum. I didn't even know he'd stayed in Yorkshire.'

There was a moment of chirping silence. Birds wheeped and twittered invisibly, and the heat of the sun continued, trapped under the envelope of sky whitened by a cloud sheet. Insects made little buzzy sounds at ground level and somewhere I could hear water running in a sullen gurgle.

'When you knew him,' Jenna began again, slowly, 'was he... *kind*?'

I'd just taken an extra-large mouthful of something that had turned out to be pork pie and had to chew ferociously to be able to answer without spraying pastry. 'Kind? I suppose so. He was never *unkind*, certainly. He was...' I trailed off, trying to remember Grant's good points. The reasons we'd ever got together in the first place. 'He was nice,' I finished. Damning him with faint praise, of course, but it was the only applicable word.

Jenna smiled slowly. 'He was always kind to me. Very sweet and gentle.' I saw Max catch her eye and raise his eyebrows and she went on. 'Sorry. Sorry, I was in a relationship before I met him and that wasn't always... very pleasant. So Grant's kindness was the main thing I will remember him for.' Her eyes clouded with tears again. 'I can't believe he's gone. Not like this.' She waved a hand, presumably intending to indicate the exploded building, but, as it was around the bend in the hill, mostly showing that Grant's death among hills blue with heat and seething with unseen wildlife was unfitting.

Another shadow passed over the sun.

'Jen,' Max said, in a concerned tone.

'Sorry.' Her voice was small. 'I'm just going to go for a walk for a minute.' She unfolded like an origami figure coming undone and was on her feet, walking away towards the top of the hill where more of the stretched, skeletal trees clumped together for comfort on the skyline.

I swallowed the last lump of pastry. 'I can't believe it either. What the hell was Grant *doing* out here?' I turned to Max, who stopped in the act of stuffing an entire miniature scotch egg into his mouth in a move that made me like him a tiny bit, despite his supercilious attitude. 'Grant wasn't that sort of person. He just *wasn't*,' I added, as though there might have been uncertainty in my words.

'Okay.' Max picked up his mug of tea. 'Well, it's fair to say he hadn't seemed particularly involved in the whole ghost-hunting thing, not at first.' He sipped. I'd gulped mine and was on to my second cup. 'But in the last – well, the last few months, he got interested in what I was doing at the Fortune House. I thought it was just a distraction.' His eyes moved up to follow the track his sister had taken. She was invisible now among the trees.

'Look, I shouldn't really say anything, but I'm mentioning it to warn you. Six months ago, Jenna lost a pregnancy. The baby was unplanned, but she was so happy about it and she and Grant were making plans, so...' He tore his eyes away and back down to the food again. 'I think that's when Grant started taking an interest in this place, they both needed something else to think about for a while, a distraction. Jenna got very into healthy eating and exercise and things – too much so, for a while, but she's better now. Grant offered to help with the some of the paperwork I had to do as part of my research.'

'Oh.' I felt a sudden burst of sympathy for young Jenna, alongside a tiny needle of something I didn't want to examine. 'That must have been awful. Poor Jenna.' Grant and fatherhood. He'd always told me that we should wait – until we'd got the house straight, until he'd set up his own business. Until, until. Until I'd realised that he really hadn't ever wanted a baby. Not with me, anyway.

'You're not a believer, I gather.' He wasn't looking at me. He was staring out over the valley to where the hills rose further and higher as they galloped towards the unseen coast. 'Ghosts. Hauntings. The paranormal. Not your sort of thing?'

I could look at him now without feeling that hot, stretchy inadequacy. He had the same long, slender form as his sister, with tapering fingers that looked as though they would be more at home playing the piano than holding morsels of food. Longish dark hair that swept down under the line of his jaw and caught momentarily in the graphite line of stubble that highlighted his cheekbones, and black eyes that stared intently at things and then moved off restlessly to study something else. He was scarily fanciable, and I was terrified that I was going to give myself away as falling for it. It was all right when he was looking away, at something else, but he seemed to be able to sense my eyes on him, and his gaze would flicker back at a moment's notice.

It was safer to keep looking at the food. I'd already eaten four pork pies and some of that filo stuff, plus two mugs of tea. Ah, well, I wasn't exactly the type to inflame a man's passions, with my round face, pointed nose and lack of chin, so I hardly had to worry. He must get stared at by plain women all the time, he'd be used to ignoring them.

'To tell you the truth, I don't think I've ever really thought about ghosts much,' I said. 'Only scary stories when we were at school and maybe the odd glance at the *Fortean Times* when someone brought one into work.'

'Too fanciful?' The dark glance swung back to me now and I felt my traitorous cheeks start to redden. 'But don't you think that is the reason *why* we enjoy ghost stories? Because they allow us to imagine what might be? That there could be more to, well, life?'

I looked down at my knees. Plain, plump, ordinary knees under jeans slightly too tight, very down-to-earth knees. No flights of fancy about those knees, or dreams of gorgeous men falling over themselves to worship them. I'd often found, during moments when my body wanted to betray my desire to dream about being loved by someone, that staring at my round, cushion-like knees would bring me back to reality.

'I thought we like to think about ghosts because they show evidence of something after death,' I said, flexing one leg. 'The whole idea of hauntings lets us think that everything doesn't end when we die.'

Max laughed. Oh, God, even his bloody *laugh* was attractively deep and throaty and a bit sexy. I killed that thought immediately. 'Well, that reduced my entire PhD thesis to one sentence, congratulations.'

The heat rose again, from somewhere around my collar right up to my hairline. 'Oh, I'm sorry! I didn't mean...'

The laugh again, which didn't help the blush. 'No. No, I know you didn't. It's all right, Alice, I'm not laughing at you.'

'You can if you want,' I muttered. 'I'm an object of hilarity to most people.' I knew I sounded bitter. The jealousy of Grant and Jenna potentially marrying and starting a family gave it a double underline in red too and I had another burst of complete disbelief that he was dead, then hated myself again.

'I'm sure that's not true.'

'Please don't do what everyone else has been doing, with the platitudes and the sympathy.' I sounded fiercer than I'd meant to, and softened my tone. 'Tell me about Grant. What on earth made him come up here that night when he...' I tailed off again as the momentary annoyance drained from me. 'Sorry. I didn't mean to be rude.'

Max gave me a direct look. As the previous blush hadn't quite completely gone, I couldn't muster a second round, for which I was grateful. 'No, you're fine,' he said, and the previous interrogatory tone was gone from these words. 'I've been treating you a bit like one of my potential research subjects here, I'm sorry. I guess the shock of losing Grant has made us all not know what to say to one another. Jenna won't stop crying either, and I don't know what to do to help her.'

'She's lost her future,' I said suddenly. 'She'd thought she was going to be married to Grant, with a family, and it's all been taken away.' I knew how it felt, that sense of the whole of life to come stretching away in a series of blank pages and unfilled diary entries. Even Grant, with his indecisive nature and his inability to say what he thought, had been something certain. Something to give shape to the days that otherwise had only contained a job in admin that gave me too much time to think, and weekends attempting stultifying housework amid the debris of undone DIY.

'So how do I make her feel better?'

I wondered why he was asking me. 'You don't. You can't. Time will do that, you just listen to her talk about him as much as she wants. She'll never forget, never really get over it, but she'll start to find she can live with the loss a little bit more each day.'

Max nodded slowly, eyes fixed on the rug. 'Yeah.' He sighed deeply. 'I thought that might be the case.' Then his dark eyes flickered up to my face and I had to bite the inside of my cheek to stop myself from reacting. 'You seem to be very sensible about all this. What about you? Who's listening to you talk?'

It was such an astonishing question that even the rising tide of attraction was taken aback. 'Me? Why would I need to talk?'

'Well, you've lost a husband.'

'One I hadn't seen, heard from or even thought much about for six years. It's like hearing someone cleared out an attic and threw away your childhood collection of *Pony* magazines.' I couldn't meet his eye. He might see the lie behind the words, the small tears I'd shed in the night. Marriage to Grant looked set to have been my one foray into life as part of a couple and, while I hadn't held out any hopes of his return – hadn't *wanted* him back and wouldn't have taken him back if he'd begged – the increasing unlikelihood of ever having anyone again had made me shed tears of desperation and a newly realised loneliness.

Max shook his head. The light caught his hair and gave it reddish highlights as it swung on the collar of his shirt, and I was annoyed with myself for noticing. 'Grant became so fascinated by this place,' he said, looking out again over the hills. 'In that last couple of months. I wish I knew why. Had he ever mentioned it to you before?'

'The first I heard of it was when the police came round to tell me about the explosion.'

'He'd come up here with the groups, and then go off wandering around the house by himself,' Max went on, keeping his eyes on the steep inclines that barricaded us into this place. 'Almost as though he was looking for something, you know?' Now he looked at me, almost thoughtfully. 'From no interest at all to spending hours peering in sheds and outhouses.'

I felt a prickle of interest. 'Did you ever go and look to see what he might have seen?'

Max shook his head. 'I asked him once what he was doing. He said he was checking for safety.'

I pulled a face. 'It does sound likely. Grant was always one for making sure all the lights were turned off at night and everything unplugged. He got it from his mum, she was the type to open windows and turn the TV off in a thunderstorm.'

The juxtaposition of Grant's careful protection against any midnight inflammability and the way he died seemed to hit both of us at once, and there was a moment of silence. Max shook his head again and then he shrugged and stood up. 'I'd better go and find Jen. You know your way back to your car?'

'I've got a map.' Then a thought struck me. 'How did you two get here? I didn't see another vehicle.'

'Motorbike.' He was already heading off up the slope towards the clump of trees.

Feeling as though I'd been dismissed by a slightly displeased boss, I stood up too, shouldering my rucksack again. Motorbike. Well, yes, he would have. He probably looked really sexy on it too, I thought grumpily as the weight of the still-damp bag settled between my shoulder blades. Bet he came down over the hill without a helmet on, with his hair blowing back like an advert for toothpaste or shampoo or something. I watched his back view striding seemingly effortlessly uphill over the broken tumbled rocks, and took a handful of the anchovy parcels and pushed them into my mouth.

I spared one last look at the pleasing way he filled his black jeans as he strode on, and then headed out for the three-mile tramp back to my car, coughing on dry gobbets of filo as I went.

4

My leave ended. Work could only stretch compassion *so* far, especially when it had been more for appearances' sake, and I hadn't needed the hours of quiet time to organise a funeral or to mourn. The week had been broken by the occasional phone call from the police, checking on details, and my somewhat unhelpful trip to the moors, but otherwise I'd mainly spent it lying on the sofa reading my way through the month's output of women's magazines and eating toast. I couldn't bear to go back to work early because I was hoping that the week would give them all enough time to talk about me and Grant and how awful it had been that he'd left me and then died – raking over the old details until there was nothing left but a gentle sympathy and an extra chocolate biscuit left on my desk at coffee break.

So I went back to the job that gave some kind of purpose to my life. Answering the telephone and emails for a company who made and fitted windows – it was hardly anything to boast about, but it was steady, I knew the work so well I could do it whilst thinking about other things, and it paid sufficiently for me not to have to share my living space with a lodger. But it also left me time to dwell. Time to linger on the past and the questions. *What the hell was the Grant I'd known doing ghost hunting? What had driven him out to that isolated spot alone late one night?* The police had pinpointed the time of the explosion that had demolished the Fortune House to around one in the morning. At this time of year, darkness only really descended after half past eleven and light was already struggling back into the world by three, so one o'clock would have been during that brief summer night. Why would Grant have been up on the moors in the dark? What was he *doing* in there?

And then I wondered about ghosts. Had Grant thought he'd seen something during a previous visit, and returned alone to check it out in the black of night? Why wouldn't he have told Max – the driving force behind the investigation?

My brain wouldn't let it go. I kept trying to dismiss all the thoughts about Grant, to stop trying to overlay the Grant I had known onto the Grant that Max and Jenna had told me about, but I couldn't. Grant had never done anything on a whim. His job as a freelance tech consultant could largely be done from the living room, and he'd maintained there was nothing outdoors compelling enough to force him into 'good' clothes and out of the door. And yet Max had insisted Grant had had an interest in the Fortune House?

When he'd only taken the most cursory interest in *me*?

The thoughts itched away in the back of my brain, like a mosquito bite that you rub away at thoughtlessly until it's the size of your hand. Niggle, niggle, niggle, waking me up in the middle of the night to remember arguments, where my desire to go out, see things that I'd never seen before had collided with Grant's desire to watch detective shows or lie sprawled on the sofa, 'meditating'.

When I got home from work the next day, there was a motor-bike parked outside my door and a black-leathered figure was sitting on it, idly poking at the kerb with a booted toe.

'Max?' I half-whispered his name as my brain ran through all the scenarios it could come up with to explain why on earth Max Allbright would be outside my house. Or even how Max Allbright would know where I lived, let alone why he should care. I had to park several houses up and walk down. I hoped it wasn't actually a lost hitman or a lookout man for a burglar.

The leather-clad figure took off its helmet. It wasn't Max, but then again, it wasn't a hitman. It was Jenna. Her eyes were red, but her hair was still blonde and long and silky. I found I was running my fingers through my lopsided 'needs a hairdresser' crop and forced myself to drop my hands.

'Sorry, Alice. I'm really sorry. I just wanted to be somewhere Grant used go. He used to talk about living here and I really, *really* want to talk about him to someone who knew him. Max is trying, but he's getting a bit tired of me, I think.'

'Grant hadn't lived here for years! And I'm not sure there's anything I can tell you about him that you don't already know.' I put the key in the door, wavering. This house had become my sanctuary, I didn't invite people round. It was my private place. Then I looked at her swollen eyes and drawn face and relented. 'Come in and have a cup of tea.'

After all, the main reason I didn't invite people round was that I didn't have anyone *to* invite round. I wanted to have a romanticised notion of myself as a lone wolf, a prowler in shadows who lived a carefully guarded solitary life, but the sight of a week's worth of dirty washing piled across the kitchen entrance and one shoe casually discarded on the sofa contrasted with the leggy sophisticated form of my visitor and made me realise that I was two weeks away from filling the place with stray cats.

'Thank you.' Jenna sat down on the sofa with a creak of leather. 'It's really nice of you to be so understanding, what with – well, our different relationships with Grant.'

'He didn't leave me for you.' I tried to tidy up unobtrusively, but her eyes seemed to be drawn to the walls and I'm not sure she'd have noticed me recovering the sofa and hanging new curtains. 'Otherwise I might be going for you with the kitchen scissors, but anyhow. None of it was your fault.'

'He used to talk about you, you know,' Jenna said. I'd gone through to the kitchen, and very nearly dropped the entire tea caddy in the sink.

'Did he? How strange. He hardly talked *to* me when we were together.'

'Grant was...' Jenna tailed off, as though she was searching for a metaphor. I, standing at the chilly, chipped sink with my feet on the crunchy edge of worn vinyl flooring, had a few I could have lent her, but I stayed quietly making tea. Being practical. Being Alice. 'He felt he'd made some bad decisions over the years. He was sad that he hurt you.'

I popped my head back through, to see her looking out of the little front window onto the narrow street. Mrs Henkus from number eleven was putting out her bin, it was hardly a view. I wondered what Jenna was really seeing. Grant, looking decisive and manly, clearing out the guttering on a stepladder? That had never happened.

'He didn't hurt me that badly.' I poured boiling water onto tea bags; the domestic smell was reassuring. 'Not really. Our marriage was pretty much over before it started, we were like a couple of housemates. We were friendly enough, we didn't argue or anything, but it wasn't a grand passion for either of us.'

'Why did you get married?' Jenna leaned forward, elbows on her knees. I wasn't sure what to say. I'd dealt with Grant leaving, I'd dealt with his death. And I didn't want any of my confidences about the fact that I'd married Grant because he was the only man to ever get close enough for me to have a sniff of coupledom to get back to Max.

'My parents were both very ill all of my life.' I put the tea mugs down on the coffee table. It never got used as anything other than a footstool, so now was its time to shine. Although it would absolutely be a figurative shine, the table hadn't seen a can of Pledge for years. 'My mum wanted to see me settled before she – well. She needed to know I'd be all right. My brother was already married and working in Scotland, she wanted me to have a life, I suppose.'

'So you got married to please your mother?' Jenna sounded a bit happier now. I wondered what Grant had told her about our relationship. I wondered how much of our relationship he had been able to remember, being that most of it had consisted of him watching football in his pants.

'It was one reason.' I sat in the never-used armchair and wondered if getting cats was really so bad as an option.

We sat and sipped our tea. A weird kind of silence had descended, broken only by the sound of the children next door to the right playing a game that involved shrieking and bouncing one another off the party wall, and I still wasn't sure how I felt about having Jenna here. She was gazing around the room as though molecules of Grant were still here and she could reassemble him.

'So, how did you meet?'

She put her cup down and stood up, restless, creaking in her leathers. 'He came to sort out our computer network at the house. We just sort of clicked.'

That was also odd. Grant didn't deal in domestic computers, he only installed company-wide systems. It had been how he'd met me.

'So do you work with computers?' I asked idly, watching her pace the floor, stare at the spines of my books on the bookcase that was starting to sag at the shelves, peer at the photograph of my brother and his wife and their children on the mantelpiece.

'Not really.' She tilted her head again and, almost unconsciously, bunched her hair behind her head into one hand. She looked very young. Then she turned around to face me and her eyes were old with a depth of sorrow and loss I could only imagine. 'Tell me about Grant, Alice, please. Tell me everything he told you, about his childhood and his family and his favourite places.'

I looked at that fragile, slim figure and those reddening eyes. 'I'm not sure it will do you any good,' I said gently. 'He's gone, Jenna.'

'I need...' She paced again and it came home to me how strange the situation was. Ex-wife, bereaved girlfriend, bonding over Grant. 'I need to talk about him.'

I'd told Max he needed to listen, hadn't I? I could hardly be so hypocritical as to refuse to listen to her request myself. So I raked back through my memory for all the things Grant had told me about his boyhood, his teenage years. His upbringing, with a widowed mother in a rattly old house in Bristol. His degree in computer engineering from York, his freelance work setting up computer networks and ensuring their smooth running. His love of football and food and his lack of ability to cook. By the time I'd finished, I almost missed him myself.

'Thank you.' Jenna breathed the words. Her shoulders had dropped, I noticed, she wasn't hunched as much as she had been on arrival. 'At least now I know he didn't lie about anything, and you've filled in some gaps for me.' She stood up. 'I ought to go. Max will be wondering where I am, and he'll be worrying. He worries about me, you see. He doesn't need to, but he does.'

Looking at her huge eyes with the smudgy purple shadows underneath, I thought she was wrong. 'You see a lot of one another?' It was a casual question, but I was really trying to establish something of Max – did he have a wife who complained about the time he was spending with his sister? A life of debauchery and recklessness broken into only by the need to care for her?

'We live together,' she said, surprising me. 'Our place was left to Max when Father died, and he's letting me stay on until...' Her voice trailed off. 'Grant and I were going to move into a little cottage,' she said sadly. 'When...'

'I know about the baby,' I said gently. 'Max told me. I'm sorry.'

Her eyes had filled again. I contemplated offering her another cup of tea, but she was already heading towards the front door, determination in her steps. 'Grant would have made a good dad.' There was a tone in her voice that sounded as though she were contradicting someone. 'He really *would*.'

I couldn't answer that. So I opened the door for her, and she passed in a swish of expensive scent, a whirl of hair and the vaguely animal smell of the leathers. When she got to the doorstep, she turned around. 'You've got questions too, haven't you?' she asked. 'I saw you, at the inquest, and you wouldn't have gone if you didn't think there was more to this than Grant being in the wrong place at the wrong time.'

Next Door Left's front door creaked open, and I waved a hand automatically at my neighbour, who passed us with a curious look, his small black dog straining at the lead. 'Well, yes,' I said. 'But then, so much had changed over the years since I saw him last, it was mostly curiosity. It sounded so unlike Grant to get himself blown up in the middle of the night out on the moors. If he'd been electrocuted changing channels on the TV with a bag of peanuts in his lap, I wouldn't have gone, that's pretty much how I always expected him to die.'

'The police will be stripping the site down completely soon,' she said breathlessly. 'Max is trying to get the last bits of research done for his book before there's no building left. Why don't you come back up there tomorrow and we can look for clues?'

'Clues,' I said flatly. 'Jenna, that's what the police are doing.'

'No, they aren't!' She was practically jittering now. 'They think it was just a weird accident with a leaky gas valve! All they are doing is making sure that the site is safe and there's nothing more...' She tailed off, stopped, sniffed and went on, '...that there's really no body left to find. *Please*, Alice, come back up and we can look around together. Maybe see whatever it was that made Grant want to go back up there that night.'

I wanted to tell her that this was real life, not an episode of *Midsomer Murders*. That we were very unlikely to see a ghost that turned out to be a smuggler hiding out in the Fortune House, with Grant trying to prove the existence of the paranormal and being blown up to cover nefarious crimes. Actually, forget *Midsomer Murders*, wasn't that actually the plot of an Enid Blyton book?

But one look at Jenna's face stopped me. Her eyes had lost the flat misery and gained a degree of animation. There was a tinge of colour in her cheeks too. I remembered what Max had said about her issues with food – if I refused to go along with her, would it send her into a spiral of not eating? Was it better to pretend there might be something to find up on the moors, purely for her mental health? Plus, well, Max might be there...

'Well, I could,' I said slowly. 'But it's a bit of a hike.'

Jenna smiled now, and never mind seeing what Grant had seen in her, I practically fancied her myself. Her whole face became rounder and more lively, she sparked with life and energy and the kind of radiant beauty that I could never have been accused of. 'We'll meet you at six, up at the parking spot,' she said. 'I can give you a lift over, save you the walk. Thank you, Alice. This means a lot.' She pulled her helmet on and even managed to look gorgeous with all her features squashed by its padding. 'And thank you for the tea and talking to me.'

She threw a leg over the bike, and it started with a roar that was going to attract the attention of everyone in the street. By tomorrow, they'd probably have constructed a story whereby I was the mastermind of an international drug smuggling ring, I thought, and then reassured myself that I was just still suffering the backwash of Jenna's *Scooby Doo* mindset, and went inside to make an attempt to clean the kitchen floor.

5

I left work early to shower and change before going up onto the moors. That tiny little heat of crush wouldn't let me appear in my creased work clothes, smelling of office biscuits and hot electrics, if Max was going to be there, so I put on a nice shirt and a swishy skirt. A little gesture to not having given up totally, even though he wouldn't notice or even care – it wasn't for Max, it was for me, for my self-respect. After all, he might not even be there; it might be Jenna and me playing at detectives. Like... I groped for a suitable pairing. Starsky and Hutch? No, more like Mulder and Scully.

Before six, I was in the narrow two-car pull-in off the moorland road. The soil was dry and sandy, whipped into little dust devils by the scudding gusts of sudden breeze that came out of nowhere, and I could see the track I'd followed the last time I'd been here, winding its beaten-heather way up and over the curve of the hill. I stayed sitting, hands on the steering wheel and the radio on low, playing some thumping beat that echoed the pounding in my head, and I could have sworn the lyrics contained the words 'stupid Alice'.

There was a roar on the road behind me and the sound of a

powerful engine going down through the gears to get up the slope. I wondered if this was Max, and I had the horrible feeling that he would be wearing bike leathers that made him look like a film star. I beat at my libido with the wet newspaper of all my past rejections and worked on my 'neutral' expression. I didn't have to look aggressively antipathetic, but I didn't want so much as the twitch of an eyelid to give away how attractive I found him.

The bike pulled up alongside the car and stopped, and I had to look up. To my astonishment, Max was clambering down off the pillion seat, looking slightly uncomfortable. He was wearing a leather jacket, but it was too big for him and made him look as though he'd got his dad's clothes on, and his helmet squashed all his features together so he was looking at me through his cheeks. 'Come on,' he said through the car window. 'Jenna will take you down to the site and come back for me.'

Jenna gave me a gloved wave.

'I've never ridden on a motorbike before,' I said, cautiously, getting out and locking the car.

'You have to hang on and balance.' Max handed me the helmet and, after a moment's hesitation, the jacket. 'Jen knows what she's doing. I hate the bloody thing, but it's honestly the quickest way to get there, otherwise I'd rather go by wheelbarrow than have to ride this.'

Cursing the swishy skirt, which I had to fold under me like a nappy, I clambered inelegantly onto the back of the bike. The jacket was enormous on me, my hands flapped halfway up the sleeves and I had to shuffle a good deal of leather up under my armpits to get a grip on Jenna's waist before we were off, scattering gravel and making me feel as though I was about to launch into orbit.

Fortunately, the ride wasn't too long. Jenna swung the bike off the road and down a rutted trackway and then off again across a featureless field of overlong grass studded with tall white daisy-like flowers, but passing through it at speed was like watching the scattering of white when you empty a pocket that's been washed with a tissue in – a blur of bits. After that, I kept my head down and closed my eyes, with my hands clutched so tightly into Jenna's jacket that she must have feared for her circulation, until we eventually bounced an arrival and the bike slowed to a grumbling stop.

I opened my eyes. We were at the head of the dale, close by the blackened circle of earth where the house had stood. I peeled myself off the seat and my skirt fell into damp folds around my legs as Jenna took the helmet and jacket from me, secured them to the bike and took off again with a waved hand, leaving me alone with the exploded aftermath.

It was very, very quiet once the bike had left. I could still hear the echo of it somewhere in the distance, but only in the same way as I could hear the distant trill of a small bird, fluttering high above me like a full stop in search of a sentence. I tried, again, to imagine Grant out here and could only conjure up a vague tone, complaining about the lack of phone coverage.

Cautiously, I approached what was left of the house. Smashed roof tiles crunched under my feet, no walls stood higher than half a metre and the rest lay in a blackened ruin in a small depression which must have been the basement that everything had fallen into to burn. Bits of glass peppered the short grass and glimmered at me as they reflected the evening sun. The site looked untouched, but accident investigators and fire people had been turning it all over since the day it had been discovered. Presumably entropy was winning out – a tendril of sticky bindweed was already inching its way over some of the scattered brickwork.

I closed my eyes and tried to feel... something. Anything. A trace of a presence, whether Grant's or some previous occupant. But all I could feel was the sun on my face, a pernicious little slice of wind coming into the gulley and the slight tickle in my nose from the smell of burned wood and hot brick, plus the heaviness of the moist cotton of my skirt. No ghosts of any kind. I opened my eyes again and lifted a loose brick from the remains of a tumbled wall. It sat in my hand, heavy and real, with absolutely nothing ghostly about it at all, while I squinted around the dale to try to catch sight of anything supernatural. There was nothing more paranormal than the shadows of the trees further up the hill, dusting the grass with darkness and then surrendering to the sunshine and vanishing.

The roar of the bike climbed back up into the register of hearing again and I turned around to watch it pulling to a stop and Max getting off with the same amount of distaste that he'd shown back on the road. Jenna pushed the bike up onto its stand and took her helmet off and the pair of them stood, looking at me. The wind flipped my skirt and I moved to tuck it between my knees. I wouldn't put it past nature to try to complete my appearance of desperation by giving a gigantic gust and revealing my knickers. Also, for the record, gigantic.

I smiled, slightly weakly, at both of them.

'This is it, pretty much the same as it was last week. What do you think?' Max dropped his helmet on the grass.

'Why here?' was all I could say.

Max ran a hand through his hair. He looked tired, I thought. A little less-than-perfect today, although maybe I'd stopped seeing him as unattainably gorgeous and started seeing him as a person since I'd seen him getting off the back of his sister's bike.

'Okay, potted history,' he said, pointing at the house. 'The Fortune House was built in 1920, by Mr and Mrs Fortune, who farmed this little patch of dale with a few sheep and grew some oats, sometimes had a cow or two. In 1925, they had a daughter, Alethia, who left the dale when she was fifteen to go into service and then on to work as a Land Girl. In 1945, they had a son, John, who left home sometime in the sixties and never came back.

'Alethia Fortune inherited the place from her parents back in the eighties and she was living here alone. I'd finished my PhD and started lecturing at York when I first heard the stories about the Fortune House, and I needed a location to form a basis for student projects and work into the psychology of the paranormal. I came up a few times, doing some peripheral work, research, photography, and one day – well, one day something happened that made me knock on her door and ask if I could use the house as a project. She said no.'

Max gave me a slightly rueful grin, which made me think there might have been a few more words than 'no' uttered, then he went on. 'We got friendly, eventually. I think she found it a bit lonely and isolated out here to be honest, although she was a spry old thing who used to cycle down to Pickering for her groceries once a week, until her arthritis got too bad. I'd do a few bits of shopping for her and call in to chat about the house and about growing up out here in the dale. Anyway, *she* died just over a year ago, and since then, I've been bringing groups out here, studying the environment and, it must be said, the people who were willing to come. It's been a valuable resource for field trips.'

Max stopped talking and stared at the ruin. I watched the way his black eyes flickered over the smoke-stained brickwork and the hole, and I wished I could see what he was seeing. A house with a few sheep grazing up against the walls? An old lady dismounting from her bike with relief and wheeling it into a shed? Dark rooms where the temperature dropped without warning and shadows moved with nothing to cause them?

The breeze had another attempt at revealing my pants to the sky and I clamped my skirt tighter between my thighs so it couldn't billow upwards. Jenna was watching me. I wondered if she'd told

Max why she'd asked me to come up here, and what she expected us to find.

'Then Grant started asking if he could come with me out here. Said he wanted to get involved in the ghost-hunting trips. I'd started writing a book about the site, and I'd asked people to send in their ghost stories, so there was quite a bit of admin work to do – he'd begun to help me with that too.'

Jenna made a snuffly little noise of acknowledgement.

'So I started bringing him up with me when the group came – he'd handle some of the equipment and make recordings for me, jobs like that. He really seemed to like it out here. Like I said, he spent a lot of time during vigils wandering around the house.'

'Did he ever see a ghost?' I couldn't avoid the tone of slightly amused sarcasm that crept into my voice. I could sense Jenna straightening up as she put Max's helmet onto the bike seat, on alert. This was why we were here, after all, whatever she might have told Max. 'Or anything that might have brought him back up here that night?'

Max sighed again. 'I'm not sure he would have admitted it if he had,' he said. 'And Grant was showing an interest in what I'd been researching at the house – the part of psychology that is my speciality, researching the *people* who see ghosts. *What* they see is all linked in to *why* they see things, you see. Grant started asking lots of questions about the place – what it used to be, why nobody had laid on mains services, that sort of thing. The things that make this place so unique for my purposes.'

'I'm not sure I—'

He cut me off. 'It was the core of my doctorate. I'm not so interested in whether ghosts exist or not, that's a side issue, I'm trying to get to the bottom of *why* people see things, why they want to see things; what kind of people get interested in the supernatural and what they are hoping to get from it.' He frowned. 'I thought that maybe Grant was starting to believe, and it would have made him valuable, from a research point of view – watching someone actually move from non-believer to fully engaged in the subject. It's surprisingly complicated and a specialised field of psychological study.' Another pause. 'The university is funding it. They're very excited about my work.'

Max didn't sound particularly excited about it himself, more as though he was beginning to wonder now what the hell he'd let himself in for, with the explosions and the deserted wife. Complications that he couldn't even have contemplated when he'd started work on the Fortune House.

He stopped talking and, for a moment, the only sound was the wind shuffling through the heather, as though embarrassed. 'You actually seem interested,' he said finally. 'Most people wander off halfway through that last bit.'

'I am. It's not something I've ever thought about before, ghosts and why people see them,' I said honestly. 'But I'm really going to give it some serious thought now. Probably at about three o'clock in the morning, thanks very much.'

Max grinned. 'Sorry about that.'

I couldn't help but smile back. He sounded so unabashed after scaring me to death, it was amusing.

'But why would Grant come out here in the middle of the night?' Jenna's voice from behind us had a top note of wail in it. 'He didn't say anything, he told me he had something to do, got up and...' She tailed off into snuffles again.

Max turned round to look at her. 'Maybe he *had* seen something. People on their way home, coming past the house, have reported things – it's a shortcut down the dale,' he explained to me. 'The Fortunes were a bit territorial, didn't like people on their land, apparently. Old Mr Fortune used to chase them off with a shotgun if he saw them, but you know what people are like. That didn't stop locals on their way back from the pub cutting through the bottom of the yard there.' He turned and pointed. I looked, although I didn't know why, there was no yard left to see, just the grassy expanse where we'd had our picnic. 'And it's quite close to a footpath.'

'It can't have been much fun for them, out here, though.' I looked around at the way the rocks broke the thin soil and the absence of anything else. 'Scraping a living and both their children having grown up and gone. Why didn't they move into town?'

'Stubbornness, I suspect.' Max went closer to the wrecked house. 'And it was their home.'

'Did *they* ever complain about it being haunted?' I asked.

He shook his head. 'Nothing I've found suggests that. No, actually, there was one report from a neighbour, someone who used to call in now and again.'

'A *neighbour*?' I looked around pointedly at the lack of anything approaching another house. 'Living in what, a tent?'

'There were other houses out here then.' He gave me another smile. 'Lime kiln workers, other farmers. This was quite a busy place up until the early seventies, you know.'

I let the silence, the air heavy with nothing but bees and the wind, do the sarcasm for me, and he went on. 'The neighbour said that the Fortunes were always a bit jittery in the house, once John had left. Didn't like letting people come in. And the place felt dark and oppressive, there was an "atmosphere", apparently.'

'Well, that's gone,' I said. 'Along with everything else. Can you *have* atmosphere, when there's nothing to be atmospheric *in*?'

Max actually laughed at that. 'Don't you feel that this whole dale has a kind of *ambience*? A weird sort of mood?'

I let the air flow around me and tried to feel something. 'Not really. If anything, it's a bit too try-hard, with all the rocks and the trees and shadows and stuff. It's a bit like those lads in town who wear big trainers and talk like roadmen and pretend to be in street gangs. You just know that they're all called Simon and their dad drives a BMW.'

'Right...' Max looked around him. 'I'm not sure I can ever do any more research here now.'

I made a face. 'Sorry about that,' I said, echoing his earlier words. 'But you're right, it does feel lonely here. Isolated. No wonder Alethia left at fifteen.'

'And her brother left when he got to a similar age.'

'Ah, the blissful rural life,' I said, and my tone was so weighted that Max raised his eyebrows.

'You sound a bit cynical.'

'Thirty-four years living in Pickering, listening to the tourists talking about getting a little holiday place up here, and thinking that I bet living through a few Yorkshire Februaries would change their minds.'

'Ah. Yes, the attractions of horizontal sleet and daylight that only lasts five minutes.' Max was smiling again. He seemed to have forgiven me for not being able to feel 'atmosphere', whatever that was.

Jenna made 'throat clearing' noises. She must have heard the story of the Fortune House so many times by now that there was no charm to it any more.

'Do you want me to get the camera off the bike? There's only about another hour before the sun starts to drop behind the hill and you won't get the light. And I promised to show Alice around the site, properly.'

'It's fine, Jen. I need the long shadows anyway.' Another look flicked at me. 'I'm bringing some groups up this week. Before they come, one group gets shown pictures taken in the half-dark, all brooding and gaunt, and the other group has the daylight sunny pictures.'

'So you're trying to influence what they see before they even get here?'

The look Max was giving me changed. Up until now it had been almost amused, almost light-hearted. Now he tilted his head as though to change his angle of regard. 'Oh,' he said. 'You get that?'

I was interested. I hated to admit it, because I didn't *want* to be interested in Max Allbright, with his shiny hair and his long legs and his work out here. But this was intriguing. 'What else do you do?'

Behind us, Jenna made a sort of 'humph' noise and started rummaging in the bags on the back of the bike. Max sat down on the cropped grass and looked up at me. 'Well, I have to have a control group who know nothing about the place – they're told we're coming up on a photography session. I do photography, you see, alongside the whole...' He waved a hand, meant to indicate, presumably, a haunted house investigation site rather than implying that he routinely blew things up. 'There are question-naires for them to fill in before and after. That was one of Grant's jobs, handing them out. It was good having him do it because it kept me at one remove, if you see what I mean.'

'So nobody suspected your underlying motives? I can see how that might influence a control group.'

Over Max's shoulder, Jenna was jerking her head at me and I remembered why I'd really agreed to come and that basking in the glory that was Max Allbright's attention was merely a side effect. 'Anyway. Jenna's going to show me around a bit, if that's all right.'

He looked taken aback again. 'Well, yes, of course. Why wouldn't it be?'

I couldn't think of a single reply to that apart from 'I might scare all the ghosts away', but he'd said that ghosts weren't the point anyway, so I ignored him and went over to where Jenna was rotating with anticipation at the thought of actually investigating something.

'He's all right really, Max,' she said. 'He's just a bit pompous. And overprotective. And a wuss about bikes.'

'That's quite a long list of drawbacks for someone who's "all right really",' I said without thinking as we walked closer to the demolished remains of the house. 'And at least he has a sense of humour.'

'I suppose he does.' Jenna stopped and turned around. 'But he's my brother. I'm contractually obliged to find him an insufferable dick at times.' She flashed me a smile and it was a proper relaxed, uncomplicated smile, which made her look a lot like Max. 'But thank you for coming, despite him, Alice. I'm really very grateful. It's nice to have someone else who understands how I'm feeling. Why I want to be here.'

I cleared my throat. 'So. What are we looking for?' I spared the blackened remains of brickwork a quick glance. 'There's not much left to investigate.'

Instantly the purpose seemed to flow out of Jenna and her shoulders resumed their slump. 'I don't know.' She sounded defeated again. 'Anything. *Anything*. Just some clue as to why Grant came up here that night.'

'How did he get here?' I asked idly.

'He borrowed the bike. The police found it up here and brought it back. That was how I found out about... what happened.'

I had a sudden image of the police on my doorstep. Jenna, as a girlfriend, wouldn't have been accorded that dignity. 'I'm sorry.' A loose brick under my hand broke in two and then crumbled. I sifted the dust, unthinking. 'I didn't know Grant could ride a motorbike?'

'Neither did I. Oooh, do you think that's a clue? I mean, it must have been something urgent to make him take my bike! It's not really been the same since, either.'

'Where's his car?'

'He sold it. Didn't need it, he said.'

I looked sideways at Jenna. She was scrambling over some outlying rock, past a tattered section of police tape, and didn't seem to be worried. 'So how was he getting to jobs?'

'He was doing all his work virtually.' Jenna panted into place atop a pointy boulder. 'Didn't need to be there in person, he said, remote working was better. Anyway. This bit here was the outhouse. You're standing in the middle of the kitchen. Can you see anything that looks – odd?'

I scanned the whole gulley. At the bottom of the site, I could see Max, camera in hand, resting his back against a whippy little birch tree. I tore my eyes away and looked elsewhere. Over the snaggly collection of loose bricks, shattered glass and into the dip where the cellar had been, where smashed concrete, like icebergs in a sea of rubble, jutted angular and grey. It looked timeworn and established, as though there had never been anything more than a pile of debris here. I could not imagine what the house would have looked like, occupying the middle of this little valley, a lone dwelling in the belly of the hills. A few sparse bushes paddled against the wind for a second and then were still, and a collection of ornithology fluttered skyward to become dark dots against the bright sky.

'There's nothing to see.' I tried to sound gentle. 'And what if what Grant came up for was in the house? It's all gone, Jenna. *He's* gone.'

She sighed a sigh so deep it sounded as though her lungs were turning inside out. 'I know.' A half-turn, so that she was looking out across the valley. 'Really. I do know. I feel so *helpless*. I mean, I thought I knew Grant pretty well, I thought we were a proper partnership. But he didn't tell me what it was that he came up here for and I want to know why he would keep a secret like that.'

Graceful and balletic, she jumped down off the boulder and

came over to me. I instantly felt as though my legs retracted and my bottom expanded so I stood like a boiled egg beside Kendall Jenner.

'Could he have been meeting someone?'

'Another woman?' Jenna sounded as though she'd already thought of this one. 'But why would he have to come all the way out here to do it? It wasn't as though I followed him around all day, he could have met someone in town during the day.'

'But you said he got rid of his car? How would he have got there?' I couldn't somehow conjure the image of Grant jumping on the 128 bus to go on illicit excursions.

'Oh, there are cars he could have used,' Jenna said vaguely. 'And besides... Grant... I can't see it being someone else. Not like that, anyway.' She flicked me a look, as though she hoped I hadn't understood, and I fought hard to keep my expression neutral. Grant had never been the most sexual of men and it looked as though it hadn't been entirely my fault. A little weight of guilt that had hung from my heart like a pendulum, swinging from 'he didn't really fancy me' to 'he probably had low testosterone', snapped off and fell.

'But I doubt he was admiring the view.' I scanned the little site once more, trying not to look over to where Max had set a tripod low down against the grass and was crouching to take pictures.

Jenna picked up a burned brick and turned it over. 'You admit it's a mystery?' She scraped at the blackened surface with a nail. 'You can see why I think it's not as straightforward as everyone seems to believe?'

I looked out again. Wind-bent grasses hissed the passage of a breeze that also hushed its way through the branches of the weedy birches. Nature hummed into the otherwise silent air. Imagining Grant out here was like trying to imagine a killer whale at a Pilates class. 'It does seem out of character,' I said. 'But I hadn't seen him for years. Nobody is going to take any notice of anything I say. Have you mentioned your doubts to the police?'

'I'm the bereaved girlfriend. Plus I – well, when my previous relationship broke up, and then when we... when I miscarried...' She stopped and then looked at me as though trying to work out whether I was trustworthy enough to tell her secrets to. 'I had a few mental health issues,' she said to the ground. 'I mean, I'm fine now, I'm better, but it's the kind of history that follows you, if you see what I mean.'

Max had packed away the tripod now. He was sitting, looking dark and moody, by a pile of stone that might be the remains of a wall or a small cairn. 'So the police are just dismissing your concerns.'

'Yes! But you feel it too, don't you? How wrong it all was for Grant to be here in the middle of the night?'

Shadows gathered and flitted. The sun was dipping behind the rising shoulder of hill behind us, throwing long shades from small objects. The heather became pillowy outlines, and the trees took on long, sinister shapes against the sky.

'It is odd, yes.' It was all I could say. 'Look, Max is packing up. Maybe we'd better go back.'

Jenna dropped the brick she'd been picking at and looked at me. I couldn't tell if she felt encouraged by my agreement or as though I were dismissing her concerns, which was my aim. I hadn't wanted to slap down her theories, but, on the other hand, I didn't want drive her any further into TV Mystery Land. After all, it *was* odd, that was no lie. But there were also plenty of believable reasons he could have been out here, if you ignored Grant's general hatred of the outdoors. After all, they'd *both* suffered the shock of the loss of their baby. It had caused Jenna's mental health to lapse, maybe it had driven Grant to seek out the peace and solitude of the moors at night? Stranger things happened. But I didn't want to drag all that up, remind her of a time so painful that it had sent her back to an eating disorder.

Maybe my mother had been right with her 'least said, soonest mended' mindset.

'I'll drop you back at your car.' Jenna disconsolately turned her back on the ruined Fortune House and led the way back across the little valley.

'You can take Max first if he wants.'

She gave me a look I couldn't fathom. 'He'll be fine here on his own. He likes sitting here while it gets dark. It's probably all part of being a psychology professor. I've met some of his colleagues. They're all rather prone to wearing too much black and trying to look mysterious.'

Max didn't even look up as we returned and climbed onto the bike. His eyes were full of the dale, staring out across the fold in the hills and the tossed-about brickwork. He'd lain the camera down beside him and didn't seem to register us leaving by so much as a twitch of the hand.

But then, I thought, as I peeled myself off the bike seat, flapped a farewell to Jenna and got back into my car, did I really expect any different?

* * *

Personal communication, first person, Bertram Salter, experiencer of event. Transcribed from recorded conversation.

It were round 1970 or such. Me and the boys were getting in a hay crop from the daleside, over near to the Fortune place, and I'd warned the lads not to get over onto their land. Old Jack Fortune, he were a devil if he thought his land were being trespassed; he'd come out with his gun, waving it about and firing. He were never really right since his lad went off to that London, he'd been a right mardy bugger before that too, but once his kids left, he just got worse and worse.

So we're turning the hay and putting it up onto the trailer. I were out on the far hedgerow. I were a lad of about fifteen, and there were a couple of lasses out with us that day, so we were all having a bit of a flirt and not paying too much mind to what we were doing, but then I realised that I needed to piss. And obviously I doesn't want to do it right there in front of the lasses, so I puts my rake down and I went off t'other side of hedge, into the little thicket of birches and firs over there, between us and the Fortune place.

I gets in there and has my piss. Now, we've been working since dawn and it were a hot old day up there and we'd taken some cider, so I reckon that the dark and the cool of the wood made me come over a bit strange, because I suddenly comes over a bit mazed and I had to sit down. I don't know how to tell it, really, it sounds a bit strange, but it were like the whole wood went black just then. Like it were the middle of the night. I'm sitting with my back against this tree, waiting for the feeling to pass, and it's so dark that I can't even see the far edge of the wood and it's not a big forest or nothing, about half an acre of copse that Jack planted up during the last war. I should have been able to see right clear through to the field where we were haymaking.

All of a sudden, this man runs past me. Quick as you like, I hardly had time to notice him. But he's running, running through the trees like he's running for his life. And then I realises that, for all he's running, he's making no sound. He should have been crashing along, going through branches and breaking twigs and such, but there's nothing. And then he's gone. Not gone out of the wood, just – gone, like he fell into a big hole in the ground, disappeared.

I don't mind telling you, it put fair put the wind up me. That weren't no flesh-and-blood person, not running so quiet like and gone like someone put a candle out. I came over all cold and I shut my eyes and I sat there and then all the sound came back and I could hear the birds singing again and the lads shouting in the field, and when I opened my eyes again, the daylight were back, and the wood were just the little copse I've known near enough all my life. Well, I ran out of there like the hounds of hell were after me and everyone come over cos I were white and shaking and kind of trying to get my words out to tell them what I seen. Mr Sleightholme, he were in charge of the haying, he sent me home after that. Said I'd probably got a touch too much of the sun and I should wear a hat and knock off drinking the cider while I were working. But you asked for anyone who'd seen anything up round the Fortune place, and that were what happened to me.

6

Work was quiet that week. People tend not to think about their windows when the weather is sunny and warm, so new orders were thin on the ground and my main responsibility was making sure our team of fitters were in the right place, replacing the windows of the cottage at number nine, rather than stripping out the unwilling windows at number eight amid the shouted admonishments of the residents – it had been known to happen.

But I found I was bored, as though my exposure to the Allbrights had flipped some kind of switch in me, and made the familiarity of spreadsheets and emails no longer enough. Chatting idly with Malcolm or Sheila, who ran the boss's office in a rather old-fashioned way, no longer had any charm, nor did the daily cake run to the baker's in the Market Place. My mind kept coming back to Grant, to Jenna, to that house on the moors. And, yes, all right, to a little bit of pleasant daydreaming about Max Allbright too, but that got pushed into the background of general musing.

What the hell had Grant been doing up on the moors that night? *Had* he seen something he couldn't explain? If so, why had he not taken it to Max? Was it something he didn't want Max to know about? But what the hell could that have been, given that he'd been helping Max out at the site?

All I could come up with was that Grant had been there for a reason he didn't want Max, and presumably Jenna either, to know about. Something he felt he'd had to hide from them both. What on earth could have been so mysterious that he couldn't even mention it to his girlfriend? None of it made any sense.

I browsed around on the internet but didn't really learn any more than Max had already told me about the history of the Fortune House, although I did find some of Max's published articles, which I read with a touch of wonder. I actually *knew* someone who'd got stuff published! Whose work appeared, peppered with words like 'peer review pending' and 'possible patholigisation of psycho-traumatic incidents', some of which I had to look up.

The articles were interesting. They seemed to boil down to 'people see what they expect to see', influenced by not just what they'd been told about a site but also by their past experiences and upbringing. Total disbelievers generally saw shadows and sought a logical explanation for anything odd that happened, whereas those primed to see ghosts saw 'mystery and the inexplicable' at the same place and time. I began to follow up references and found myself forgetting about the mystery of what Grant had been up to, in favour of reading the journals of the Institute for Parapsychological Research and the writings of James Randi. It was fascinating.

Unfortunately, all the tales of mysterious shapes and voices and figures that appeared and disappeared wouldn't leave my brain and I found myself wide awake in the middle of Friday night, listening to every creak on the landing in a fever of dark expectation, much as I'd told Max I would. My little terraced house was well over two hundred years old – what if ghosts really *did* exist? What if they hung around places they had known in life, and were, even now, massing at the top of my stairs?

I turned resolutely away from the wall by the door and faced the wall that lay between me and Next Door Right, through which I could hear the faint wail of the baby crying for its three o'clock feed. Or was it? Was it a *real* baby? Or the spectre of a long-mourned child, dead in some outbreak of typhoid or cholera but doomed forever to cry out for its parents in the deep watches of the night?

Oh, for goodness' sake, Alice! This was no time for a dormant, and previously unsuspected, imagination to come roaring to the fore. I sat up and put on the light.

It was that peculiar hour that is either very, very late or much too early, and outside all was quiet, apart from the slight buzz of the street lighting and the distant sound of cats fighting. No traffic ruffled the air, even the early workers hadn't got going yet, and the air hung heavy and oppressive under the night. I was never going to get back to sleep. I dared the possibly phantom-strewn landing and went downstairs to make myself a cup of tea and turn all the lights on to try to drive the dreams away.

Whilst I was waiting for the kettle to boil and tidying the kitchen in a desultory way, I had a sudden thought. *I could drive up and look at the site of the Fortune House in the dark.* Then I'd have a chance to see if there was anything that could have drawn Grant's attention that only lingered in the crepuscular shadows or under the depths of midnight. And if I found nothing, then that would help to reassure Jenna. I could check it out and report back that there were no ghosts, no weirdly moving lights or haunting wails; no half-formed creatures creeping through the low grasses...

... actually, no. The idea was far too scary. It would be dark and dangerous, and I might twist my ankle and lie there until someone found me, a rotted corpse, flyblown and – for goodness' sake! Stop it! There was nothing there. Nothing existed out there on the moor that I couldn't personally poke in the eye. Fear lay all in the mind, wasn't that the central tenet of Max's research?

Before I could talk myself out of it, I put a jacket on over my pyjamas, locked up the house and took a firm grip on my phone, in case I *did* twist my ankle. It was bad enough Max seeing me all pink and sweaty, but the possibility of his falling over my hefty corpse didn't bear thinking about. Then I got into the car and drove up onto the moor.

I didn't park in the pull-in. Instead, I drove carefully along until I found the beginning of the rutted track down which Jenna had taken me on the bike, and parked there. It still meant a good mile of stumbling progress over tiny snares of bush, but knowing that nobody could see me through the thick dark made it easier to accept the constant falling over. By the time I arrived at the lip of ground where the moor dropped into the gulley, my pyjama trousers were studded with fragments of undergrowth and my hair had come down from its night-time bun in wisps and straggles. I was puffing, too.

The sky stretched, star-strewn and perfect, above me. I'd got my night vision now too, so I could make out the line of the old house amid the shattered remains. Somehow it was easier to see what would have been, in the dark. That line along there, that would have been the outside wall, and Jenna had told me that the little square at the back had been the outhouse. A tattered bunting of wallpaper showed where an internal wall had once stretched across the middle and not been completely obliterated by the blast. I'd thought it was quiet in town, but the quiet up here was something solid. It felt as though my ears had been stuffed with the night. There was a faint whistle from the wind passing through the dale and a shiver of leaves, but that was all.

I sat down with my back to a boulder and my knees under my chin. The thought of Grant up here, searching either for something corporeal or ethereal, still didn't compute. I couldn't see anything that might have called him from a warm bed to this silent, shadow-filled scoop in the landscape. Plus, it was cold, even on this summer night. I could almost convince myself that there was something supernatural about the chill, except that the practicality I'd been born with assured me that sitting on the ground in the small hours wearing only a thin coat and pyjamas this high up was never going to be balmy. The shadows that seemed to move, masses of blackness that flowed and writhed around the stumps of wall still standing, weren't paranormal visitors either. They were the result of what little light there was from the stars and the falling moon being blocked by brickwork and flickering in the breeze.

No. There was nothing here.

I stood up and ricocheted off something behind me. With a mind full of ghosts and skin already pricked to goose pimples with cold, I had a brief moment of total terror. My mouth felt as though it were being sucked towards my stomach, my heart squeezed its way up into the veins of my neck and all my limbs flailed a panicked retreat, tumbling me over backwards into the heather.

And then the very unparanormal swearing started.

'What the fuck...? Who the bloody hell are you? And what the fuck are you doing up here?'

It was Max. I'd only gone and cannoned off the person I least wanted to walk into whilst in my current state of sartorial inelegance and with middle-of-the-night hair. Hell, I'd even have preferred some kind of supernatural visitation than this very corporeal incident. 'It's me. Alice,' I said, trying to stem the torrent of abuse he was currently unleashing in my direction. 'I came up here to... well, Jenna said Grant...' I tailed off. There wasn't really a good, sensible reason for my being here, I now realised. I'd let the generalised megrims of a three o'clock in the morning waking get the better of me. 'I just am,' I finished. 'There's no law against it, is there?'

The previously apparently unperturbable Max was staggering around clutching at his chest as though he was having some kind of cardiac incident, but at least he'd stopped swearing now. 'You – Alice?'

'Yes. Alice Donaldson, Grant's ex-wife.'

'Yes, I know who you are.' Another moment of fist to the sternum and he flopped to the heather, a shadowy outline in front of me. 'It's more *where* you are. Up here? In the middle of the night?'

'It's four o'clock, actually,' I said, trying to force myself to be factual and yet helpful at the same time.

'Still with the where, rather than the when.' He sounded rather breathless. I wondered if I'd driven the wind out of him with the body-impact. 'What the hell are you doing here?'

'But you've only ever seen me here.' I couldn't shut my mouth up. It was trying to follow the 'reasonable' right to its conclusion, when I really wanted it to stop talking and let me breathe through it for a moment. 'So, for all you know, I live down the dale.'

Max's face was a pale circle. He was wearing black and with his dark hair it was giving him the look of a levitating head. 'No, you don't,' he said. 'You live in Pickering, Jenna told me she'd been to your house. And that you were very kind to her. Thank you.' He clambered to his feet. It was, I was glad to see, a very inelegant manoeuvre.

'That's all right. She was very unhappy, and with what you told me about her mental health, I didn't like to just dismiss her, even if I think she's talking rubbish about Grant.'

'It was still kind. Given that you and she have a somewhat complicated reason for knowing one another.' A pause. 'You do seem a very kind person, Alice.' His voice was softer now.

I was flustered and it made me babble. 'No more so than the average person, I don't think. And I do have frequent daydreams of doing Malcolm a mischief when he "helpfully" tidies up my paperwork, which definitely do *not* contain any kindness. More a degree of stuffing him in his own filing cabinet, really.'

'Well, regardless of that. You still seem kind.' There was a moment's pause. 'But, of course, I don't know Malcolm. He may be utterly innocent and undeserving of whatever mental punishment you've devised.' A hand came out towards me. 'Why are you lying down?'

I took it and hauled myself to my feet, not worrying for once about my weight and how much effort it might have cost him. 'I fell over. It's really dark out here and I didn't see you.'

'Right. And who's Malcolm?'

'Malcolm?'

'You were just talking about him. Is he here with you?' Max's shadowed outline seemed to survey the surroundings as though in search of a lost accountant.

Now I was upright I could see that he was wearing a dark trench coat, black boots and a black beanie style hat. He looked like a manga version of a paranormal investigator. 'No! And why are *you* here?'

'Um, it's my job?' There was a tone of almost sarcastic amusement that instantly made me feel every inch of my sloth-printed pyjama-clad body.

'But your job is writing about the psychology of ghost hunters, isn't it? How much of *that* can you do at four in the morning on a deserted moor?' My reply was snippy in consequence. 'There isn't anyone *to* analyse.'

'There's you,' came the equally snippy reply. 'And, possibly, the mysterious Malcolm. Who either is or isn't here, I've not quite got to the bottom of that one.'

'Malcolm is our accounts person. He is most definitely not here.'
I was beginning to feel a bit baffled. 'I only mentioned him because
– actually I'm not really sure how he came into the conversation
now.'

'So what did *you* expect to see out here?' The sarcasm was gone
now, his tone was pure amusement, almost as though he was
enjoying himself.

As the adrenaline of our physical encounter drained out of me,
so did my attitude and my energy. After all, I'd hardly slept, it was
the small hours of the morning and here I was, in my PJs, facing off
with a man I had only just reasoned myself out of having a crush
on. It was *painful*. 'Nothing,' I said, heavily. 'Absolutely nothing.'

'Then I'd guess that's exactly what you did see. I've got a PhD in
this, you know.'

Jenna was right, I thought. He *was* pompous. So certain of
himself and his rightness, sure that his assumptions were correct.
Just because he was writing a book, that didn't make him any better
than me, really, did it?

'I'm not sure,' I said, wanting to puncture his certainty. 'I
thought I saw something moving, over there, for a second.'

'A shape? A figure?'

Again that tiredness, that rearing up of the part of my personality that made me wonder what the hell I was doing, trying to talk
to people more intelligent than me. 'Shadows,' I said. 'Just the dark.'

'Nothing that might have brought Grant out here?' Max was
looking at me. Although his face was little more than a circle,
slightly paler than the sky, I could feel his close attention.

'I don't know the place well enough to know,' I said, matter-of-
factly. 'It doesn't look like the kind of place that drug-dealers would
use – too far out from civilisation. And anyone hiding anything out
here would run the risk of ramblers falling over it, which rather
rules out the chance of it being used to stash stolen goods. And

besides, we're talking about Grant here, not Hercule Poirot.' I waved a hand at the night. 'It's all just shadows.'

More silence. I couldn't see where he was looking, if his eyes had gone in the direction I'd indicated or whether he was staring out over the moor in general. Then he spoke again, and his voice was different now, it had lost the gently humorous, almost teasing, edge. 'Jenna's really unhappy,' he said. 'I don't know what to do. She got a little better after she brought you up here, but I'm worried about her again. She's so caught up in what she thinks Grant was doing up here – she told me that you both came up to "investigate".'

'Yes, I'm sorry. I didn't mean to encourage her.' I felt better talking to him when his tone was more normal. 'But she does have something of a point. What *was* Grant doing up here?'

'It's the explosion that bothers me.' Max shrugged himself down into his big coat. I was starting to really feel the cold now. Cotton pyjamas aren't really moorland wear, and I was praying to any deities which might be hanging around out here that he hadn't noticed the cute sloths. 'Some of those propane cylinders had been up here for years. I left them because we sometimes had overnighters up in the house and it was useful to be able to cook breakfast in the mornings and put a bit of heat through the place now and again. In a somewhat more controlled fashion than eventually happened,' he added, turning to look over the remnants of house.

'So the cylinders were full?'

'I got them replaced when they ran out.' He turned around now, I saw the flick of his coat and hair. 'Alethia left this place to me, you see.' Hands in pockets, he was just an outline against the lightening sky. 'If there'd been any insurance, I'm fairly sure the police would still have me in an interview room, but as it stands, there's no profit in the destruction.' A sigh. 'It's a shame. I could have lived here.'

'Was there electricity?'

He shook his head, and I saw the hair flick again. 'Nope. Only the gas, powering everything. No mains water or sewerage either.'

I had a momentary image of this dark man wandering around a large, unlit house. Holding a candle. 'How Victorian.'

'Well, yeah, I would have had to run mains power out here, of course.' The dismissive way he said this told me that he came from money. From privilege. From the sort of background where dropping a few thousand pounds on electrifying an isolated property miles from the nearest supply was more a matter of inconvenience than a financial impossibility.

'So it's not beyond the realms of possibility that Grant came up here, went into the house, lit a match or a candle and...' I raised both hands in an 'explosive' gesture. 'Which is what the police think happened.'

'And that's exactly what happened.' Max sounded fierce now. 'It *has* to be. But Jenna won't have it. I think, deep down, she knows it's as simple as that. But she wants there to be more to it, she wants it to be a mystery, and that's what's so worrying.'

'Where's your car?' I asked suddenly. 'I didn't see one up at the track. How did you get here?'

A faint tinge of brightness was highlighting the hills now, I could see. The merest dusting of illumination, as though someone was very slowly turning up a dimmer switch on the world. I could see Max more clearly, see the detail of his eyes and his chin. He was looking at me, but thankfully I didn't blush, although I did shuffle the sloths about a bit to try to conceal the worst of the cuteness.

'I'm parked a bit further down,' he said at last. 'I like walking over the moors at night.'

'How very Heathcliff of you,' I said without thinking.

'I like to think I'm nicer to my women.'

Now the blush came roaring in, heating my chin, my cheeks and my forehead, as though I'd been standing under a sun lamp. Even though he hadn't meant anything by it, I still blushed. God, I felt pathetic.

'Well,' I said, awkward as usual. 'I ought to go.' Hopefully the oncoming dawn still wasn't bright enough to reveal my pinkness. Maybe, I thought optimistically, it was adding some interesting shading to my face. Giving me cheekbones. 'Now I'm positive there's nothing mysterious going on up here at night.'

'Apart from you and the invisible Malcolm roaming the moors.' There it was, that slight tone of teasing again. Weirdly, it stopped me feeling so overwhelmed by Max, made him more human.

'Obviously.' I tugged my inadequate jacket further towards my knees. 'Come along, Invisible Malcolm, let's go.'

Max laughed, a proper deep laugh, as though I'd been really funny, rather than responding to his ridiculousness. Then he said, 'Come over,' really quickly, as though he'd only just thought the words and they were bursting out of his mouth without any consideration. 'Tomorrow. Oh, well, today really, I suppose. Come and talk to Jenna,' he added, as though I might have thought he was inviting me to see him. 'You've got that mix of pragmatism and empathy that might help her to get to grips with losing Grant and understanding that he wasn't up to anything out here.'

Had I? Pragmatism and empathy? 'Well, I...' I hastily tried to think of a previous engagement but couldn't come up with anything. I had been going to wash the sofa covers, but as I wasn't taking them to the local river and banging them on a rock, that was hardly an all-day excuse. Plus he really did sound worried about his sister. 'All right.'

'Here.' A tiny square of card thrust out from one of his pockets under my nose. 'This is us. See you at about three?'

Jenna had said she was living with her brother, hadn't she? I took the card without looking at it and pushed it into my pocket, then shivered. There was a chill down my spine – whether to do with the sharp coolness of the early hour, a particularly localised breeze or the stern words I was having with myself about noticing Max's fingers brush mine as he handed me the card, I didn't know.

'You're not really dressed for it up here, are you?' He took a couple of steps back and raised his eyebrows. 'In fact, aren't those your pyja…?'

'Thank you, tell Jenna I will see her this afternoon,' I said, as haughtily as I could manage. The light level was increasing fast, and my nightwear was becoming far more apparent. Any minute now, the sun would come up and I would be highlighted in all my jungle-animal glory. Some of the sloths were wearing nightcaps and I didn't think I could stand the humiliation. I turned around to begin the stomp back across the meadow and up the track to my car, feeling the cold beginning to spread between my shoulder blades now. Maybe I could run, to warm myself up? But the thought that Max could be right behind me, watching me, and my bra-less state that would mean discomfort and the sound of slapping flesh, kept me to a decorous walk.

I'd got about a hundred metres when there was a flash of black beside me. 'Here.' A sudden draping warmth descended over my shoulders. 'You look frozen. Bring it back later.' And then Max was gone, as though he'd evaporated into the scenery, leaving me with his coat wrapped around me and the birds beginning their early-morning vocal routines from the gorse bushes and the heather. I stood for a moment, as though I suspected a joke, then carefully, without turning around, continued on my way over the stunted grass. I was almost sure I heard a voice carried on a snatch of wind say, 'Nicer than Heathcliff!' but I couldn't be sure whether it had been Max or my inner monologue.

I arrived back at the road, in a state of wonder that Max had invited me over. It had hardly been 'assignation of the century', I was going there for Jenna, but even so, it was the closest I'd come to being asked out for some time. I wanted to hold that feeling for a little bit longer. A gorgeous man had given me his number and his coat, had teased me lightly, and in my world, that was up there with 'being swept off my feet', fanning the embers of my imagination into the tiniest spark of potential.

Then I sighed as the weight of reality and practicality settled itself around me again and forced that little spark back into the darkest regions of night-time fancy. The sun was coming up now and I was profoundly glad of the coverage of the large coat. I hadn't really considered dawn when I'd set out, and my nightwear was clearly visible to any and all cars coming down the moorland road as I headed back to my parking space. I would have looked like an escaped hospital patient hiking along in my quickly slipped on shoes and inadequate jacket, but the flapping length of the big black coat covered the worst. I probably still looked like I was heading for the nearest soup kitchen for a good meal, but at least I was decently covered.

The sun breasted the distant rise of hills and inched its way vertically, clearing the last of the night from the sky and making the tarmac steam. I stood and watched morning arrive over the undulating acres of moorland. Birds began to flutter and scoop above me, the occasional car dashed past, ripping noisy holes in the fabric of the quiet dawn and the wind carried fragments of torn sentences from early walkers. The dark, loaded atmosphere of the night had gone. Even the site of the Fortune House was invisible from here, beyond a hump of hill and dropped into its little gulley. No wonder nobody had noticed the destruction for days.

I gathered Max's coat more closely around me and got into the driver's seat. The coat smelled of strangeness, of different cupboards and houses. A hint of orange peel, a smoky smell like incense – I realised that I'd dropped my chin under the collar when the stiff fabric scratched against my cheek and pulled myself upright again with a quick look to see if anyone had noticed. There was no one *to* notice. Just a sheep that had wandered out to sit in the middle of the road, placidly chewing its breakfast.

I made a face at myself in the mirror, and drove home.

7

The address on the card said 'Hatherleigh Hall'. It sounded grand but I'd never heard of it, and my satnav took me down lanes of decreasing size until I ended up in a village on the outskirts of York. I say 'village', but the whole place had the uniform look of an estate, built by a lord of the manor to house his cap-doffing underlings in slightly less squalor than might otherwise have been the case, and I became increasingly uneasy as the coordinates brought me closer and closer to an enormous grey stone building. It had a square and uncompromising frontage, with the occasional pillar breaking the lines, as though it had been designed by someone handy with a ruler and uncertain about curves. Max and Jenna lived *here*?

Maybe the place had been divided into those posh flats that historic buildings all seemed to be turned into these days. High ceilings, moulded cornices and an impossibility of dusting; all carefully furnished and decorated 'in keeping', and horribly expensive. I reassured myself with the prosaic thought of Max standing on a chair to remove cobwebs from a ceiling rose and then berated myself for thinking of him at all, but somehow my imagination wouldn't put Jenna and dusting together. She seemed too ethereal for housework. Born to languish, was Jenna, drooping pale and solitary on a chaise, with a small handkerchief and a slight cough. But then I remembered her confident in leathers, riding that powerful motorbike, and wondered which version of Jenna Grant had seen and fallen for.

There was an absence of marked parking bays on the expanse of gravel outside the columned and porticoed front of Hatherleigh Hall, so I left my car lowering the tone beside a Range Rover and went to the front door. There was no row of buzzers and intercoms either. It made me uneasy. I didn't know whether I was supposed to knock and wait for a butler or fling the door open and yell, 'Flat number nine, I'm here!' There was something about the formality of the building that caused me to hesitate, but the informality of the scattered parking let me know there were people about, they just weren't *here*. In the end, I spotted a huge bell-pull behind a pillar, and gave it a couple of diffident tugs.

Nothing happened for long enough for me to think I should get back in the car, when Jenna appeared around the side of the house, wearing an apron which was covered in flour. 'Oh, hi, Alice! Sorry, I was baking, we don't really use the front door much these days, come around the side.'

She was holding her hands out in front of her, scattering grains and gobbets of dough as she came, and I wondered if *this* had been the Jenna that Grant had found so intriguing. He'd loved food but hated cooking and I'd always wondered whether it had been my winning ways with a chocolate muffin that had swung him round to marrying me. I followed the trail of flour and finally caught up with her heading in through a small door in the side of the enormous building. 'You live here? The whole *house*?'

We pattered on down a long corridor lined with paintings and tapestries and eventually ended up in a large kitchen, where the bronze and copper pans gleamed like an outback sky from hangers on the ceiling and everything was super-scale, as though we were Lilliputians trying to make a go of it in the regular world. Jenna filled me in as we went. 'Well, no, we have a flat upstairs. But we open the house on Sundays in summer, and we start next week, so I'm trying to make a job lot of scones to freeze, for the teashop.' Jenna knocked a stray wisp of hair away from her face with the back of a wrist. 'Sit down over there, I'll get these in the oven and then I'll take you up. Max is around somewhere, he said he'd asked you over, and I really should repay you for your hospitality the other week when I dropped in unannounced.'

I sat and enjoyed the smell of fresh cooking and industrial cleaner. Jenna was following a recipe on an iPad, trying to scroll down the page without touching the screen with floury fingers, and it gave me a sudden idea. 'Jenna, did you check Grant's computer?'

'Mmmm?' She added some milk to a bowl. 'What for?'

'Well, he may have had something on there that gave him a reason for going up to the site on the moors.'

Now she was focused on me. 'You've been doing more investigating? Alice, that's wonderful! Did you find anything out?' In her eagerness, she picked up the iPad, smeared its surface with sticky offshoots of baking, and put it down again to wipe her hands on her apron.

'Not really.' Just that it's really cold on the moors before sunrise, I didn't add. And your brother isn't Heathcliff, I didn't even dare *think*.

She subsided again and sat on one of the many high wooden stools that dotted the echoey space. The whole room was tiled, and huge scrubbed oak tables took up much of the floorspace, like a cross between a Victorian dairy and a mortuary. 'The police had a quick look at his computer, but they said there was nothing there.'

'But did they look thoroughly enough?'

Jenna was picking strings of yeasty flour off her arm. 'I don't know. They weren't here very long, they just switched on his computer, had a quick look at Grant's things – they were looking for a suicide note, I think, from what I overheard. They didn't say as much to me, of course.'

'Could I have a look?' The police thought it was either an accident or that Grant had blown himself up on purpose, that much was clear. I wondered if they'd gone through his passwords. 'I mean, I used to know all his logins. He never told me, but I spent so long watching him on the bloody thing...' I tailed off.

Jenna seemed energised now. 'Of course! That's a brilliant idea!' Her words echoed off the walls, powered by enthusiasm. 'Let's go up now!'

'But you need to get your scones in.'

'I'll do them later. They're scones, not soufflés, they'll keep.' And she was off again, me tailing her through obvious servants' quarters; endless winding corridors and panelled spaces where ancient bells hung rusted and unrung and the floors were stone flagged and uneven. We climbed stairs, jigged around corners formed from walls several feet thick, and eventually burst through a door onto a hallway with actual carpet and where the walls were painted in chalky colours rather than looking as though they suffered from a particularly disfiguring disease.

'This is our flat.' Jenna hurtled her way along until we came to an open living space. If I'd expected something boxy and scattered with old newspapers, I was wrong. It was entirely in keeping with the rest of the house, long windows letting in sunlight, billowy white curtains, floor-to-ceiling bookcases and, I was amused to see, plenty of mouldings. Jenna went to a corner, pulled a lever, and what had seemed to be an ordinary piece of walnut furniture folded in on itself to form a desk. There was a laptop in the middle, slightly dusty, and a huge monitor and illuminated keyboard on the top. I presumed the actual computer was in the bottom bit, hidden by Louis XV doors and gilt handles.

'This is where Grant used to work.' Jenna stroked the laptop casing gently. 'We don't often use this room, so he had it all to himself most of the time.'

This life must be nice, I thought, as I opened the laptop gingerly. I had one or two saucepans I didn't often use, and the back door didn't get as much exercise as I'd like, but to have whole *rooms* you didn't use? And where was the dust, the smell of shut-in woodwork and damp? This place smelled as though someone had gone berserk with a tin of beeswax recently. Then I realised that Jenna and Max must have a team of cleaners to keep a place this size from becoming ninety per cent cobweb, and felt slightly better.

Praying that Grant had still been set in his ways after six years, I switched on the laptop. When it asked me for a passcode, I typed in his date of birth and everything opened.

'That's what the police did.' Jenna was watching over my shoulder. 'Grant told me his code, in case it was ever needed.'

All normal. Emails, all standard, basic admin. Some internet orders, work. Nothing suspicious. Nothing on any of the other sites either. I flipped through to check. 'Did they check his other account?'

Jenna stared at me. 'What other account?'

I felt my heart drop. Jenna didn't know. How much did I tell her? Would it make her feel differently about Grant? Oh, what the hell, he was gone anyway... 'His account under his gaming name? You knew he gamed?'

'Oh, yes!' Her laugh had relief in it, as though she'd been as worried as I momentarily had. 'Every Friday night, online, with his cohort. I thought it was rather sweet.'

At least you got him down to every Friday night, I thought. I'd had to suffer the gaming practically every evening. 'That *Lord of the*

Rings rip-off game, where they all played characters surviving in the woods and trying to take over the Evil Kingdom?'

Jenna shrugged. 'It was something like that. I never really got involved, it was Grant's thing.'

'Well.' I typed a few more words, another screen opened up. 'He had another account under his character name.'

Jenna leaned in closer. 'LionLord? Gosh, that doesn't sound much like Grant.'

'It was the character he played in *Wilderness Assault*. He had mastery over beasts. Something like that, anyway.' And, yes, it had been as far removed from real-life Grant as it could be – a bare-thewed, kilted avatar, who could call on the power of the wild to further his aims in the game. Like Jenna, it hadn't really been my thing, and I'd let him get on with it. I never really understood the allure, but it had, apparently, been really important for Grant never to leave his computer during weekend hours, in case a rival warlord infiltrated their... something or other. I'd glazed over by the time he'd got to this bit of the explanation, and wandered off to stare out of the window at other couples walking hand in hand down the street.

There was a tension in the air between Jenna and me now. A sharpness, as though Jenna was waiting to hate me, waiting for me to show her something that made Grant a little less hers. I wished she wasn't standing there behind my left shoulder. I wanted to be able to rummage about among his files and filter out anything that could hurt her before she saw it. I was slowly coming to realise that I liked Jenna, with her odd dichotomy between the fragile and easily upset and the bike-riding badass. If there was anything on this computer that might upset her or make her think differently about Grant, I wanted to see it first.

There was nothing. A few messages, emails, all about gaming. I cranked up the big computer and found the same. Absolutely nothing – to, I thought, a suspicious degree.

Jenna breathed out a big sigh. 'Well. That's all right, then. You had me worried there, with all that talk of a secret account. Oh, here's Max.'

Max had evidently been standing in the doorway watching us. Jenna briefly explained what we'd been doing. 'But there's nothing there,' she said, sadly. 'And now I must go back to my scones for a minute. Max, will you make Alice some tea? I'll be back as soon as they're out of the oven.'

I sat awkwardly in front of the keyboard as she left. I didn't want to move. I didn't want to sit in the wrong place or touch the wrong thing and, whilst I'd felt quite at ease up here with Jenna, with Max it suddenly all felt different. Formal. I was worried about knocking antiques with my elbow or ripping the cover of a first edition, as though I'd turned into the Incredible Hulk in the last thirty seconds.

While I pulled myself together, Jenna had gone. I could hear the echoes of her leaving down several floors, scuffing feet on stone, until a final door slam and silence.

The whole house was silent. Apart from the computer and laptop buzzing and beeping in front of me, there was nothing. Even Max, standing beside me, was quiet. Finally, I had to say something.

'Why do you go up onto the moors to look at haunted houses when you live in something out of an Austen novel? Couldn't you research ghost hunting round here?'

He pulled up a chair that looked as though it had started its life in a Sheraton catalogue and made its way here via Blenheim and Laura Ashley. 'Because I have to walk these hallways at three in the morning, when someone's left a window open or the cat's got stuck in a sideboard,' he said, leaning forward. 'The last thing I want is to have had a bunch of students telling me they've seen a dark shape walk through a wall in the dining room when I've got to go in there in the dark.'

'I thought you didn't believe in ghosts?' I turned round rather sharply and cracked his knee with the leg of my chair. He was sitting closer than I'd realised.

'Ow. No, I don't. But all bets are off at 3 a.m. when there's a gale blowing and mysterious noises in the library. It's amazing what you can believe in in the dark.'

'Sorry.' I wasn't sure if I meant to apologise for hitting his knee or challenging his beliefs.

He smiled. He seemed more relaxed here, less dark and moody. It could have been because he was on familiar territory, of course, but the change of clothing helped. He was wearing a shirt so lairy that it looked as though it would offer to sell me six genuine Chippendales for a fiver, a pair of shorts smeared with creosote, and hefty work boots. 'It's fine.'

There was a lapse in conversation. Max was looking at the computer screen. 'Did you find anything?' he said at last.

I twitched, checking the doorway to make sure Jenna hadn't tiptoed her way up four storeys. 'No,' I said slowly.

'And? You sound as though that's giving you pause for thought.' Max leaned back. Hairy legs jutted into my field of vision, but it was fine. I didn't feel as though I was about to blush or cover myself in confusion today, as though seeing him in his natural habitat made him more normal. Or it could have been because the shirt was so awful that it threw his appeal into the shade of dreadful clothing choices.

'It's... strange,' I said, hesitantly. 'I'd have expected lots of gamer chat, searches for kit – Grant always likes... *liked* to look the part. He was constantly trading for in-game stuff – I don't really know the terminology, but his search history should be full of stuff. And it's not.' I glanced at Max. 'Almost as though he's deleted a lot of it.'

Max leaned forward now, so he could see my face. 'He's deleted parts of his search history? Anything else?'

'I don't know. I mean, this is a new machine since he left me, I don't know what he might have done. Maybe he's archived his searches or put them in an inaccessible file. But yes. There are things I would expect to see that aren't here. And Grant knew how to go dark, he knew how to search without leaving a trace, which means he must have deleted anything he thought would be suspicious. Or, at least, put it somewhere it wouldn't be found by anyone doing a cursory search. But because he's got rid of stuff I would have expected to see, it probably means he deleted it in a hurry.'

'But what would he be deleting? What the hell could he have been looking for that made him go up onto those moors?'

Max and I exchanged a look. I felt a moment of quiet triumph, not only that I was managing to look at him as a human being, not the single most desirable man I'd ever met, but also that I'd managed to impress him.

'Don't say anything to Jenna.' I switched both machines off. 'She might start on with the Famous Five stuff again, and I really don't think there's anything to "detect". Grant's gone. Whatever he was doing, it's over.'

Max nodded. There was paint in his hair, I noticed. 'Yes. You're quite right. But at least *we* can be pretty sure he was hiding something from her. From me, too. There was something up there, something about the Fortune House that he knew and didn't want anyone else to find.'

'And it killed him,' I said shortly.

'Something did, certainly.' Max leaned forward, arms on his thighs. 'Grant never struck me as particularly…' He trailed off, looking at me sideways.

'Are you waiting for me to fill in a word there? I've got lots.'

He raised his eyebrows. 'I bet you have. And yet, here you are, helping Jen, being kind. You didn't have to do any of this, you know, Alice.'

'Well, it's too late to say that now. Before, when the police told me, I was just "accidents happen". Since I've met you and Jenna, I've practically got Grant down as a criminal mastermind,' I said. 'Well, criminal, anyway.'

'So it's my fault?' He was teasing me again, I realised, with a slight shock.

'I haven't ruled you out.'

'Good.' There was a bit of a pause, and then Max seemed to mentally shake himself. 'The police team are up there now.' He shuffled his chair back. There was the careless noise of expensive furniture squealing along carefully polished floorboarding. 'If there's anything suspicious, they'll find it, but there's been nothing so far.'

Our eyes met. 'What was he *doing*?' we both asked at the same time, as though interrogating one another. I stopped, embarrassment had finally caught up with me, but Max continued, 'Jenna must never know. She's having a lot of wobbles, just when I think she's doing better she goes back downhill again. I can't wait for the site to be cleared and nothing found. It might help her.'

I didn't know what to say. All I could do was reassure him. 'Don't worry. I'm not going to say anything, and she *will* get better. As the memories fade and everything gets less sharp, she'll stop dwelling on Grant so much.'

Max jumped up. 'I was going to show you this,' he said, stomping heavy-booted to a side table. It was scattered with photographs in frames, all carefully arranged to give maximum exposure to the pictures, and I wondered who did the arranging as I followed him over. He picked up one photograph, but I was scanning the others. Most of them seemed to feature a couple, a man like Max but older, with shorter hair and less watchful eyes, and a woman very like Jenna, with flowers in her hair. 'Our parents,' Max said shortly. 'But this is what I got out to show you. This was the Fortune House. This is the picture that got me started.'

It was a black and white shot of a four-square house built of brick and roofed with Yorkshire stone. An ordinary, unremarkable house, with a small stable-type outhouse to one side, it looked grey and dour and about as North Yorkshire as it was possible for a house to be. If it had been a person, it would have been wearing a flat cap above a worn, wrinkled face. And probably smoking a pipe.

'I took this picture when I was out on the moors one day. Only Alethia lived in the house then, her parents had been dead for a good number of years; she let me into the kitchen for a glass of water, and that was the first time we met.' Max tilted the frame so that the picture winked out of existence, merging with the light from the window. 'I wanted to show you what it looked like in its heyday.'

I didn't know what to say. It looked like – a house. Windows to the left and right of the front door, one above it, all blank and black, with only a hint of reflected sky. The front door was enclosed in a deep porch, making the front look unwelcoming. Bare, unleafed trees jutted from either side and I wondered why I'd not noticed them on my visits and then realised that they must have been blasted from the ground by the force of the explosion. There was a tatter of curtain remnant at the window above the porch, but the others were bare.

'Why is it in a frame?' I asked suddenly and Max, who had been looking down at the picture with me, turned his head slowly to look at me. It was a very deliberate movement. 'You must have loads of pictures of the house. Why is this one different enough to keep?'

'You...' He started to speak, stopped, cleared his throat. 'Do you know, no one has ever asked that?'

There was nothing I could say to that.

'This picture is special. Yes, you're right, I've got lots, but this one...' He came in closer. I could smell the wood preservative from his shorts, the smell of something sweetish from his hair which I presumed was shampoo. His shoulder bumped mine. 'What do you see?'

I looked again. 'Why is that the only room with curtains?' I pointed to the little window above the porch, where the flash of something lighter on one side of the window was the only feature.

I had Max's full attention now. Those dark, dark eyes were staring into mine. 'There are no curtains at the window,' he almost breathed the words. 'There was absolutely nothing in that room. I got Alethia to let me have a look around.'

'So what's that, then?' I flicked at the white smear. Max's only reply was silence. 'It's obviously something inside the room, you can see where the window frame cuts it off.' I looked at his face. 'Oh, come on, you're not going to tell me it's a ghost, are you?'

He said nothing for a bit longer, then breathed out a sigh. 'You know I told you that I saw... something one day up there? This was it. *Something* at that window. There when I took the picture and then, the next minute – not there. I didn't know what I was looking at, and I thought it must have some obvious explanation, so I went to the house, got talking to Alethia and asked her to show me around. I *think* she thought I wanted to buy the place. When I went back later and asked her about using the house for some ghost research, she – well, she got quite angry. Threw a saucepan at my head, actually.'

I imagined Max running from the house, pursued by a little old lady flinging cookware, his carefully cool image in tatters. It made me grin.

Now he was smiling back at me. 'It was the beginning of a beautiful friendship. Well, it was, when I finally got the courage to go back, anyway. She told me that when she inherited the house, that was the only room that was empty. All the rest were furnished; it was almost as though her parents didn't want to acknowledge that space.'

'What about when she was growing up?' I looked at the image of the house again. Blank, black windows, giving nothing away. Rather like Max's eyes, I thought, and then had to cough to force the blush back down.

He inclined his head as though acknowledging that I'd said something clever. 'Just another room. Her parents used to use it as a storeroom, she said. Old furniture, things her father was going to mend, stuff like that. But when she took the place over, after her mother died, the room had been stripped. Just an empty room, not so much as an old painting on the wall or—' he flicked a finger at the picture, two-dimensional yet threatening, 'curtains.'

'Maybe she was up there dusting when you took this? Or looking out the window at you?'

Max gave me a level look. 'She had crippling arthritis. She couldn't even get up the stairs. She slept on a pull-out bed in the room next to the kitchen,' he said.

'Well, maybe there was a cat.'

'Are you sure you've not done this ghost-hunting thing before?' Max leaned back now and put the picture carefully down on a little bureau. 'You're asking all the right questions. No, no cat. The door was closed when I went up there and there were no animals. Nothing there at all, except Alethia, living on a pension. She thought that maybe it had been her brother's room, and they wanted to remove all traces of him for some reason, when he moved away. What do you do for a living, Alice?'

He'd gone to stand by one of the long windows now and was gazing out over the fields with his hands behind his back. The effect of the shirt was blunted by the sunlight, but the shorts still looked anachronistic and slightly grubby. It was like being interrogated by a Mr Darcy who'd got dressed in the dark.

I swallowed. 'Admin,' I said shortly. I definitely did *not* want to feel any more out of place by explaining what kind. I already felt two degrees and an alphabet of qualifications short of his standard. 'Plus, I have to torment Invisible Malcolm.'

'Any chance you'd feel like giving it up and becoming my researcher?' He was still talking to the agricultural view. 'You seem to see things that other people don't, and that could be really useful.'

I almost flopped down onto the nearest sofa with surprise. Only the worry that it might be a genuine antique, and unable to support my considerable bulk hitting it at speed, stopped me. Change my *job*? But I'd been there since I left school! That was nearly eighteen years! It was a job I could do competently without needing to think! I settled for gripping the back of the nearest chair to keep me upright.

'Er,' I said. 'No, thank you.' I mean, how *could* I? I knew that office inside out. I knew where Sheila kept the secret supply of paperbacks that she read in the boss's office when no one was about. I knew about Malcolm's habit of slightly massaging the figures, and the fact that our workforce of fitters quite regularly used their lunch breaks to head to the nearest betting office, having spent the whole morning discussing form and handicap, when they weren't supposed to leave the site.

I knew that job in the same way I knew how to breathe. I'd gone there on work experience week aged fifteen and they'd told me to get in touch when I finished school and they would have a role for me. 'A bird in the hand, love,' Mum had said. 'It's a guaranteed job, good money. You could train for years and not get anything as reliable.' So I'd gone straight into Welsh's Windows and run the photocopying until I'd worked my way up to being allowed my own computer.

'No, thank you,' I said again, a little more firmly now. 'I'm fine where I am.'

Max turned around and made a face. 'Okay, if you say so.'

Silence descended again. There was nothing but the sound the curtains made, brushing softly against the back of expensive upholstery and far, far off, a faint sound of hooves on a tarmac road. I began to feel like a maid who's not come up to scratch in the fire irons cleaning department and is about to be chastised by the master of the house. Sometimes I sneaked a read of some of those books Sheila thought were hidden, and the stories had obviously rubbed off on my psyche.

'Tea,' Max said suddenly.

'I'm sorry?' Thinking about those books had made me go back to thinking about my job. About the familiarity of it; the way my office chair had moulded itself to me so that I was the only one who could sit on it with any degree of comfort, the fact that I was the only person who could work the blinds in the front office. The predictability of the Monday morning chat, the smell of old soup and sandwiches in the tiny kitchenette.

'I told Jenna I'd make you a cup of tea.' He was moving now, crossing the carpet, which occupied the middle of the floor with highly polished boards all around its edge, as though the carpet was afraid of the walls. 'Come on, we'll go and sit in the kitchen, it's a bit more homely than this room.'

I followed him out and down the corridor to a room that could only be described as 'homely' by someone who lived in a house with floorspace that was measured in acres, with pale oak cupboards, a range cooker and an island which accommodated a butler's sink and a wine rack. 'It's like falling into an edition of *Ideal Home* magazine,' I said, without thinking.

Max blinked at me. 'It's just a kitchen,' he said, filling the kettle.

'It's *a* kitchen, certainly.' I looked around. 'I don't think there's any "just" about it.'

He was half smiling to himself as he filled the kettle, as though he was enjoying himself. 'It's got all the normal kitchen things in it, though,' he said. 'I can't start calling it anything else, not after thirty-odd years. My head might explode.'

'No more exploding,' I said firmly. 'One person a lifetime is quite enough.'

Max swung away to a beautiful oak-surfaced worktop. 'I shall bear that in mind.'

I remembered Jenna staring at my walls when she'd visited my house. She'd probably been wondering where the rest of the room was. But thinking of Jenna reminded me of Grant. 'Did Grant live here?'

'Well, yes. He moved in with Jenna after they'd been together about six months. They were going to move out to a little place up near the carriage house, but...'

'I'm going to have to stop you there.' I held up my hand. 'I was getting on all right with the "it's just a kitchen", but mentioning that you have a carriage house is gratuitous, I'm afraid.'

Max grinned and I felt proud of myself. As though turning down his offer of a job had somehow swung the pendulum of power in my direction, I no longer felt in awe of him. I mean, yes, I was still madly jealous of the big house and the qualifications and the fact that he was writing a book and could look sexy and appealing in horrible clothes, but – I didn't want to work with him. I could say no. I could tease him and pull him up on his privilege. I wondered if this was what that empowerment I'd heard so much about felt like, and resolved to try it more often.

'Yeah, sorry.' He plugged the kettle in. 'But to properly answer your question, yes, Grant lived here. Jenna used to live – well, she lived with her utter shit of a boyfriend and when that broke down and she was so...' He tailed off, as though searching for the right word.

'Fragile?' I supplied.

'Jenna's not fragile, she's as tough as steel,' he replied. But he had his back to me, shuffling through mugs in a cupboard, and I wasn't entirely sure that he meant what he said. 'Don't let the waifish eyes and the tears fool you.'

He's trying to make himself believe that, I thought. He doesn't want to acknowledge that she's not strong at all. The insight surprised me.

'She was upset, that was mostly it. And it kind of triggered an eating disorder, so I brought her back here to live with me so I could keep an eye on her, and she's, sort of, stayed. Like I said, they were going to move to the cottage when the baby arrived but...' He stopped talking again and plonked two mugs down on the surface, harder than was really necessary.

I did a slow rotation, taking in the walk-in larder, the huge fridge, the dresser with the collection of what was probably very expensive china displayed on its shelves. 'It's a lot of kitchen for only two people. Well, three, I suppose, if Grant was living here too. Unless you're also accommodating a herd of buffalo, because there's room, you know.'

'Nope, no buffalo, although we do get silverfish, according to Mrs P.' I didn't ask who 'Mrs P' was. Max dropped her name in so casually that I thought I was already meant to know. 'Jenna likes to cook, she just doesn't always like to eat.' He closed his eyes slowly and there was a slump to his shoulders that made me worry he was about to drop to the floor. 'I don't know what to do, Alice. Everything is so fucked up. I need help, here.'

The change of tone, from lightly amused teasing to this, was abrupt, as though Max couldn't keep the façade of cheerfulness going any longer. He sounded so desolate and looked so dejected that I felt a burst of sympathy. He had all this – the house, a *carriage house*, for God's sake – and yet he could still feel out of control and miserable in his life. But then I didn't know really know what to say to a man who didn't think his kitchen was anything out of the ordinary, when you could have played competition netball in there. Angst whilst rich is a whole different thing to angst whilst just getting by, I'd had personal experience of that.

'How nearly done is your book?' The kettle was boiling, but he was ignoring it, so I started making the tea.

'It's... okay. I mean, I've written up most of the stories. I've had to stop taking groups up to the Fortune House while the police are investigating, but we can resume once they're done and the site's cleared. There's a clear demarcation between those people who've had what they consider paranormal experiences up there and a past belief in the subject, I've just got to write up my conclusions, really.' He sighed. 'I never thought it would take this long to write a bloody book. Or, to be fair, that it would include explosions and a dead potential brother-in-law.'

I pushed a tea mug closer to his hand, found milk in a jug in the fridge and fetched it out. The fridge was the size of my entire kitchen and had *samphire* in. I hadn't realised it was a foodstuff until now, I thought it was a paint shade. 'Right. So that's progressing as well as can be expected, then. So what else is, as you so delightfully put it, "fucked up"?'

He lifted his mug and looked at me through the rising ghosts of steam. 'You really like to put things into proportion, don't you?'

'You have to. Otherwise it's too easy to dwell on what might happen, and then it's easy to get overwhelmed,' I said carefully, keeping my tone even. Trying not to flash back to years of lying awake when things had been really bad, fears of what would happen to me, if Mum didn't make it through the night.

'Yes, but am I not allowed to feel a bit overwhelmed? I've got a sister who may slip back into not eating, I've got Hatherleigh Hall to run, thanks to Dad thinking that the place should stay in the family rather than doing the decent thing and leaving it to the National Trust. I've got a book to finish, despite the subject of said book having been obliterated, and a study of the psychology of ghost hunting to write up, plus about a hundred students' papers to read through and comment on before term ends next week.'

Max took a sip of his tea, made a face, and then poured the contents of half of the milk jug into the mug. 'Don't let all this fool you.' He jerked his head at the kitchen ceiling. 'Big house just means it's more expensive when the roof leaks.'

'You could hire people? It sounds as though it's all down to organisation, and there are companies that specialise.'

'That's why I was hoping to persuade you. You're practical and you think laterally, which is what I need.'

I gave him a look over the rim of my mug. 'You've just told me all the bad points. Don't go into the recruiting business, will you? You make it sound as though only someone who untangles Slinkies for a living could organise your working life.'

Max lowered his mug and grinned. 'And you have an interesting perspective on things. Seriously, I like the way your mind works, I don't think I've ever met anyone who sees things the way you do.'

I bit the inside of my cheek and concentrated on the awful shirt for a moment to stop me from taking such an enormous gulp of tea that I would probably drown.

'Ah, well.' Max shrugged and a little bit of milky tea slopped onto the work surface, where it blended with the wood. 'I'll work something out. I usually do, I've had a fair bit of practice.'

I moved away a little, so as not to do something wildly disorganised, like putting my elbow in his spilled tea, and ruining his opinion of me. These confessions were making me feel uneasy.

None of it was my business. I was only here because of Jenna and, now I came to think about it, *that* was a weird reason. She was my ex-husband's girlfriend, we were hardly united in grief about his death. I'd got sucked in to her beliefs that he'd been up to something out at the house. I suddenly had no real idea what I was doing here.

'Look, I'd better go,' I said. 'I'm not doing any good, I'm just reminding Jenna of what she's lost. It's been nice meeting you both, but – well.' I put my half-drunk tea down on the scrubbed oak of the table. 'Anyway.'

Max was scratching at incipient stubble with his paint and wood-stained fingers. 'And you're sure you won't come and work for me? I really, really need someone who's organised and sensible to help get this book to be an actual *book* and not a collection of experiential evidence with pictures.'

I stared at him. 'I don't know what that means.'

'I need – I want – *somebody*.' He sounded frustrated, although he hadn't so much as raised his voice. 'And I like you, Alice.'

Like. Oh, I was used to that. Like was as good as it got for people like me, apparently. But I was still riding that crest of being able to be assertive, not giving way beneath someone else's aspirations. 'Well, I'm sorry,' I said. 'But I think I'll leave you and Jenna to it from now on.'

It wasn't exactly a hard 'no'. It wasn't me taking charge and putting him firmly in his place, but I'd only just discovered that I could say no at all and be listened to, so it would have to do. I left Max sitting with his tea steaming its way to coolness while he put his head in his hands and stared at the immaculate worktop in front of him. It took me several goes to find my way out of the house, and when I did, it was out of a door so obscure that it took me another few minutes to find the parking area. But when I did, I started my car with unnecessary savagery and spun my wheels, flinging gravel at the house in a passive-aggressive leave-taking that nobody would even have noticed.

I was halfway home before I realised I still had Max's coat on the back seat.

* * *

Personal communication from Miss Deborah Wilson, experiencer of event, received via email.

I don't know if this is the sort of thing you mean, but I saw your letter in the *Yorkshire Post* asking if anyone had had any kind of paranormal experiences up on that part of the moors, and this is mine.

To this day it remains the oddest thing that has ever happened to me. I am sixty-three, in good health and not given to flights of fancy or hallucinations, and I am at a loss to explain what I saw that day.

This was the long, hot summer of 1976. A friend had come to stay and we'd decided to take a drive and a short walk up out onto the moors. I'd known this friend for years, we'd been at college together and now, at nineteen, we were about to separate. She was off to teacher training college down south and I had a job in a typing pool. I had recently passed my driving test, so we were taking this last chance of a day out together.

We'd parked the car on the roadside and walked a little way out along the dale. We could see the house that I now know to be the Fortune House, but we walked past that and out onto the moor proper, to try to get a bit of a breeze as we were so hot.

After we'd walked about another mile, we sat down to have a drink and our picnic. I was talking and taking my sandwiches out of my rucksack, when I turned to look at my friend, who'd gone a bit quiet. She was sitting with her back to me, looking, I thought, out at the view across the moor. I said her name and she turned. And her face was not that of my friend. Instead, it looked to be a much older person, and she wore a smile that I can only describe as 'evil'; a kind of fixed rictus grin, above which her eyes were staring in the most horrible way.

I jumped up and screamed, my friend turned away again, smoothly, and untroubled by my evident distress. She did not speak. When, after a few seconds, she turned back to me again, her face was restored to that of my friend, and she was puzzled at my obvious terror. She told me that she had been looking at the view, that she hadn't heard me say her name nor turned around. She had simply heard me scream, presumed I was fighting off one of the many wasps that were continually buzzing around our picnic, and only looked away from the view when I had, apparently, called her name loudly after I had jumped to my feet.

8
_____

The office continued its normal summer flurry of inactivity. Everyone tried to look busy to justify being there at all, but there really wasn't a huge amount to do. Orders were low, there was work on the books but that was all arranged and dates pencilled in. The only people really working hard were the fitters.

In previous years, I'd used this season to sit and catch up with women's magazines. There was always a large pile in reception – Mr Welsh's thinking being that the wives could sit and flick through articles about hair and dieting whilst their men talked the serious business of windows. Mr Welsh, now in his seventies, had a rather fixed idea of gender roles, and I'd tried to tell him that, nowadays, the wives were often out-earning their husbands and wanted a say in what kind of windows they had put in their homes, but he still refilled the magazine rack every week and got Sheila to put the nice cups out.

This summer, however, I took to bringing in books I'd borrowed from the library. First of all, I'd searched for books about ghosts, but found I scared myself too much reading those. It had been bad enough imagining every creak of my old floorboards to be otherworldly presences, but when it got to the stage that I was having to leave the downstairs light on and sleep with Mum's old crucifix under the mattress, enough was enough. I turned to the psychology section instead, found a series of books on beliefs and parapsychology, and I was reading my way slowly through Pickering library's thin collection on the subject.

I kept away from the Allbrights. Although Max's coat was practically burning a hole in the back seat of my car, and I had the card he'd given me propped up on my bedside table, I told myself that if he wanted his coat back, he knew where I was. The card was... well, the card was propping up my alarm clock, that was all.

I drove up onto the moor once. Absolutely not hoping to run casually into Max and maybe give him a cool, contemplative smile and look winsome and mysterious, but, to my disappointment, he wasn't there to be winsomely smiled at. So I sat and looked over the ruins of the Fortune House, watched a small police forensics team hard at work and wondered again about Grant's final visit. I was still trying to come to terms with the fact that we'd probably never know what had called him up to that isolated little dale in the middle of that short summer night, and the 'unfinished business' nature of it rankled.

A couple of weeks passed. I became better read in the subject of ghost hunting, despite the teasing I got from the rest of the staff, and the police kept phoning me to tell me that they hadn't found anything 'of note' up at the Fortune House. Whatever Grant had been doing up there had died with him, I had to learn to live with that. I imagined, when I thought of them at all, that Max and Jenna were busy with their weekend openings; the baking and repairing and generally keeping up appearances in that huge old house. None of it was anything to do with me.

But I couldn't ignore the sense that, for some reason, my life had started to feel smaller, somehow. Not physically, of course, the house was still the same size, as was I, but metaphorically. I cursed myself for it. Now I'd seen 'how the other half live', I'd got a weird kind of an itchiness in my soul. An impatience with the normality of my day-to-day existence; get up, go to work, come home, cook something, go to bed. I found myself getting a bit snappy at work, prompting raised eyebrows and choruses of 'Oooooooooh!' when I berated a team for lateness where normally I would have let it slide on these long, hot days.

I expanded my reading outside the parapsychology section of the library and slid a bit further along the shelf into psychology. I began to inwardly analyse everyone in the office under my breath and probably incorrectly, but there was something infectious about the headings in those books. When I found I'd reduced the perfectly inoffensive Malcolm to 'passive-aggressive, mother issues, stunted emotional growth', I decided it was probably time to move along the shelf a bit.

And so it was that, on this sultry, humid Sunday evening, I was sitting outside in my tiny backyard with a book about the cases of Oliver Sacks, some of them quite horrifying. The heat had increased with the darkness. All around me, families were barbecuing or just sitting around, drinking and trying to keep cool. Nobody could go to bed, it was too hot.

Someone knocked on my front door. The knock was barely there, it sounded more as though someone had brushed against the door in a skirmish of drunken passing, so I stayed in my seat until it came again.

Definitely a knock this time. I looked at my phone. It was 10.30 p.m. Who would come calling at this time of night? The brief thought that Max might have come by to pick up his coat flashed into my head, but I forced that one down under the weight of the sensible thought that it was far too warm for him even to have missed the coat, let alone suddenly find a need for it, unless someone wanted to do a photoshoot of him looking mean and moodily ghost-hunterish somewhere. The only way to find out was to answer the door.

When I first saw the knocker, I thought it was a homeless man, trying to use my porch as shelter, and was about to offer him some change and the leftover beef joint in the fridge to move on, when he stepped into the light and I nearly fell over backwards.

'Grant?'

'Er. Hi, Al. Hello.'

'Grant?'

Not a ghost. No ghost would smell quite so hot and unwashed. He'd gained a beard and was wearing a fishing hat and stained clothes that looked as though they had been stolen from a random selection of washing lines. My heart was somewhere in the back of my eyes, forcing them wide with the sheer speed of its thumping, but the rest of me had gone empty.

'Grant?'

'Yes. Yes, it's me.'

'But you're *dead*!' I almost wailed, as though I'd been personally disappointed by his reanimation.

'Ah. Yes. *Bit* of a long story. Can I come in?'

Well, what do you say when your previously exploded, unseen for years ex-husband turns up late at night on your doorstep? In my experience, nothing. There are no words. I just stood back and let him over the doorstep, shuffling in his ill-fitting shoes and baggy tracksuit, until I could close the door behind him. Between the beard and the hat his cheeks looked sunken and sunburned and there were deep shadows under his eyes as if he hadn't slept in a while. Well, good, I thought, because the memory of this reappearance was going to cause me sleepless nights for months.

We went into the living room and Grant stopped and looked around. 'It looks nice in here,' he said. 'I like that lamp.'

'You,' I said with difficulty because my teeth were gritted and beginning to chatter in a sudden chill, 'have got a *lot* of talking to do and I shouldn't think any of the words you are about to use feature light fittings.'

I still couldn't really take it in. Grant, dead Grant, was here. Walking, talking and evidently very much alive. My brain wouldn't stretch as far as the implications, it was having trouble making sense of the simple fact of his continued existence.

'And sit down,' I added. 'Before your trousers beat you to it.'

Grant sank, looking rather thankful, into the armchair that had been his chief repository when he'd lived here. I tried not to think 'when he'd been alive'. I was freaked out enough already.

'Look, Al,' he said, taking off the fishing hat to reveal matted hair. 'I've done something a bit stupid and I need your help.'

I inwardly congratulated myself for not screeching that he'd done a *lot* stupid by the looks of him and how dare he come to me for help when he'd cast me off like an outgrown T-shirt so he could go off and explore himself. I just said, 'Go on,' and perched myself on the edge of the sofa.

'I don't know if you've heard,' he began, but my expression must have indicated that I had, indeed, heard, because he moved on swiftly. 'I set up the explosion on purpose. I planted my belt and wallet so that I'd be identified – and I blew the place up and tried to disappear.' He ran out of breath and stopped.

'Why?' I asked weakly. I wanted to go and make myself a cup of tea, or, even better, pour myself a stiff gin, but I had a horrible feeling that if I took my eyes off Grant, he'd vanish. Too much parapsychology, that's what that was.

Grant was sitting hunched forward, hands between his knees. He looked abject. 'There was this girl,' he said slowly.

'Jenna?'

His head came up. 'You know Jenna?'

'You blew yourself up. It kind of brought us together.'

He hissed out a long, deep, sigh. 'Yes, Jenna. And she... we...' He stopped again.

'I know about the baby,' I said, surprised that the words came out gently.

Grant flicked a look at me. I was slightly taken aback to see that his eyes were still that greenish blue, very bright in his shadowed, burned face. 'Oh. Right. Sorry, Al.'

So he remembered too. Those long nights where I'd put the case for having a baby and he'd shot down all my arguments. I'd wanted a baby before my mum died, wanted her to have a grand-child, to see life going on. My brother and his children lived so far away, she'd had no input into their lives. I thought a baby here, now, would have given her something to hold on for. Grant had thought otherwise.

'It was an accident,' he carried on, muttering to the carpet now. 'I wasn't... sure. But Jen was so happy and we were going to move to this little cottage—'

'Near the carriage house, yes, I've already done this bit,' I said, somewhat testily. 'Can we move directly to the blowing up?'

Another sigh. 'After that, Jen sort of – she wanted to get married, have more babies and I... I still wasn't sure. But she kind of went from really happy and looking forward to stuff to really sad about, well, about losing the baby and all. How could I say to her that I didn't really know what I wanted?'

'Like a normal person!' I almost shouted. 'Like an adult!'

'Yeah. Sorry. I didn't *want* to do that to Jenna, I couldn't bear to see her upset and all, and I'd been out at the Fortune House with Max – I guess you know Max as well, then? – and I'd seen all the gas cylinders and it got me thinking. I did a bit of research and...' He did a fast and expressive movement with both hands. 'Boom.'

I rubbed my face. My skin seemed to have become very elastic all of a sudden. 'And you didn't think that you being dead might not upset her more than a grown-up discussion about the future of your relationship?'

'Well, yes, but she'd get over it faster if I was dead. Wouldn't she?'

I stared at him over my fingers. Grant had never had a great deal of imagination or empathy. Or, it now became apparent, common sense.

'Right. Skating over the immense problem of you having destroyed Jenna utterly for the sake of not wanting to have a difficult conversation, what – and I want you to think very carefully before you answer this – what the ever-loving *fuck* has made you decide to reappear on my doorstep?'

Grant looked taken aback. I didn't often swear, but I thought if any situation warranted a quick F-bomb, this was it. 'Er,' he said. 'I've had a rethink.'

'A rethink.'

'Mmmm. Turns out it's not that easy to make yourself a new life, even if you're good with computers. And... and...' He tailed off, took a deep breath and started again. 'And I've discovered that I really, really do love Jen,' he finished in a rush.

I stared at him until he started speaking again.

'You and me, we were just mates really, weren't we? I mean, we got married cos of your mum being so poorly and all, it was never this great romance, was it?'

Well, no, I thought. Not when you wouldn't leave the house or your computer, or take me out or go anywhere with me or even have a proper conversation. It seemed churlish to bring that up at this point though. 'Go on,' I said again.

'And there were a few girls after we split, I mean, not many. One or two. But they didn't work out and then I met Jen.' To his credit, he really did get a tiny bit more sparkle when he said her name, but then it would have been hard to get much of a sparkle from Grant, without cutting him into facets, and don't tempt me... 'And I wasn't sure before, but I am now. I want to marry her and settle down and have children.'

I bit my tongue to force myself not to mention the cottage, the big house, the evident financial status of the Allbright family.

'And I thought,' Grant went on, 'who do I know who's really sensible and can sort things out when they all go totally tits up? There's the guys I game with, and they're great if you need a crew behind you to win the Sword of Afara, but for this? You're the only person I know who could sort this kind of thing, Al. Plus, you know, you're local. So I came here.'

'Thank you so much,' I muttered, tightly.

'And I thought... I wondered if you'd tell Jenna I'm here. That I'm back.'

* * *

I paced. I made tea, I drank tea. I gave Grant a sandwich, which he swallowed almost in one gulp, and I thought. Mostly what I thought was, 'This is way, way above my pay grade,' and 'What the hell do I *do*?' Would Jenna be happy to see Grant? Or would she want to kill him for what he'd put her through? What on earth could I possibly tell her? That he'd orchestrated his own death with such care and attention to detail, just to avoid telling her that he wasn't sure he wanted to marry her, and blown up Max's book project location to make it work? That he'd deleted his computer history to prevent anyone finding out that he'd been researching how to do it? Anything I could think of saying to explain what Grant had done would destroy her completely.

I needed help. I was probably also going to need therapy to get over this. Grant was being of no use at all. He'd sat back with a mug of tea and the absolute certainty that he'd always had when we'd been together, that however awful something was, I would sort it out.

I paced a bit more and then decided there was only one thing to do. I fetched down the little bit of card from its position alongside my bed, and dialled the number.

'Hatherleigh Hall.' It was Jenna. She'd answered the phone. My mouth went dry and I made some little croaky noises.

'Hello?' Jen sounded nervous. Did she think this was a dirty phone call?

'Hello, Jenna,' I finally managed. 'Can I speak to Max, please? It's Alice.'

Jenna laughed, relieved, by the sound of it. 'I think he's down in the Queen's Drawing Room,' she said, sounding completely oblivious of the fact that most of us don't have a drawing room at all, let alone a royal one. 'Can I tell him why you're calling? It might make a difference between him coming to the phone now or calling you back in the morning.'

'Tell him...' I groped for something. 'Tell him I've had a rethink about coming to work for him,' I said on a flash of inspiration. 'Tell him I want to talk about the job.'

Jenna laughed. 'Oh, good! He *so* needs someone to get this book organised! He told me he'd asked you and you'd shot him down – he was quite upset about that, actually. He really wants you on board, you know.'

'Yes,' I said weakly, wondering how much more upset Max was going to be when he found out why I really wanted to talk to him.

'Give me two minutes.' And she was gone.

Grant sat, expectant as a Labrador over a biscuit tin, until Max came to the phone. 'Hey, Alice. Jen says you've had a rethink...'

I cut him off. 'I need you to come here, Max.' My voice was low, urgent. 'I need you here, at my house, *now*.'

A moment's silence. Then, 'This doesn't sound as if it's to do with the job.'

'Please.' I couldn't even *begin* to explain over the phone, I just couldn't. 'Please, come, Max.'

I hear a breath. A soft, almost sympathetic noise. 'Are you hurt? I'm coming now, I'll find my keys.' He moved away from the mouthpiece for a second. 'Jen, I've got to pop over to Alice's, have you seen my keys?' Then back to me again. 'I'll be there as soon as I can. Don't worry, Alice, whatever it is, we can sort this out.' And then the phone went down, leaving me with Grant eating the contents of my fruit bowl, and me trying to tidy up the living room a bit so that Max wouldn't think I lived in a hovel. Then I realised I hadn't asked him definitely, absolutely, on no account to bring Jenna with him, and made Grant go and sit upstairs in the spare room in case she came along.

I was trying to work on a plausible excuse for having dragged Max over, in case Jenna *had* come with him, when there was another knock on the front door and Max was there, alone, with his Range Rover squeezed in behind my car.

'Ah, good,' he said, when I opened the door. 'This is the right place, and you've got all your limbs attached and no evident blood. So, what's this about?'

Then Grant came down the stairs and Max reacted in the same way I had, only with more swearing. And louder, because Next Door Left banged on the wall.

'Sorry. Sorry.' Max had collapsed onto the table I kept in the hall to drop all the post I didn't want to cope with. 'But... no, I'm sorry. I'm stumped.' He looked at me. 'You could have given me a heads-up,' he said, reproachfully.

'How? What the hell could I say, over the phone with your sister in the room to give you a heads-up about *this*?' I gestured at Grant, who was arrested in the act of stepping off the fourth stair. 'It's not really a heads-up kind of thing, is it?'

'Well, no, I suppose not.'

A heavy kind of silence fell over us all. Teamed with the heat, it felt like being under a very thick blanket. 'Look. Let's go and sit in the living room, where at least there's an open window. Grant can explain and I can make myself a very stiff drink.' I moved as Max stood up and we kind of jostled against one another in the narrow hallway for a moment. He had that slight smell of orange peel about him that I'd noticed on his coat, and I wondered if it was a very expensive cologne or whether he just ate a lot of oranges. Then I cursed myself for even noticing, when events were, quite clearly, getting away from me.

I left them and went through to the kitchen. Out of the window, I could see the smoke and glow of Next Door Right's barbecue dying down, my discarded chair and book and the twinkle of solar lights on Next Door Left's slightly over-ambitious rose arbour. Everything looked normal outside. Straightforward. Uncomplicated. I poured myself a glass of cold water and drank it, knowing that I was using it to waste time. I didn't want to go back into the sitting room, didn't want to see Max all glorious amid my peeling furniture and dusty carpet. I also didn't want to see Grant, because I'd just got used to the thought of him being dead and I didn't want to snap and bludgeon him to death with a rolled-up copy of *Prima* magazine to save me from having to cope with this not being the case.

But eventually I couldn't hover about in the tiny kitchen any longer. I filled a big jug with water, added a few sad ice cubes and, trying not to compare and contrast my randomly self-defrosting fridge with Max and Jenna's enormous American fridge, carried it through to where the two men were sitting in differing stages of relaxation.

Grant had slipped right back into his 'at home' persona. He'd got his feet up on the coffee table and was furtively scratching his navel. Max was hunched on the sofa, hands around the back of his neck as though he was trying to pull his head inside his body. He looked up when I came in.

'What the hell are we going to do?' he asked.

'I was hoping you would think of something.' I put the jug down on the table and pushed Grant's feet back onto the floor. 'Do we tell Jenna, or what?'

'Oh, you have to tell her,' Grant said eagerly. 'That's the whole reason I came back!'

'That and running out of money,' Max observed dryly. 'What were you living on, incidentally?'

'I sold my car for cash. Told Jenna I'd put it in the bank, but I kept it. I thought I'd be able to pick up some work, but it turns out it's hard without any ID.'

'Where did you *go*?' I asked, eyeing him sternly. 'Somewhere that outfit fitted in, evidently.'

'I was trying to get to London. But train tickets are really expensive,' Grant whined. 'I only got as far as Peterborough.'

Max and I looked at one another. There was nothing to say.

'I've been staying in a B&B, but the money was running out and I was afraid that the police would be watching my accounts and looking for activity online, so I had to keep my head down. I bought the clothes in a charity shop, because I'd only got the stuff I had on when I went up on the moor and I needed to change. I hadn't dared to pack anything, because Jen would have noticed.' Grant talked quickly, as though he wanted to get the story out.

Max collapsed his head again. 'Oh, God.'

Outside, a threatening grumble indicated an oncoming storm. There was the sound of a thousand barbecues being wound up speedily and next door's dog was escorted past the window for a comedically fast late walk. Rain must be forecast, I thought, and wished it could have arrived in time to have soaked Grant to the skin on my doorstep. Then I had a word with myself about this vindictive thinking. Grant had just been being Grant, looking to other people to solve his problems. The fact that those people were Max and me was almost incidental.

'And how were you going to work things if I didn't already know Jenna?' I asked Grant, who was looking hopefully from Max to me as though waiting for us to slap our foreheads and yell 'Eureka!' 'Give me her address and ask me to pop over one afternoon? Somehow casually raise the subject of her boyfriend still being alive?'

Grant's expression told me that, yes, that had pretty much been his plan. I didn't know whether to be glad that my already having met the Allbrights would make this easier for him, or whether to declare this was all beyond me, move to Scotland and join my brother on an oil rig.

The first fat drops of rain smudged the street lights against the window. 'Damn,' I said. 'My library book's outside.' I knew I had to go out and get it, but I was paralysed by the current situation.

'Fetch it in.' Max spoke to his lap. 'We promise not to decide anything without you.' His words were heavily sarcastic and Grant wriggled in his chair.

'I'm really sorry,' he said, still with that top note of whine. 'I didn't know what else do to.'

'One, stay dead. Two, not be dead in the first place. Three, oh, I dunno, set up home in Peterborough and never mention any of our names again?'

'I'm sorry,' Grant said again. 'But I'm in love.'

'Oh, God. Jenna.' Max resumed his attempt to pull off his own head and I slipped outside to the yard, where the sky had begun to rumble impressively and gigantic drops of rain were falling in that steady, determined way that says a downpour is only seconds away.

I picked up my book and turned my chair up so that the seat wouldn't get wet, collected the assortment of bowls and cups that I'd been snacking out of, and turned to go back indoors, just as a tremendous crack of thunder erupted overhead and the night flickered as though the lighting man in the sky was experimenting with effects. The streets echoed to the sound of people shouting and laughing as the deluge started, and then went quiet as they all sought shelter. I went back into the living room.

'I've got work in the morning,' I said, inconsequentially, but as a hint that I didn't want this to go on all night.

Max raised his head and his eyes met mine. There was real desperation in them. Grant was fiddling with a loose thread in the arm of the chair, looking as though he was waiting to be rescued from this situation of his own making.

'What do we *do*?' Max half-whispered. 'Do *we* tell her, or what?'

I bumped my head gently against the door frame in the hope that the pine would knock some ideas into me. Tell Jenna that Grant was back? Well, we'd have to. The shock of running into him otherwise could send her over the edge. But how could we explain it? Telling her the truth wasn't an option, not at this stage, how could she possibly deal with knowing that Grant had planned to disappear forever from her life? It wouldn't be kind. My book, still in my hand, jabbed me in the hip and I had an idea.

'Amnesia,' I said.

'Oh, I want to forget any of this ever happened,' Max said fervently.

'No, no, look.' I flicked through to the appropriate chapter. I'd read it only yesterday, sprawled out on my miniscule lawn listening to the neighbourhood having water fights. 'A man, brain damage, no memory...'

Max's eyes widened. He looked at me and then at Grant, who was still picking. 'Could we? I mean, could it work?'

'Grant, when the house exploded – for a reason you've totally forgotten and it was probably an accident anyway – is there any chance you could have been hit on the head by a brick and knocked into a fugue state, from which you recently recovered to find yourself in Peterborough, with no memory of how you got there or who you were?' I asked.

Grant frowned.

'But, as your memories gradually started to come back, you remembered this house, so you came here, and talking to me brought back the rest of your memories?' I carried on prompting.

'Er.'

'And you realised that it was going to be a shock to Jenna to find that you're really still alive and so you asked Max...'

'And you,' Max broke in. 'I'm not doing this on my own. I can't. Oh God, *Jenna*...'

'...and me to break the news to her carefully.' I finished and eyeballed Grant sternly. 'Isn't that what really happened? Grant?'

The light of understanding gradually crept across Grant's face. It was accompanied by another flash of lightning, as the world's most appropriately timed thunderstorm continued overhead. 'Oh!' he said. 'What, I pretend to have had amnesia for the last six weeks?'

'It's remotely plausible.' I gazed around at the two of them. 'And you can always gradually "remember" later, if you feel yourself ever able to tell her the truth. But for now, let's stick to the amnesia storyline and hope it works.'

Max suddenly jumped up from the sofa, took me by both shoulders and kissed me. It was a proper full-on kiss too, not just a quick peck on the cheek, and I knew I'd hold the memory of his slight stubble grazing my chin, the fresh-orange smell of him and the taste of his mouth on mine close to my heart for a long time. 'You are a genius, Alice,' he said, and it was heartfelt but obviously his heart didn't feel like mine. Because mine felt like a cushion that's been sat on and then replumped. 'An absolute frigging *genius*.'

My face was flaming, but luckily, at that moment, the lights went out. You could probably still have read the small print on a ticket stub by the glow from my cheeks, but we were all too busy swearing and I managed to hide away by grubbing in a drawer for the battery-powered candles.

At last we sat, crowded around the tiny flickering candles, most of which had a slightly desperate Christmas theme and had shed cheap glitter all over the carpet. The insufficient light, coupled with the flashes of lightning and the unnaturally lengthened shadows that resulted on the walls of my living room, were giving a definite Macbethian vibe to the moment.

'We'll have to do this carefully,' Max said, elbows on knees and hunched. 'It's going to be a huge shock for Jen, whatever we say.'

'She'll still have questions.' I addressed Grant, who was fiddling his fingers and watching the shapes against the light. If he started doing 'this is a rabbit', I would definitely have to kill him. 'You have to make sure you've got your story straight.'

'I don't remember anything. I remember being in bed with Jen, the next thing I can remember is suddenly finding myself in a B&B in Peterborough with no idea how I got there.' Grant grinned at me. 'Will that do?'

'It's good enough for now.'

'Okay.' Max took a deep breath. 'When do we do this? I need you there, Alice.'

'Oh, but I...'

'Look, I dashed over here tonight and I didn't even know *why*! You owe me one.'

I looked at Max, all hollows and shade, like a carved head. He was right, I did owe him. And then I looked at Grant, who was smiling, and sighed. 'I know. And yes, we have to break it to Jenna carefully, not just wheel Grant out with a "look what we found". Oh, this is complicated.'

'Come and work for me.'

'What?' I tried to see the expression on Max's face, but the stupidly insufficient and unseasonal lighting effects meant that he was largely a pool of dark. 'I can't. I've got a job.'

'You can change jobs. Honestly, I'll give you a great package, good pay, all that. I really, *really* need help with the book, and research, and then there's all this—' He gestured at Grant. 'Someone needs to be around to keep an eye on Jenna, and make sure the story doesn't slip. And besides,' he gave me a grin, 'when you rang you told Jen it was about taking the job. What are we going to tell her, if you *don't*?'

'I'll tell her we couldn't agree on a salary!' I hissed. 'I'm not giving up a job I've had for...' I calculated quickly, 'eighteen years for some fly-by-night one-off book research. I've got a retirement to plan for!' I finished, realising suddenly how sad and thin my excuses sounded. Retirement was looking to be a good forty years ahead and that was a long, long time to be answering emails about the arrival times of a fitting team.

'Oh.' Max sounded taken aback by my sibilant refusal. 'Oh. Right, yes, that's very sensible.'

Sensible. Was that what I was reduced to being? Big, sensible Alice, living in the house she grew up in, doing the job she'd done since she left school. Complaining that nothing ever happened in her life? I opened my mouth to say something else, but realised that I couldn't. Just *couldn't.* Give up the regular salary, my little office, my job where I knew everyone and everything? No, no, no. But then a tiny tickle of rebellion wormed its way into my soul. 'Look, I've got a lot of time off owing, we're really quiet at the moment, let me go in on Monday and sort things out and I could maybe take the rest of the week off? I could give you a hand with the book and help you break the news to Jenna.'

Max looked at me, a direct look in which the candlelight flickered, reflected in his eyes. 'How the hell,' he said slowly and clearly, 'have I managed without you in my life all these years?'

'Badly, I suspect.' I took refuge in briskness, in practicality. 'Now, if you two will excuse me, I've got work in the morning and a lot of organising to do.'

Max stood up. The lights came back on, spotlighting him in all his tall, dark glory, and from outside, we heard the cheers and whoops of the neighbourhood getting its late-night telly back. 'Yes, of course. You're right, it's late. So, it's decided, I'll wait to see you on Tuesday and we can break the news to Jenna together?'

Grant looked up.

'Not you,' I said. 'We're going to have to do this gently and slowly, not say "Guess who?" and wheel you out of the back of the car.'

'But where should I go?' He looked forlorn. 'I mean, I've got no money, nothing.'

Max and I exchanged a look of utter exasperation. 'All right, you can stay here for a couple of days,' I said. 'The spare bed is made up. And I can coach you to make sure you've got your story straight.'

I began to pick up the candles, one by one, very slowly. Max bent beside me to help. 'Thank you,' he whispered, so close that it made the hair on my neck prickle. 'You're a lifesaver, Alice. I mean that.'

After Max had gone and whilst Grant was in the bathroom chiselling off the worst of Peterborough, I relived the evening. Well, bits of it. Max kissing me, Max and I being partners in this conspiracy, Max whispering to me. Then I wondered if it was really such a good idea giving him a hand with his book, even if it was just for a week.

But the thought of how delicate, slight Jenna was going to react to the reappearance of Grant kept me from changing my mind again. At least I could be there to help her adjust to him being back. Or I could hold her coat whilst she attacked him with every sharp object to hand, I was good either way.

And then I listened to Grant singing 'My Way' in the shower, using all my hot water, and I opted for handing her the knives.

9

Work seemed oddly relieved for me to take the week off. Sheila looked at me with her head on one side and asked if there was a man involved because, apparently, I'd become 'argumentative' and, obviously, there was only one reason that a perfectly amenable – for which read 'absolute pushover' – woman would get tetchy and that was because there was a man in the offing. When I said that, no, it was nothing to do with a man, she sucked her teeth and talked about hormones and offered a coffee and sit-down chat to talk about HRT, which, since I was thirty-four, I thought was bloody cheeky.

I'd lied, of course. The only reason I needed this short-notice week off *was* because of a man, even if that man was Grant. And Max too, but I didn't count him. Not because he wasn't a man, he was sufficiently male to be causing me sleepless nights, but none of this was his fault.

So on the Tuesday morning I pitched up at Hatherleigh Hall in my little Fiesta, feeling out of place and out of my depth. Technically I was on holiday. Did I *really* want to spend one of my rare holidays knee-deep in someone else's angst?

Then Jenna dashed around the side of the building to meet me, and I remembered why I'd agreed to this. She was so slight she was practically invisible. Wearing trousers with huge flowers on them and a white shirt, she blended in with the garden that was blossoming almost audibly around her. 'Alice! Oh, I am so glad you've agreed to do this! Max is throwing papers around and swearing again, I think he's lost his notes.' She lowered her voice, taking my arm to lead me through the side door. 'I mean, he's a lovely guy, my brother, but he's really not very organised. It takes all his energy keeping this place running, I think, and I know he'd really like to sell but Dad was keen on the whole "family name" thing so he's doing his duty and it's really hard to keep all the plates in the air.'

'What about your mum?' We made our way up another staircase. I'd never find my way around this place. I'd have to stay wherever Max put me and never move; I'd better make sure it was close to a kettle and a toilet.

'Oh, she died when we were both very little. Dad brought the estate back from the brink, apparently, after the war it was going to have to be broken up, but he worked and worked to get it earning. Then he left it all to Max.' We rounded a corner that was vaguely familiar and were back in that carpeted corridor. There was the sound of vigorous language being used at volume from one of the rooms.

'Max! Alice is here!' Jenna tapped on the door and the swearing stopped. The door flew open to reveal Max, looking dishevelled and distraught, with a notepad in one hand and an iPad in the other. He was wearing a shirt that was half tucked in and half trailing from his belt, some kind of trousers like a cross between running and yoga wear, and his hair was on end.

'Good.' He scooped me into the room and kicked the door shut.

Jenna called, 'I'm down in the rose garden if you need me!' and padded away.

Max and I looked at one another.

'You're overdoing it,' I observed mildly. 'Either the swearing *or* the papers *or* the random writerly get up. You don't need to do all three.'

'Oh.' He sat down. 'Too much, you reckon?'

'Way too much,' I agreed. 'You could just have told Jenna you needed help with research, you don't have to lay on the "distracted author" thing quite so thick.'

'I need her to believe that I'm in such a state that you're coming over for a few days to help me get to the bottom of it.' Max tucked in his shirt all round. 'In case we can't work out a way to reintroduce Grant quickly. I mean, yes, I *do* need you, but we needed a reason for it to be short-lived so you can go back to your – other job.' He began straightening his hair. 'If you're sure…'

'I'm sure,' I said firmly and looked around the room. It was a study. In fact, it looked as though it had been carefully staged as A Study by an overenthusiastic props manager for a play. Big desk, check. Large leather furniture in shades of brown, squatting around the floor like tanned musclemen doing poses, check. Walls lined with bookshelves and globes and decanters and rugs, also check. 'Good grief, this place looks as though it fell out of a Sherlock Holmes novel.'

'Does it?' He stared around, distractedly. 'It's my work room, I don't really look at it.'

A huge computer with see-through innards beeped and flashed on a more sensibly sized desk near the window with a cardboard file labelled 'Psych York', which I assumed contained students' work.

'So.' I perched on the arm of one of the well-muscled chairs. 'How are we going to do this? Pretend to get a sudden phone call, or gradually drop hints, or what?'

Max sat on the desk and swung his legs. 'Where's Grant today?'

'I've told him to go to the police station to report himself undead. He's giving them the memory-loss story too.'

'Good. Maybe that will mean they'll stop sifting around in the remains of the Fortune House and I can get back up there again. I've got a ghost vigil planned for next week and I don't want to have to cancel, because it's the group that I've been working with for the last two years.'

'There won't be any reason for the police to be there any more, though, will there? They've just about concluded that the explosion was an accident, and without a body, it becomes "one of those things" presumably.' I looked around the study again. There were piles of papers in corners, all differently sized and tottering, propped against walls and furniture with occasional drifts and slips slumped further onto the carpet. 'What on earth is all this?'

Max rubbed at his arms as though the mess made him itchy. 'When Alethia left me the house, she also left me all her papers. Everything. There might be something of interest in there some-where but...' He made a face. 'She kept everything,' he repeated. 'Shopping receipts, notes to the milkman, paint samples, recipes – everything. I threw away the more obviously veterinary-related stuff, but...' He scratched his arms again. 'I told you I need an assistant,' he finished, rather forlornly.

'You need a bonfire,' I said sturdily. 'A quick go through to make sure there's nothing valuable, and burn the rest.'

'Well, an assistant could do that job.' He gave me a significant look.

'Oh, no. I'm here to help break the news to Jenna and make sure she's all right, with a side order of gradually reintroducing Grant into polite society and trying to make sure he doesn't shoot himself in the foot and upset her again. I am *not* here to tidy up your messes.'

'But you'd be so *good* at it.'

We looked at one another for a moment.

'Does that kind of flattery ever work?' I asked, eventually, with interest.

He shrugged. 'Sometimes. Students can be surprisingly gullible.'

Plus, I thought, I bet they're under the spell of your good looks and charm and wanting to be 'in' with their lecturer. I was surprised he didn't have teams of them in here already. I had a brief moment of imagining a collection of young women in short skirts wielding feather dusters and 'falling', having to have Max examine their twisted ankles, like a cross between a French farce and one of Sheila's lurid romance novels.

'But I don't have the students here,' Max went on. 'It would be unethical. So this mess—' a waved arm indicated the slowly subsiding piles, 'is all down to me to sort.'

'Anyone want a coffee?' Jenna arrived in the doorway, carrying a tray bearing a cafetière and a milk jug shaped like a tiny Jersey cow. 'I thought Alice might need a drink to help get over the shock of the state of this place.'

Max looked at me, raised his eyebrows, and I nodded.

'Jen,' he said gently, taking the tray from her hands, 'sit down a minute. Alice and I have got some news for you...'

Ten minutes later, Jenna had stopped crying, just about. She'd got her hands cupped around a mug of coffee and was sipping at it as though she needed something to do with her face. 'He's alive,' she kept saying. 'He's *really* alive?'

I thought of Grant, whom I'd left making a huge amount of mess in my kitchen and toasting himself the last of my loaf. 'Oh, yes,' I said fervently. 'He's really alive.'

'And his memory is coming back?'

Max gave her another hug. 'Yes, in bits and pieces. Like we said, he remembered where he used to live so he turned up on Alice's doorstep.'

'Did he think he was still married to you?' Jenna's eyes were very wide, but she seemed to have gone for our story, despite a few inconsistencies where Max had had to cover up the fact that he'd already seen Grant. We didn't want Jen to even suspect there was a hint of collusion between us.

'No. He remembers you.' I refilled her mug. 'He wants to see you, but he's still – recovering.' With the aid of all the food in my cupboards and all my hot water. 'His memory is still a bit patchy, and he doesn't remember why he was up at the Fortune House, he just remembers suddenly waking up in Peterborough.'

'But the head injury has healed up all right?' Jen was almost pleading. 'His personality and everything aren't affected? Just his memory?'

I *wanted* to say that Grant had so little personality that it was very hard to tell, and wished I'd thought of mocking up a head injury, preferably by hitting him with an actual brick, but I didn't say anything, I could only nod.

Jenna began crying again. 'When can I see him?' She turned to Max. 'Can I see him today? I want to see him as soon as possible.'

'And he wants to see you,' I said soothingly, trying not to catch Max's eye. 'We think it might be best to give him a day or two to… to…' I flailed. 'Get his story straight' were the words I was trying not to let slip.

'To recover,' Max filled in smartly. 'It's been very traumatic for him, losing his memory, and he wants to make sure that he hasn't forgotten anything that might cause you upset.'

Gosh, he was so smooth at this that I might almost imagine Max spent all his days fibbing wildly about supposedly dead people. But he'd had Monday to think about the details, I'd been at work, fending off Sheila's menopause literature.

'Yes. He was in pretty bad shape,' I added, absolutely truthfully. 'He's asked me to pick up some of his clothes today, and he's going for a haircut and shave.'

'So he looks like the Grant you remember,' Max said.

Jenna stood up. 'I'll go and get you some of his things.' She put the mug down so quickly that a little bit of coffee slopped out over the rim. 'I just can't believe...' More tears. 'I don't know whether I want to kiss him or kill him for putting me through this!'

Kill him, go on, said my thoughts, but my mouth was under firm control as usual. 'It wasn't his fault, Jenna,' I lied. 'He probably went up to the house to clear his head, the explosion was an accident, and the amnesia couldn't have been foreseen.' Unless you read Oliver Sacks. 'Grant is still Grant.' Unfortunately.

'Yes, I know.' Jenna sniffed. 'I don't know what to feel, I'm so... right, I'll go and find his favourite jeans and some other stuff.'

Still sniffing, she went out. We waited. After about ten seconds, Max crept to the door and peered out. 'She's gone. She'll be in her room, it's down at the end.'

I let out a huge breath. 'How did we do, do you think?'

He began to pour our neglected coffees. 'Pretty well. Good thinking on your part, to say you'd rung to warn me. And that bit about Grant going up to the house to clear his head...' He handed me a mug and I added milk to it. The cow's tail was the jug handle and the milk poured out of its mouth, which I thought was odd, since it had been given a gigantic udder, but maybe milk coming direct from the udder was a bit too 'on the nose' for the upper classes. 'Inspired,' he finished.

'So, I'll bring him over tomorrow.' The bitterness of the coffee seemed fitting. 'Then we can introduce them slowly and leave them alone but under observation.'

'Like a couple of mating dogs,' Max said, obviously without thinking, and then dropped his head so that his hair covered his face. 'Oh, God. I didn't mean that. I've no idea why I said it. The family used to breed English Setters, I can only assume that one of my ancestors possessed my body there for a minute. Sorry.'

I laughed. The fact that Max, posh, good-looking, intelligent Max, could let his mouth run away with him was reassuring. 'Yes, very much like mating dogs. Only without the bucket of water at the ready.'

'You don't actually need…' Max began, then raised his head, met my eye and started to grin. 'Oh.'

I rolled my eyes at him and stood up, my mug grasped firmly because this carpet was probably an heirloom. 'Right. Well, since we've got the rest of the day to get through, would you like me to make a start on those papers for you? I may as well make myself useful while I'm here, and backup the story about coming to work for you for a while, although I think Jenna has completely forgotten about that little ruse now.'

'I can't even remember where we stand on the "you coming over" storyline,' he said. 'Not that you even really need a reason, you know, Alice. You're always welcome here.'

I stood for a moment, as out of place in this over-furnished, dramatically masculine study as Max would have been among my window fitters. 'Thank you,' I said, somewhat stiffly. More words brewed up in my head, words about only being here because of Grant and Jenna, about this, all this, not feeling natural to me. I belonged in a cramped, stuffy office that smelled of Malcolm, in a Portacabin on a trading estate. I belonged in a tiny terraced house with a rowdy family one side and a middle-aged couple plus dog on the other. My house and office were small. My life was small. Not *this*.

But Jenna was kind and emotionally volatile and needed someone. Max was – well, he was Max. Attractive and intelligent and in need of my help and, if this was going to be as close as I got to a good-looking man wanting me, well, I'd take it for as long as it lasted. It was, I had to admit, but only very, very quietly to myself in the darkest part of the night, nice to be needed again.

'Thank you,' I said again, in case Max had seen me thinking all this. 'Now, just point me at the most immediate of the papers and I'll get sifting. Anything in particular you want to keep?'

He looked hopelessly at the heaps. 'I don't know, that's the problem. I'm not a social historian, I don't have the faintest idea what may be important to someone who's recording life in the 1930s in a farmhouse on the moors.'

'Right.'

'But I need to keep anything that relates to the past of the house itself. Building records, planning papers, notes on renovations, that kind of thing.' Max flicked me a dark look. 'Apparitions are often reported around buildings undergoing structural work,' he said. 'I need to cross-reference.'

'Okay.'

'And anything obviously personal, like diaries or journals, although I hardly think the Fortunes are going to have been writing extensive memoirs of life out there. But there may be letters from Alethia and John, and I'd like to give those a once over in case they mention any kind of paranormal activity.'

I looked again at the slithering mounds of paper and card that dotted the carpet. It looked as though he was trying to house-train a library. 'Right,' I said again, with slightly less enthusiasm. 'And what are you going to be doing?'

'*That* pile,' he pointed to a slightly more domesticated heap of cardboard files stacked under the computer desk, 'is my research and notes on the house. I shall be putting them in chronological order and checking that they are there in the outline for the book.'

He went to move towards the window, where the curtains hung, velvet and heavy, under the weight of the sun that was obliquely illuminating the room, then stopped. 'Thanks, Alice,' he said, very quietly. 'Really. Thank you.'

He wasn't looking at me. He seemed to be staring inexplicably at the floor and his tone was what I could only describe as 'intimate'. I felt the sickening pulse of heat building at the base of my throat and fought it back. 'No problem,' I replied briskly.

'But you...' He stopped. Cleared his throat. 'You've put your life on hold for me. For Jenna. You're going above and beyond for my family.'

'To be fair, it's my ex-husband that's caused the drama, I do feel a *little* bit responsible.' I turned my back, I didn't want him to see how pink and sweaty I was getting. I didn't want to give myself away, so I knelt down by the nearest pile of papers and began sifting.

I saw him move out of the corner of my eye, but it was just a twitch, I couldn't really tell what he was doing. It looked a bit as if he took half a step towards me then thought better of it. 'You're a really lovely person, Alice.'

Ah, this was more familiar territory. The implications that had come from words like those in my past shoved the raw fuchsia colouring back where it belonged. 'In two minutes, you'll be telling me that I've got a great personality and you bet I'm really fun with a couple of drinks inside me.' I was surprised at the acerbity in my voice. It was a shame, I hadn't wanted to think that Max was this shallow, yet here he was—

'What? No, I won't! Er. I mean...' He sounded flustered, and I chanced a quick look. He was half-crouched next to the file pile, head turned towards me, arrested in movement. He looked like Gollum protecting his Precious. 'Sorry. Sorry if I sounded patronising. I really didn't mean to, I just wanted you to know I appreciate everything you're doing for me. For Jenna,' he corrected himself.

I muttered a toneless acceptance of his apology, and started sorting my allotted papers into piles that I mentally labelled 'throw away', 'burn' and 'burn *then* throw away'.

* * *

Personal communication from Douglas Andrews, experiencer of event, received via letter.

Apologies for sending you this so long after your initial request, but I live in Derby and my friend, who lives in York, has sent me the clipping of your letter from her local paper. Knowing of my experience, she suggested that I write to you and I hope I am not too late for my story to be of any use to you.

I see that you are asking us to be as accurate about the date and time of our story as possible. I'm afraid that I don't remember exactly, I know only that it was during the early autumn and I think the year was 1978, although it could have been 1979 or even as late as 1982. I was very interested in bird-watching, and took many holidays up on the North York Moors during those years, prior to my marriage and other life events, which took me away from my hobby. I can, however, be sure of the time of year, as I had been watching out for migratory species, particularly short-eared owls heading from northern climes to winter in the UK.

As far as I remember, I had just disassembled my hide, having been lucky enough to see a flock of waxwings passing through the dale in search of berries. It was early evening, with the dusk starting to come in, and my car was not too far away, as I packed up my gear. However, as I passed by what I now know to be the Fortune House, I was overcome with a great thirst. I'd only had a flask of coffee with me and that was now fully drained. I have a medical condition which requires me to be well hydrated, and I had left my bottle of water at my lodgings, due to an oversight whilst rushing to leave.

The house was fully dark, with no lights showing, but I decided to knock on the door anyway, reasoning that someone might be about in the outbuildings at the back, or that I might find an outdoor tap from which to take some water. So I knocked and, to my surprise, the door was answered by a young man. He was wearing a cap and jacket, as though he had just come in from the farm, and I asked him for some water. He did not speak but held the door to allow me inside, and I found myself in a large kitchen.

Reasoning that the young man might be either deaf or unable to speak, I indicated the sink and asked, by means of gesture, if I might help myself to water. There was no reply but, as I had been allowed inside, I supposed it would not be begrudged. I refilled my flask with water, took a large drink, and turned to find that the young man had vanished, leaving me alone in the kitchen. I made my exit, closing the door behind me, and went back to my car.

It was only the following day, whilst talking to the lady who owned the lodgings where I was staying, that the mystery surrounding my water gathering mission became apparent. She informed me that the Fortune House was currently empty, the daughter and son of the family having grown up and left, and Mr and Mrs Fortune being down in York, where Mr Fortune was in hospital and Mrs Fortune was staying with her sister to be near him. There were, my landlady informed me, no animals requiring care, and no reason for anyone to be at the house. She investigated further on my behalf, and the house was found to be locked up securely, with no one resident or in evidence.

I can only say that the young man who let me into the house seemed familiar with the layout and also seemed to have no fear of being thought to be a burglar. His lack of speech, as I said, I put down to a disability, although I cannot attest to how 'solid' or 'real' he looked, as I only glanced at him, and the house was both dark and gloomy, so his appearance was not clear.

I add the note that, when I arrived back at my lodgings after this encounter, my flask was empty, which I attributed to my not having screwed the cap back on securely, and my thirst was completely slaked. I had no recurrence of my health problem, which leads me to believe that I drank whilst in the house. Some to whom I have told this story have told me that I must have seen a ghost, whilst others believe a more mundane explanation. I leave the decision in your hands.

10

The next day, I took Grant over to Hatherleigh Hall with me.

He'd scrubbed up reasonably well, I had to admit. His hair looked tidily cut and he'd lost the beard to reveal a thinner face that made his lack of chin less noticeable. He sat bolt upright next to me all the way there, almost vibrating with eagerness.

'You will stick to the story, won't you?' I turned into the driveway. 'You're not going to blurt anything out?'

'No! No, honestly, Al. I really do realise now what I could have lost. I just hope Jen will let me come back.'

I stayed silent, so as not to let out a sarcastic comment about his realisation of loss being linked to our driving along a gravelled approach that went on for about a mile. Fields either side held the tarnished bells of oats behind black railinged fences and the house sat in the distance, rising like a mirage on the horizon. Grant's words about all that he could have lost packed a little less emotional punch when illustrated by this bucolic splendour and evident landed wealth.

Jenna must have seen the car approaching, because she was out in the car park before we pulled up. Her cheeks were flushed, and she looked very young and very impressionable in a sunflower-patterned dress and bare feet, seeming not to feel the ridging of the gravel under her soles.

Grant got out slowly. 'Hey, Jen,' he said. 'I'm really sorry.'

Jenna let out a squeal and threw herself at him. He caught her and the two of them locked into an embrace. Grant hid his face in her hair, and she had her arms wrapped so tightly around him that she looked as though she was trying to merge herself with his body. There were no words, just the hug.

I got out of the car now, finding that I had to swallow hard to force down the lump in my throat. The emotion looked genuine on both sides. Jenna had her eyes screwed shut but she was visibly crying, Grant's shoulders were shaking too, and I berated myself for my previous cynicism. This was what love should look like. A sunlit clasp of arms, a reunion of tears, hair tangling together, cheeks pressed close. I'd never had that. Grant had never greeted me the way he was murmuring softly to Jen, had never held me as though he was afraid that I'd be snatched away at any second. Nobody had.

But then, I reminded myself, I was built to be sensible. I was not the kind of girl who inspires devoted longing in men. All I seemed to inspire was the desire to see me organise the hell out of their lives whilst cooking edible meals with one hand and filing their tax returns with the other. As soon as they realised that they could organise themselves and that ready meals and accountants were a thing, I was redundant. So I took a deep breath, shook my head and straightened my shoulders to stalk past the moulding together of bodies that was taking place on the drive.

Max was circling, worried, inside the nearest door. He was peering out of the little side window whilst pacing on the spot and practically wringing his hands. 'Jenna seems to be forgiving Grant,' I observed dryly as I practically cannoned into him.

'I know, I know. It's just – she's so liable to start overthinking. Do you think she believes all that "amnesia" rubbish? Isn't she going to ask about the wallet and the belt buckle? And the tooth?'

Today Max was wearing a torn sweatshirt over paint-stained jeans. His trainers were flapping at one sole and he looked far more as though he'd spent six weeks on the streets of Peterborough than Grant did. His hair was scruffed up on one side and he hadn't shaved. It was appalling that someone so badly turned out could look so attractive. I clearly hadn't shaken off my crush as much as I wished I had.

'She wants to believe his story,' I said. 'So she'll put herself through any amount of mental gymnastics to make it fit. And, though I say so myself, it's realistic enough to be credible. All Grant's lacking is any sign of a head wound, and even *Grant* can remember to go "ouch ouch" once or twice.' I looked at Max, with the worry drying his skin into little creases around his eyes and mouth. 'Try to relax.'

'They really do seem very fond of one another, don't they?' Was that the hint of a tone of wistfulness in his voice? Or wishful thinking on my part, because Max must have had his share of devoted love in the past. And, perhaps, in fact, in the present. I knew nothing about his private life at all. He might have a partner tucked away somewhere in this house, for all I knew. The place was big enough to accommodate a bevy of lovers with none of them knowing about the existence of the others, unless they managed a fluke meeting on one of the million staircases one night.

'They do.' I wondered if I sounded as wistful.

Grant and Jenna had broken out of the clinch and were standing, face-width apart, staring into one another's eyes.

'I think I may vomit,' Max said. 'Shall we go upstairs and leave them to it?'

'I think,' I said slowly, 'that we ought to stay out here. Leave the flat to them for a while. I'm sure they've got a lot of, er, making up to do and I'm pretty sure that they won't want her brother and his ex-wife listening in. Maybe I should go home.'

Max looked taken aback. 'But you've only just got here!'

'Max, I live in Pickering, not Melbourne. It's only half an hour.'

'Yes, but...' He looked around, wildly. 'I thought you'd be here all day! I was going to cook lunch!'

I patted his arm gently. 'It's fine. I won't fade away during the drive.'

'I'm not rich, you know,' he said, apropos of nothing. As he was staring out across the acres that bordered the enormous house he lived in, I couldn't really take this seriously.

'Well, in that get-up, I never would have guessed it,' I said briskly. 'Did you mug a tramp and steal his clothes?'

Max seemed to shake himself, as though he was pulling himself back from a vision that he'd been seeing that he wasn't at all sure about. 'What? Oh! No, I was hauling some rubbish out of the old icehouse, we're thinking of getting it repaired and making it part of the tour.'

I raised an eyebrow and pursed my lips. I hoped that my look encompassed everything I felt about people who say they aren't rich but own an icehouse, and it seemed to, because he laughed, suddenly. 'I know, I know, it's all relative.' He looked down at his flapping trainers. 'When I said I'm not rich, I mean, it's a struggle to keep this place ticking over and, now I come to think of it, that's a bit insensitive really.' Now that dark glance flicked up to me and I forced my neck not to go red by sheer mind power. 'Would you like to come and see? The icehouse, I mean. If we can't go inside, we may as well do something else.'

'Max, I really ought...' But I made myself stop. There was absolutely *nothing* I really ought to be doing.

'Please, Alice. Please don't leave me alone with my sister all loved up and having to pretend that Grant has amnesia. You're the only other person who knows how bonkers this whole set-up is – and, in fact, now I come to think of it, it was your idea – so you're the only person I can really talk to. Besides, watching the pair of them doing the whole romantic reunion is making me feel dreadfully inadequate and a little bit lonely.'

He was back to looking at his trainers again.

My stomach was doing curious things. It felt alternately hollow, as though I hadn't eaten for a week, and fizzing with acid, as if I were excited. Max was trying to keep me here. He wanted to talk to me. I would stop him from feeling lonely. That was activating the effervescence. The knowledge that he was so far out of my league, that he was in the Premier Division whilst I languished at the bottom of the Sponsored By The Local Carpet Manufacturer And Everyone Works On Their Dad's Farm During The Week amateur league tables kept the hollowness. The best I could ever hope for was Max feeling so desperate for company that I might get offered a half pint of cheap cider, some chips and a quick fumble on the back seat of his car.

Oh, well, I could always go along with the fumble and then plead amnesia. We'd got a precedent.

'All right. Show me the icehouse, then.'

We started to walk around the house on the crispy gravel, before Max broke off to lead the way along a grassy terrace towards a small clump of trees set into the side of a hillock, which formed a 'feature'. We walked in silence, broken only by the slop-flop of the sole of his trainer.

'It's nothing special,' he said, as we reached the trees.

I stopped, opened my hands and turned around to indicate the vast acres, the house, the carefully groomed terracing. 'Max, you have an icehouse. All I have is a place where the toilet freezes solid in cold weather. Believe me, it's special.'

But at least about the icehouse he was right, it wasn't special.

Apart from being attached to a bloody great big house with gardens plural, it was a brick-lined hole in the ground inside an echoing cavern. There was a prosaic ladder leading into the hole and rubble sacks full of junk inside the little gate that led in, obviously where Max had been clearing it out.

'You see? It's a big dark pit into which they used to pack ice from the lake in winter. They'd cover it with straw and it would stay frozen into the summer.'

'That's a lot of trouble to go to for out-of-season snowballs,' I said, trying to lighten the mood.

Max gave me a stern look. 'You are far too intelligent for that remark,' he said, leading me back out and closing the metal gate behind us.

I wanted to simper 'Am I?' and fish for compliments using fluttered eyelashes as bait, but that sort of behaviour didn't wash from someone who has SENSIBLE practically carved into her forehead, so I just said, 'Yes, sorry.'

He rested his head against the bars of the gate and leaned in a defeated way. 'I don't have enough disposable income, I don't work out, I care too much about my sister and I spend too long working,' he said, slightly muffled, yet his voice echoed hollowly around the brick cave. The echo gave his words the sepulchral nature of one denouncing their entire life, which, I suppose, he was.

'What?'

'That's the litany of failings that past girlfriends have given as a reason for breaking up with me. Oh, apart from one who was lovely but definitely didn't want children. And I do.' He kept his forehead pressed against the gate as though he were staring into the darkness beyond.

I had no idea what to say. And, even worse, I had no idea why *he* was saying *this*. It was none of my business. Then I wondered if seeing Jen and Grant had shaken up old memories. 'Relationships can be hard,' I said, channelling the Reddit relationship forum, which was about the only knowledge I had of interpersonal connections these days, apart from borrowing Malcolm's rucksack, which was hardly tawdry threesomes in cheap hotel rooms. 'If your exes broke up with you for those reasons, then they weren't the right person for you,' I added, now channelling Dear Deirdre, whose advice column Sheila insisted on reading aloud for the edification of the office.

Max took a deep breath and straightened up. 'No, they weren't. That is becoming apparent,' he said. When he turned to face me, the pressure of the gate had formed a giant red groove down the centre of his forehead, like a solipsistic brand. The thought made me laugh.

'What?' it was his turn to ask.

'You look like you've got "I" on your face.'

He raised his hand and felt the mark, then started to laugh too. 'Well, that'll teach me to be so self-pitying, won't it? Self-obsession makes you look like a dick.'

We moved away from the dark oppressive hole and out into the sunshine, which seemed brighter in contrast. Somewhere away to our right, water sparkled, and I presumed this was the lake that had produced the ice for the icehouse. But somehow the grounds didn't seem so overdone now, more like an extension of Max. After all, someone had to own places like Hatherleigh Hall, so why not him? It was an accident of birth that had given it all to him. He'd hardly gone out and bought the place, like an overpaid footballer desperately in search of somewhere to put his money, had he?

'Did you grow up here?' I asked casually, as we walked, and in his case flopped, back along the smooth lawn towards the house.

'Until I was eight.' Max looked across at the square chimneys and stolid portico, set firmly into green acres as though someone had pressed a Lego house onto a board. 'Then I went away to school. Then there was university – I didn't really come back until I started my PhD, just before Dad died.' I noticed he didn't mention his mother. That struck me as odd, but there was something about his manner, the brisk way he picked up the pace until we were virtually sprinting over the lawn, that told me that the omission was deliberate. 'Do you think they will have finished consummating their relationship again yet?'

'I'd give them a bit longer,' I puffed.

'Oh, well. I suppose I can make us some coffee in the house kitchens.' Max set off along the corridor that I'd followed Jenna down before, past the obvious 'below stairs' décor of whitewash and flagstoned floors. 'It's what the public expects,' he said, seeing me looking at the dreary paintwork. 'They want things to look original, otherwise I'd have got the place plastered and properly heated years ago. The crowds come for the whole *Downton Abbey* vibe and the history, so that's what we have to give them. Costs a fucking fortune,' he finished slightly dismally, turning through the doorway into the huge room where Jenna had made scones the first time I'd been here.

'We don't have to light the range to heat the water, do we?' I asked, slightly warily, as I stared around the echoing space. 'Or find a flunky to do it for us?'

'Nope.' Max bent to a low-level cupboard with a wooden door thicker than the one that kept my house secure. Inside, there was an electric kettle and jars of coffee and sugar. 'The staff use this as their kitchen when we're not open. Well, they use the housekeeper's room through there, but this is where the kettle lives.' He nodded to a door almost concealed in the wall.

'This place—' I looked up at the ceiling, racked with beams from which hooks of varying sizes hung. 'It's almost as if it's not real – I've never been anywhere that felt so much like a film set. I can't imagine a family growing up here.'

'It's just a house, Alice.' Max plugged in the kettle. 'I'd really rather hand the whole thing over to someone else to manage and get on with life, writing books and teaching, but managers cost money and the finances are pared to the bone as it is. It's duty, not love, keeping me here.'

'Would Jenna take it on?' I thought of the dichotomy of Jenna, the emotionally frail and the bike-riding badass. Then I imagined Grant as the other half of the team and instantly could see him as the ineffectual lord in every TV drama ever, foppishly wandering around in baggy trousers with a spaniel at his heels.

'I dunno. Maybe.' He changed the subject. 'So, how did you get on with all the papers yesterday? Anything interesting in there? Sorry I didn't see you off, I had to go down to Home Farm to see about some fencing.'

We entered a more neutral discussion about what to keep, what to throw away and what to possibly donate to the Beck Isle Museum in Pickering, where they'd made the just-gone history of local life a tourist attraction. It kept us busy until there was a sudden appearance in the doorway of Jenna looking radiant and Grant with his arm around her.

'I've proposed,' he said proudly. 'We're going to get married.'

A sudden flashback to my wedding day filled my mind. Registry office in winter, my mother very frail by now, Dad long gone. All my workmates had attended, Grant had had two of his gaming friends, and we'd gone for a fish and chip supper afterwards. It had felt like a day brushed under the carpet, a formality to be gone through. Grant had looked smug that day, though. Happy enough but with a tiny tinge of 'now I don't have to try at all any more'.

Today he looked genuinely delighted. Almost handsome, in fact, with his new haircut and slightly rakish sideburns.

'Wow. That's – congratulations, both of you.' I stepped in and hugged them both. 'You'll have to divorce me first, though, Grant.'

A fleeting expression of slight panic crossed his face, but Jenna beamed. 'It's fine. I'll take care of the details,' she said. She was absolutely radiant, her skin flushed and her eyes sparkling. Despite the unlikeliness of the pairing, Grant and Jenna genuinely seemed made for one another.

I pushed down the thought that he'd need to work on his desire to fake his own death to avoid difficult conversations.

'We should have champagne,' Max suddenly announced. 'There's some in my study.'

'I can't,' I said. 'I've got to drive.'

'Er, Al, there's about fifty million bedrooms in this place.' Grant, still surfing the wave of recent sex and having proposed to a half-share of the estate, waved a hand. 'I'm sure you can stay over.'

'Oh, yes, do stay!' Jenna, still clutching Grant's arm as though she feared he might be swept back to Peterborough if she let go, beamed at me. 'Let's open *all* the champagne and have a party!'

Max met my eye. He made a 'this is out of my hands' sort of face and spread his hands wide. But now a lot of the tension had gone from him, there was a little bit of amusement in his face and a spark in those dark eyes that told me that seeing his sister so happy was buoying him up too.

'Oh, all right,' I said, probably sounding a bit grumpy. After all, what did I have to dash home for? An evening in with the TV, listening to Next Door Right's attempts to persuade her unholy triumvirate of children to actually go to bed, at full volume? Waiting for the slam that indicated that Mr Next Door Left had taken the dog for its final walk? Everything that served to double underline my single status, my lack of any dependants. Sensible Alice, there behind her drawn curtains with a cup of tea, whilst everyone else threw caution to the winds. Except, possibly Mr Next Door Left, whose well-trodden evening walk route I could map in my head. 'Why not?' I added, with a little bit more animation.

'Party *on*!' said Grant, that well-known party animal.

We went up to the flat, into a room I'd not seen before. A piano sat beside an open window with a balcony jutting beyond, like a book cover for a novel where the musical hero goes deaf and spends the whole book wafting around being angsty and handsome. A far more prosaic television took up one corner, faced by a saggy sofa. Someone had left a pair of downtrodden slippers and a badly folded copy of *The Guardian* on the floor, which reassured me that the flat was actually lived in and not kept visually pristine whilst everyone lived in hunched squalor in the attic.

Max fetched champagne and glasses and we all got rather tipsy rather quickly and very giggly. I tried to moderate my intake – I wasn't at all sure about staying over, and *someone* needed to make sure that Grant didn't become drunk enough to blurt out the truth about his amnesia – but it was useless. The champagne was far too drinkable, buttery and vanilla-y, with a hint of strawberries. We drank a couple of bottles before deciding we were hungry and went en masse to the kitchen, where I had confused memories of laughing hysterically at Max's attempts to make risotto while Grant danced on the table...

... and the rest of the evening was all a blur. There was some kind of memory, or it may have been a bad dream, of my playing the piano and singing an indecent song that I'd learned at school, but it was all fragments. As though everything after the risotto was a jigsaw with the pieces broken up and scrambled and only parts of the picture being whole. And, from the feel of it, as I gradually swam into consciousness, someone had sat on the box.

It was dark, for which I was grateful, and I didn't have a headache, for which I was practically ecstatic. But my mouth tasted as though I'd licked those worn slippers, I had a strange pain in one ankle, and I was lying on something soft with my head dangling in space. There was a telephone ringing somewhere.

'Assa phone,' I mumbled indistinctly.

When a voice beside me said, 'Yeah. Noisy phone. Make it shut up,' and there was the sensation of someone turning over, sobriety returned with an almost audible whoosh.

'What the hell? Who are you?' I jack-knifed to a sitting position, clutching what turned out to be an eiderdown to my fully dressed chest.

There was a moment of silence, presumably as a similar level of awful dawning memory arrived at the figure beside me. Then, 'Alice?'

'*Max*?'

The distant phone stopped ringing. The silence was almost worse.

'Er,' said Max. 'Have you got clothes on?'

I felt around a bit. 'Yes. All of them. Even my shoes.'

'Me too. So that's a good thing?'

I had no idea why he made it a question. 'Where are we?'

'Hang on, I'll find a light.' There were sounds of groping, then the bed dipped, there was a lot of blundering and swearing and then a weedy illumination appeared. At first, it seemed that I was in a tent with no flap, but as my vision cleared, it became apparent that it was a four-poster bed, with the curtains partly drawn around it. There was an enormous wooden cabinet by the bed but that was all I could see. Even Max had become invisible.

'Is this...' I had to clear my throat. I really, *really* needed a glass of water. 'Is this your bedroom?'

From somewhere in the Stygian gloom, Max snorted. 'No, of course it bloody isn't,' he said mildly. 'I may have delusions of grandeur, but I've got a perfectly ordinary bed. I *think* we're in the Blue Room. I vaguely remember something about giving you a tour of the house yesterday – this must have been as far as we got.'

'Why is it dark?'

'Because it's three o'clock in the morning.'

'Oh, God.'

'And we don't have big main lights in these rooms, it's bad for the furnishings, so I've turned the emergency lighting on.'

'This *is* an emergency, and I need a bit more light than that.' I swung my legs over the edge of the bed but couldn't feel the floor. 'And I need water. Lots of water.'

Max came into shadowy view at the end of the bed. He looked rumpled and half-asleep still. 'If this *is* the Blue Room, then we're not far from the main staircase. We can go up to the flat.'

'Right.' I couldn't quite muster the bodily organisation to get myself up off the bed and instead just slumped backwards, realising that I was still quite drunk. 'Or stay here.'

'I'm glad you said that.' Max crawled onto the bed beside me. 'I'm not sure I can find the door. Maybe, maybe we should camp out here until it gets light.' He shuffled a bit closer. 'Unless you feel sick. This bed is Elizabethan and I'm not sure we'd get vomit out of the hangings.'

'No, I'm fine.' More than fine, in fact, with Max's warmth against me, feeling his breath puffing against my cheek. He seemed to be very close, but it was too dark to see. He must have pulled the curtains around the bed again when he got back in.

'Good.' There was movement and his voice got a little further away from my face. 'The Blue Room,' he began in the tones of one reading from a tourist brochure, 'is in the original part of the house, which dates from the reign of Henry VIII. Most of the rest of that house was demolished and rebuilt in the reign of Queen Anne, leaving only the central portion as original. The furniture and hangings are mostly Elizabethan, the exception being the chinoiserie cabinet by the bed, which dates to the early eighteenth century, the beginning of the popular Rococo movement.'

'Why are you telling me this?' I wanted to go back to sleep now. The lingering remnants of the champagne had caught up with me.

'Sorry. Force of habit. I do the house tours, y'see. And I think I'm still very drunk.'

'Well, let's sleep it off and try to tiptoe up to the flat as soon as it gets light enough to see. Before Grant and Jenna are awake, anyway. With any luck, they'll think we crashed out in separate rooms,' I said, trying to inject some sense into the situation. 'And then, when I am sober enough to see, I can make an early start on sorting the papers again.'

There was a pause. I thought Max had fallen asleep, his breathing was regular and soft, and I wanted to make sure he was fully asleep before I let myself drop off, in case I snored. When he spoke, it was so unexpected that I jumped. 'I really like you, Alice.'

'Don't start that again,' I said sternly.

'But I do! Why don't you believe me?'

There was enough alcohol in my system to disable my usual speech filters. 'Because you've got a big house and an estate and you're gorgeous and clever and I live in a terraced house that my parents left me and I'm big and plain and I make sure that windows go in the right houses.' The words came out in a machine-gun burst. 'Now, shut up and go to sleep.'

Another moment, broken by some wriggling. 'Alice,' he said eventually. 'I want to show you something.'

'If it's your dick, then prepare to say goodbye to the Elizabethan bed, because I will tear it apart and batter you to death with one of the posts,' I said briskly. I wasn't afraid, I'd had more willies waved at me than I knew what to do with. The fitters' humour could be somewhat robust and the #MeToo movement hadn't really made much of an impact in our tiny square of North Yorkshire.

'Of course it's not my dick! Good God, woman, what do you take me for?' said Max, sounding so upper class that it made me laugh.

'And stop laughing. My reproductive equipment is not something to be sniggered at.' He somewhat spoiled the effect of this haughty retort by sniggering himself. 'Sorry, sorry. Like I said, I'm still really drunk. But *in vino veritas* and all that. And please don't pretend not to know what that means, you're better than that.'

'All right, sorry. What do you want to show me?'

This time, the pause went on and on until I realised Max had fallen asleep again. Carefully, I crept my body a few centimetres further away, just in case, because I didn't want to snore in his ear, and let myself drop back into a grateful stupor again.

11

————

We crept back up to the flat in the early daylight, hung-over and greedy for tea and toast. There was no movement from Jenna or Grant and we sat in the kitchen with mugs of tea so strong that it was almost soup as the toaster popped regular slices at us.

We hadn't really spoken much since the conversation in the night. I still got little heart-thumps when I thought about the way Max had said, 'I really like you,' but reasoned that posh champagne was probably no bar to the drunken 'I bloody love you' syndrome. He'd been affectionately drunk, that was all. Nothing to it. He'd hardly known what he was saying. But none of my best rational thinking could quite drive away the feeling those words had given me, and I was hugging them close to me as I downed another mug of best Yorkshire tea and an unflattering amount of chunky toast. I had no idea what bread it had been made from, but I had the awful feeling that the word 'artisan' would be in the description somewhere.

Gradually the liquid and carbohydrate intake did their work and we straightened up a bit and opened our eyes properly. Max let out a little sigh. 'How much did we drink last night?'

'I have no idea. You were in charge of the bottles. Where did it all come from?'

'Dad had quite a stash. He only drank champagne, apparently, and I *think* we may have seen off most of his collection.' He sighed again. 'Oh, well. His daughter just got engaged, I think he would have approved.'

'I'm not sure he would have approved of his son and heir crashing out on the antiques, though,' I said. 'With a woman of the Lower Orders. That's the sort of thing that used to get sons disinherited faster than you can say Georgette Heyer, you know.' I refilled my mug.

Max looked at me. 'Right,' he said. 'I said I'd got something to show you and now might be the time, before anyone else wakes up.' He stood up and wielded his mug. 'Bring your tea.'

I followed him out of the flat and down the main staircase this time. We walked past a young woman in an overall who was vacuuming an acre of carpet with a Henry Hoover, who looked up as we passed. 'Morning, Max.'

'Hi, Daisy.'

I could feel Daisy's curious eyes following me along the corridor and even the Henry had turned to look my way as I trailed behind Max to the end of the passage, where he threw open a double door and bowed. 'This is what I want you to see.'

I stepped past him and into a room that ran the entire width of the house. Black-shrouded windows made up one whole wall because the room had obviously been built to make the most of natural light, although now it was only illuminated by some subtle wall-lighting. Polished wooden flooring smelled of beeswax beneath me and I had a sudden schoolgirl urge to take off my shoes and slide as far as I could in my socks. Then I looked up. 'Bloody hell.'

'This is the Painted Room,' Max said. 'Or, as we know it in the

family, the Boobie Room. It's eight-times Great Grandad's equiva-
lent of a mucky photo album.'

The walls and ceiling were covered in paintings of naked
women. There were occasional naked cherubs in there too, presumably to detract slightly from the numbers of boobs, but they didn't
dilute them much. I had never seen so much naked flesh on display,
and that was including the showers after hockey. 'It's...' I had to take
a mouthful of tea to find the words. 'Er. Quite striking.'

'The legend goes that Eighth Great Grandad had all his lovers
painted here.' Max pointed to one. 'This is Lady Elizabeth Weir,
whose family owned the estate next door. This is Carlotta of Venice.
We *think* this one may be the Duchess of Devonshire, but we aren't
entirely sure.'

Despite the fact that most of the ladies had been painted in
provocative poses, there was something entirely unerotic about so
much nakedness. A bit like a naturists' convention, I thought, trying
to comprehend the vast swathes of flesh. 'I wonder if the artist ran
out of pink?' I mused, staring at the large painted sky, which
extended down two walls. 'He must have enjoyed doing the clouds,
for a rest.'

Max walked into the centre of the room and put his tea down on
the floor. 'But do you get my point?' He looked around at the walls.
'Alice?'

'No,' I muttered into my mug, trying to ignore the fact that there
were about fourteen breasts immediately above my head and the
number of cavorting thighs didn't bear thinking about.

'You said last night that you didn't think I could like you
because you were big and plain.'

'I was hoping you were too drunk to remember that,' I said,
somewhat waspishly. 'Or too much of a gentleman to mention it
ever again.'

'Well, I wasn't and I'm not. Just look.' He waved a hand at the billowing mass of fuchsia, watermelon, salmon and coral, interspersed with darker shades of both skin and hair. 'This is what Eighth Great Grandad found sexy. These girls were the pin-ups of their time. Just because nowadays it's fashionable to weigh the same as a large carp, not every man finds that attractive, and in Great Grandad's day they would have been seen as starving waifs living in poverty.'

'So you're trying to tell me that I'm a great beauty, four hundred years out of my time?' I stayed near the door. There was altogether too much 'female' in the room already.

'Alice, I'm telling you that not every man finds the same thing attractive. Not every man values a woman for how tiny her waist is or the fact that she can get into clothes made for a ten-year-old. Some men, *lots* of men, want a woman they can talk to, who's kind and interesting and clever and doesn't want them to be ripped gym-fanatic billionaires.' He gestured at the ceiling. 'If all men liked the same kind of women, then there would be one very smug super-model in the world and the human race would die out in two generations.'

I kept my eyes on the floor. Was he saying what I *thought* he was saying? He couldn't be. It wasn't possible. Not a man who fitted the 'tall, dark and handsome' mould as though it had been constructed around him. Not a man who owned all this. Not, basically, *Max*. How could he like someone like me, without being intrinsically flawed?

'Nobody's perfect, Alice,' he said gently, as though he was reading my mind. 'Nobody. We all have our baggage and our hang-ups, mine are in my head, that's all.'

He came in a little bit closer. Not too close, maybe he didn't want to risk getting my tea thrown over him. 'But...' I was floundering. 'How can you? I mean... I'm *me*.'

'Well, Beyonce was busy and Christina Hendricks is spoken for.'
Max flashed me a grin. 'You were third on the list.'

'But...' I said again and stared down at myself.

'Looks all right from where I'm standing.' He was definitely
smiling now. 'Plus you've got a brain and you're not afraid to use it,
and that's the number one fascination for me.' He came in closer
still. 'There's no rush. Just, please, believe me.'

Max reached out a hand and touched my hair. His eyes were
very dark, I noticed, meeting them properly for the first time. So
dark that I could feel myself pulled in, watching his pupils expand
and feeling his hand touch the side of my neck. My skin reacted, as
though all my nerve endings were pushed into that tiny part of me
that was under his fingers, and I could feel nothing else but the
sensation of his fingertips under my jaw.

The door burst open. 'Oh, thank God!' Jenna erupted into the
room. 'Daisy said you were in here. Hi, Alice. The police are on the
phone, Max. They say they need to talk to you, urgently. They've
found a body under the Fortune House.'

12

The hole was enormous and there was tape and plastic fencing round the entire dale now. It had stopped looking like an exploded house and begun to look like an archaeological site, with a digger arrested in motion and three suited-up assistants sitting on a bank with a flask.

Max and I stared into the hole. 'We decided to clear right down to the foundation level,' said Digger One, the forensics manager. 'More to give the guys some experience at sifting for evidence than anything. Now your misper has turned up alive and well, there was no more need, but we'd got this far, so we thought we'd keep going and once we got the basement floor up... well. *This* turned up.' He pointed with the end of a trowel at a glimmer right at the bottom of the hole.

'And it's definitely human bones?' Max asked. He sounded a bit queasy.

'Oh, yes. We reckon there's a complete skeleton in there. We're going back in, once the lads have finished their tea. You had to be notified, as the owner of the land.'

'But it's *under* the house, right?' I found my voice. 'As in "older than"?'

The forensic investigator, who, to my slightly disappointed eye didn't look anything like the characters in *Silent Witness* and, in fact, bore more of a resemblance to a bank manager on his day off, looked at me appraisingly. 'We're not certain,' he said. 'Could have been buried down there, or could have been there when the house was built. He's been there a while, certainly, we're not treating it as a crime scene.'

I felt Max relax a little. 'But the site is sealed off again, I suppose.'

'Until we get your lad lifted and back to the lab, I'm afraid so.'

'Oh, bugger.' Max put a hand on my arm. I felt every finger pressure, every degree of the heat of his skin. 'That's the final ghost vigil written off then. It was going to be my concluding chapter too.'

'Can't you do it somewhere else?' I tried to ignore the weight of his hand.

'But the book is about the supposed haunting of the Fortune House. It's going to look a bit bloody daft if I finish it somewhere else.'

The policeman who'd driven us over, having had to pick us up from Hatherleigh Hall as none of us had wanted to drive in case the champagne was still in our bloodstreams, shifted his weight. He was obviously expecting us to have A Domestic, and looked fully prepared to shove the pair of us into the big hole.

'Why not change the focus? Make it more about the whole "who sees ghosts and why" than about the place?' I asked, channelling Oliver Sacks and the half dozen other books I'd still got piled beside my bed, accumulating a library fine. 'Not so much haunted house, more psychology.'

Max's head came up, he stopped staring at the partly uncovered bone in the hole and gazed out over the moorland horizon. Several disgruntled sheep stared back. 'Oh,' he said. 'Oh. Now that's an idea.'

'Look, shall we let this poor man drive us back? He's clearly fed up with standing here, and we may as well be sobering up somewhere useful. If we're allowed to go, obviously.' I glanced towards Forensic Man, who nodded.

'We needed your permission to excavate the skeleton,' he said cheerfully. 'You didn't even really need to come over.'

Our driver took his hat off and wiped his forehead. I had the feeling he was swearing inwardly.

'I wanted to see,' Max said. 'And take a few pictures.' He raised his camera. 'For the book.'

Besides, it had got us out of the house, where Jenna had begun wedding planning with a vengeance, and neither Max nor I had been able to stand more than ten minutes of conjecture over a suitable location for the ceremony. Not while we were hung-over, anyway.

'Can you drop us in Pickering?' I asked the driver, when we got back into the police car.

'I'm an on-duty officer, not a bloody taxi,' he muttered, but did concede to drop us outside my house, where Mrs Next Door Right took great delight in noting our arrival. By the end of the day, it would probably be all over the neighbourhood that I'd been arrested for whatever crime they thought I was capable of. I had no idea who they would assume Max was, in the dramatic story they would construct. My carer, possibly.

The house smelled hot and stuffy. I suspected I did too.

'You can come and stay at the Hall,' Max said. 'Just for the rest of the week,' he added quickly. 'While you're sorting the papers.'

I couldn't think of a single reason why I shouldn't. There was nothing to stay here for, and I had to admit that the champagne party of last night had been a lot more fun than my usual evening activities of TV and magazine reading. I wanted to make a protest, something to justify my solitary existence, but Max was currently looking at the way I lived. I didn't think he'd believe that I had to come home to attend to my million admirers. 'I'll pack some stuff then,' I said.

'I'll get Jen to come over and pick us up in a bit.' Max began to walk around my living room. 'After they've drunk a lot more water and maybe had a bit of a nap.'

I now realised that I'd given Max carte blanche to be in my house and looking at my things. It hadn't mattered so much on Sunday night, when we'd all been too shaken by Grant's sudden arrival to observe the niceties of checking the skirting boards for dust or only choosing the most flattering photographs to display. But now, in the cold light of a Wednesday, I wished I hadn't brought him back here. He was looking at my parents' wedding photo when I went upstairs to fetch a holdall and fling a few of my clothes in, in a way that was as unlike packing for a holiday as was possible, and consisted of all my clean underwear and the jeans that someone had once complimented me on.

When I got back downstairs, Max was still looking at the photos. 'Are these your parents? You're very like your mother.'

Mum had been eight stone two on her wedding day. I only looked like her if you imagined Mum after a decade of really good dinners.

'Yes, that's Mum and Dad. That's my brother, Stewart, and his family.' I pointed at the group on the bookcase. 'They live in Aberdeen.'

'He's a lot older than you?'

I wished Max didn't sound so interested. It meant I was going to have to explain my family set-up, and I hadn't really had to do that since I was at school. 'My mum and dad met in hospital,' I said, trying to sound factual. 'Mum had a degenerative illness and

Dad had a form of cancer from where he worked when he was young. They got married but were told there was no chance of children. Stewart was a total surprise, and ten years later, I was an even bigger one. They both got insurance payouts for...' I stopped. Max was looking at me with an expression that I didn't want to analyse.

'For terminal illness,' I said, trying to be factual. 'Dad died first. Stewart had already moved up to Scotland with Morag then. I looked after Mum. When Grant and I got married, we all lived here together for six months, then she died. I was left the house, Stewart got the money that was left from the insurance payouts. That's why I own this house.'

I stopped. It had been ten years ago, but my voice still caught on the memories.

'Ghosts,' Max said softly. 'There are always ghosts.'

'I'm sorry?' I went to straighten the curtains so he couldn't see my face. Mr Next Door Left gave me a cheery wave as he passed, just his upper half and the dog's tail visible over the top of the small wall at the front. He was probably on his way to pick up the gossip about my arrival from Mrs Next Door Right.

'Oh, not in the spectral figure on the stairs sense. I meant ghosts in your head.' He looked as though he was speaking about both of us now. As though my upbringing with frail parents, constant hospital visits and doctors' appointments and never quite knowing what I would come home to was something he understood. 'I'm so sorry, Alice.'

'Memories. Just memories, Max. We've all got them. Some are good and some are – not so good. It's the way we react to them that gives us the ghosts, I think.' I looked down at Mum and Dad, all flowers and contented smiles. 'I try to choose to remember the good stuff, which doesn't always work, but it helps.'

There was a bit of a pause. Then Max said, 'That sounds very sensible. Are they really not ghosts somewhere in your imagination? Watching you, trying to communicate?'

'The only thing they'd have to tell me is that I ought to dust more often. Oh, and Dad would probably have things to say about the amount of gardening I don't do. But that's all. No ghosts. No need for them to hang around here when they could be—' I shook my head and took Mum and Dad's picture from him and put it back on the shelf, where a narrow groove in the dust revealed its exact resting place.

'Our mum died when I was eight,' he said, unexpectedly.

I remembered the photographs, that smiling young woman who'd looked like Jenna, the much older husband with Max's eyes. 'That must have been hard.'

'Hard for Dad, yes. That's why he sent me away to school. He couldn't manage two young children on his own.'

'Did you not have nannies and housekeepers and, oh, I don't know, nursery maids?' I suddenly realised that I ought to rewatch *Downton Abbey* and make notes.

'Not really, there wasn't the money for that. She was killed. Fell off her horse.' Max was keeping his eyes on my parents' photo, determinedly not looking at me.

I could see the motes rotating in the air around him, where the sun shone in and the disturbed dust was still settling. It gave him a shimmery outline, as though he were a ghost himself. 'I'm so sorry,' I echoed his words to me. They didn't help, I knew that, but it was better than saying nothing.

'Jenna was only three,' Max said, staccato. It sounded as if there were many, many more words that he wanted to say, built up around the experience in layers. I just needed to unlock them.

'Max, sit down and talk to me.' I touched his arm and he swung round to look me in the face.

'I don't know if I can.'

'Well, if you move that magazine and those newspapers—'

'I *meant* talk about it, not sit down.' There was a tiny lift at the corner of his mouth. I only noticed it because I'd studied his face so closely. At least having a crush came in useful sometimes.

'I know.' I let myself smile in answer. 'I'm trying to lighten the moment.'

Now he laughed. 'Oh, I do like you, Alice! You really don't let me get away with anything, do you? Including self-pity.'

'Tell me what you need to and then I will decide whether or not a degree of self-pity is to be allowed.' I spoke softly but tried to keep the tone of levity. Max seemed to respond better to being challenged than he did to sympathy. Maybe he'd had enough of that over the years; insincere sympathy, that artificially gentle pity that people put on to pretend that they understood, when how could they? How *could* they understand what it felt like to be a child who had to cook and clean for herself because her parents were too ill? Who couldn't go out and play after school because Mum needed someone to go to the shop and pick up her prescriptions or needed help counting out her pills because her hands were bad that day, or Dad needed lifting and turning? I'd *had* to be sensible back then, and I'd got stuck in that persona.

It was an uncomfortable realisation.

Max sat and I perched myself next to him. 'Jen used to see Mum, you know,' he said. The words were casual, but the tone wasn't. 'She said Mum used to come into her room at night and kiss her and tell her to be a good girl. After she died, I mean. And part of me wants to believe that Jen was only three, she was at that age when dreams and reality aren't always easy to tell apart, maybe she was dreaming of Mum? Or she was remembering and she didn't have the language to explain that this was all memory, all things that *used* to happen. Of course, I only realised that later, once I was studying psychology. At the time, I was just angry.'

'You were angry with Jen?' I put my hand over his. His fingers were cold.

'I thought – God, this is ridiculous, I've not even thought about this for years – I thought, why did Mum come to Jen and not to me? Didn't she love me enough to come back and tell *me* to be a good boy?' Max shook his head and then used his spare hand to rake his hair back. He didn't move the one I was holding, I noticed. 'So I took it out on Jen. I was horrible to her, Alice.'

'She doesn't seem to bear a grudge,' I said.

'I'm not sure she even remembers.' Max looked at me directly now. His eyes were slightly red. 'We don't talk about it. But Dad sent me away to school. Oh, it wasn't entirely because I was fighting with my sister, or because our mother had died, I mean, I'd just finished pre-prep school and Dad was obviously having to decide whether to keep me on there or send me on to boarding prep, but I made the decision easy for him.'

'You're talking posh-people talk again,' I said, gently squeezing his fingers with a sense of amazement at how easy it felt to touch him, how comfortable to sit next to him with our shoulders brushing. He didn't fidget further away or get up and head to the kitchen; we could actually *talk*, properly exchanging information in an emotional way and I realised, with a slight sense of shock, how I'd never had this with Grant. Any show of emotion to him had been met with a joke, a silly face pulled, a quick attempt to change the subject. Or even that 'zoning out' expression, where he'd stopped listening and started thinking about something else before I'd even got to the thing I was worried about.

Was *this* how it was meant to be? Was this what all those romantic books were on about? Was this what Dear Deirdre meant by 'honest communication'? It felt – sad, yes, listening to Max talking about his mother, but also somehow as though these things had to be said. How could we have a relationship if we didn't understand these things about one another?

Then I realised I'd thought *relationship* in association with *Max* and nearly dropped his hand. As though he'd felt me react, he curled his fingers through mine. 'Sorry about that. But yes, Mum had just died and Jen was telling me that she'd seen her and then Dad sent me away – it all kind of curdled in my head into feelings about Mum not loving me as much as she loved Jen and her ghost not even bothering to visit me.'

'I thought you didn't believe in ghosts.'

Max dropped his gaze away from me now and looked at our linked fingers. 'I don't know,' he said. 'I don't know. If I believe, then I have to acknowledge that Mum never came to me. If I don't, then I can think that Jen was mistaken, that it was dreams and memory and not really understanding the situation – she was only a toddler.' He gave our combined hands a little shake. 'It's more comfortable not to believe. To be able to disprove experiences; to say it's all psychological and to do with expectation and priming and fantasy-prone mindsets.' He gave my fingers a squeeze. 'But do you know something? I can't believe how good this feels. How *right*, somehow. To be telling all this to someone and for that someone to be you.' His attention was back on my face now, eyes moving, scanning.

I had to look away. 'Maybe I should make some more tea. This stuff will be cold.'

'Alice...'

'No.' I stood up and gently uncurled my fingers from around his. 'It would never work,' I added briskly. I couldn't even look at him, with his dark hair all tousled, the slight line of stubble on his cheeks, the curve under his lower lip – he was all my dreams rolled into one man and I couldn't bear to be let down again.

'Why not?' He sounded genuinely curious.

I kept my eyes on my parents' wedding picture. 'Because it wouldn't. We're too different. I'm boring, sensible Alice of the size 16 jeans and the floaty tops that are supposed to make you look a size smaller but make me look as though I fell through the curtains. I've never been to boarding school – hell, I've never even been to *France*. I was born here and I'll die here and I'm only cut out to organise window fitters and listen to Malcolm's tales of walking holidays in Scotland. This is *me*, Max. And it always will be.'

There was a moment of silence. Then Max said, 'I'm sensational in bed, you know.'

'*What*?' I couldn't help myself, I started to laugh. It was so unexpected.

'I am. Apparently. So I've been told. Just in case that influences your decision.'

When I let myself flick a glance his way, there was a deadpan expression on his face, but a tiny spark of mischief in his eyes. He was doing what I'd done, adding some humour to stop a situation from circling into doom.

'In that case, I am sure you will have no shortage of women to relieve you of your no doubt phenomenally high sperm count.' I tried not to grin. 'You don't need me.'

'Oh, I'm sure I don't *need* you.' He picked up that wedding picture again. 'But I want you. I want your way of looking at things, I want your intelligence and your down to earthiness and I sure as hell want your body, whatever you might think of it. It's sex on legs from where I'm standing.'

'But I'm...'

'Remember the Boobie Room? All those gorgeous women? Not a thigh gap amongst them.' Now he turned and gave me such a direct look that I felt that heat rising at the base of my throat again. 'Maybe that influenced me at an impressionable age. But you are my idea of perfect, Alice, you're clever and you're kind, you have emotional intelligence and you're funny. You're also bloody gorgeous. If you don't want me, that's fine, I will live with your decision.'

I looked at the smile on my mother's face, on her wedding day. Neither of my parents knew how long they had left, even when they'd married. I'd often wondered if it wouldn't have been easier for them to never have met, never have had to suffer one another's pain, never had to worry about Stewart and me being orphaned. But they had met and they'd gone for it. Marriage, and then the surprise babies, and, despite the daily treatments and the medication and the suffering, I knew they'd had a happy time together. 'Seize the day', wasn't that how it went? And here was this amazing man who didn't seem to see me as I saw myself and whose very presence made me feel as though even my more generously cut clothing was a size too small and heavily insulated.

'I didn't say I didn't want you,' I said slowly. 'Wanting you is the least of it. It's more that I'm... outclassed.'

'I'm just a person, Alice. Okay, I've got an education and a big house. So what? I've also got a sister with an eating disorder, no money, a book that, despite my best efforts, isn't writing itself, a study full of someone else's shopping lists and your ex-husband as my incipient brother-in-law. Class has nothing to do with it.'

I looked again at Mum and Dad. Smiling at the camera, as though they had all the time in the world. 'Well,' I said slowly, 'I suppose we could give it a try. But I want to take it gradually. See if it works out.'

'As gradually as you like, Alice,' Max said earnestly. 'I'm good at taking things gradually. I've been painting that fence for three months already.'

'Plus it might all be an illusion. You may be trying to convince yourself that you... that we could... because of this whole thing with Grant. Crisis bonding or something, I think they call it.'

He turned round and stared out of the window. A small knot of neighbours had collected at the end of the road near the paper shop, and I *knew* they'd be talking about me. 'That's actually a little insulting, Alice,' he said to the smear on the pane. 'You're implying that I don't know what I want. That I'm free-floating, looking for a woman to attach myself to and any woman who drifts into my orbit will do. I have quite high standards, in fact.'

'I don't mean it to be an insult,' I said quietly. 'It's nearer disbelief. Nobody has ever really wanted me, not like that. There was only Grant, and he only married me because he was too lazy to do anything else. Oh, and a few teenage fumbles with the boys nobody else wanted to go out with, and I thought we were going to the cinema but it turned out that they thought "cinema" was a code word for "sex in a Vauxhall". I'm not really the stuff dreams are made of, you see.'

Max turned round and came in close. 'You've got beautiful, creamy skin. Your eyes are a kind of greenish gold and your intelligence shines out of them. Your lips are, I have to say, *very* inviting, you've got curves in all the right places. You're not afraid to challenge me, you're not rendered mute by looking at my house, you've got a down-to-earth attitude that I find most attractive and, all round, I really enjoy your company. *Please* don't insult me by telling me that I'm wrong because, despite frequent indications to the contrary, I know my own mind.'

'You've gone all posh again,' I observed, trying for a neutral tone.

'Sorry. Hugh Grant possesses my body when I'm trying to sound romantic.'

'Well, at least you aren't talking about mating dogs. I was a bit worried for a minute there.' We looked at one another solemnly, then his lips twitched and I couldn't suppress the giggles any longer. 'Sorry, but you *are* posh and you have shown yourself liable to drop dog-breeding references into perfectly ordinary conversations.'

'I can assure you that nobody has ever stood over my mating attempts with a watch and a set of kennel club forms.' He was laughing now. Properly laughing, and it reassured me that he was honest; that this wasn't all some huge wind-up to set me up on a date and then spend the evening telling me how I'd be prettier if I only lost a few stone, wore nicer clothes and put enough make-up on to render my actual face invisible. It had happened and had made Grant seem positively gentlemanly and an absolute catch in comparison.

'Leaving our possible mutual attraction aside for a moment,' I said, 'we've now got the little matter of a body under the Fortune House.'

'Mutual attraction. Yep, I'll take that.' Max gave me a tiny wink. 'But you're right. Although I don't know what I'm supposed to do about it. Even the police say it's not considered a crime scene, which means the skeleton could be centuries old. There's loads of Bronze Age barrows and things dotted all round the moors.'

'*That* was not a Bronze Age burial,' I said sternly. 'But the body could account for the stories of hauntings.'

Max sat up suddenly on the sofa, which let out a small puff of dust on contact. 'I know,' he said, and he sounded as though last night on the champagne was catching up with him. 'Folk memory of a death or a burial ground might make people more prone to building perfectly normal occurrences into something supernatural.'

'And did the Fortunes know the skeleton was there when they built the house?'

He gave me a stern look. 'Would *you* build a house if you knew there was a grave underneath it?'

'Depends how old the grave is. I mean, Britain isn't very big and it's been occupied since the early Palaeolithic, there really can't be very much of it that hasn't had someone buried on it at some point.'

'God, you're amazing.' There was a gleam in his eye.

'I just have a robust approach to things. Besides, I've had a lot of experience with death. My dad...' I nearly stopped, but the way Max smiled made me want to go on. 'My dad used to say that death is the one thing we've all got in common and being afraid of it is like being afraid of rain. You might not like the fact that it's going to happen, but you may as well dance in it when it comes.'

'He sounds like a laugh a minute.' Max was gauging my reaction, I could see. Checking to see whether I'd take the joke or be offended or upset; he was working out my attitude, my relationship with my father.

'Dad could be a touch lugubrious, yes. But spending the greater part of your life terminally ill will do that to you, I guess.' I kept it light. Death had been a release for Dad, welcomed like summer rain on a parched garden. He had, I liked to think, been dancing when it came.

'And your mum?' Max stood up and moved in closer. Away from the window, although the sun still sheeted him in gold.

'She'd fought it and fought it all the time I was young, but once Grant and I were together, it was like she could relax. I was employed, I had the house and a husband, and it was like she – stopped trying.'

'Alice.' That was all he said. Just my name. And all of a sudden, all the grief and the fury and the years and years of having not much of a life hit me somewhere underneath my heart and I burst into tears that wouldn't stop. All those years of being practical, of being *sensible*, they'd weighted me in a way I hadn't realised and now all that weight was bobbing to the surface like a corpse in a lake.

Max wrapped his arms around me and pulled me against him

and that reminded me of Mum too, so I sobbed harder. Nobody had held me since she'd become too frail. Grant would occasionally drape an arm around my shoulders and give what had always felt like an awkward hug, and then change the subject, try to get me laughing. Never this all-encompassing embrace, feeling as though my unhappiness was shared.

There were no words. Just the feel of Max's shoulder under my cheek, his arms around my back and his face against the top of my head. That orangey scent, that seemed to come from his skin, and the slight movement as he breathed, that was all. I cried myself to a standstill, then sniffed heartily. I didn't, I noted, even in my grief, move away.

'Better?' The word thrummed up from his chest, I felt it more than heard it.

I nodded.

His arms loosened slowly, and he took half a step back. 'My lovely, lovely Alice,' he said softly, which I thought was very gallant of him because I had snot streaming down my lower face and my eyes felt like golf balls.

'Why do you smell of oranges?' It was all I could think of to say. I wanted to distract him, to stop him thinking about loss and death and sadness, yet this feeling of actually being held and comforted was so wonderful and unusual that I wanted it to go on forever.

'Oh. Penhaligon's. It's a mandarin cologne.'

'Posh git. You could just sit and eat oranges, like us poor people.' I sniffed again, hoping that there had been the right amount of 'subject changing levity' in my tone, and he wouldn't take it the wrong way.

'Oddly enough, I don't really like oranges, only the smell.' Another half step back, but a lighter note in his voice. 'And I'm not *that* posh.'

I indicated my living room. 'You'd probably stable your horses in here.'

'No horses. Not any more. Dad got rid of them all, after Mum...' He moved further back and I took the opportunity to scrub furtively at my face with my sleeve.

'Sorry.'

'It's fine.' It didn't sound fine but there was more than enough emotion in here already, hanging in the air with the dust. 'I think it's why Jenna turned to motorbikes, she was deprived of the pony experience in her formative years.'

'Max...' I didn't know what I'd been going to say. I think I wanted to divert his attention from my swollen and grot-covered appearance but there was a heaviness to his tone that stopped me in my tracks.

'No, it's really fine, Alice. It was twenty-five years ago, I've worked through most of it now. It's just the ghost thing left, just that tiny question in the back of my mind. Did Jenna see Mum or was it a child's interpretation of a memory? That's all.' He took a deep breath. 'And talking of Jenna, it's time I gave her a call and got us a lift back to the Hall. They should be sober enough and have had enough shagging time, surely.'

He slid his phone out of his pocket and moved away out into the passage by the front door. A politeness, a courtesy I wasn't used to – my fitters would whip their phones out and bellow imprecations to their partners practically under my nose. It made me wonder, again, if the gulf between Max and me was really one that could be breached just because we wanted it to be. But then the tactile echo of the feel of his arms around me, the warmth of his body and the swell of his breath, came roaring back in. Any man who held me like that had to be worth a *bit* of pretending that our class differences didn't matter, surely? Plus, if my piecemeal memory was anything to go by, he could cook – at least, we'd eaten the risotto; he was practical enough to paint fences and sort out the icehouse, to keep Hatherleigh Hall ticking over. If there was a downside to Max, it seemed limited to his desire to write a book outstripping his ability to *organise* writing a book, and that was only a downside if he was going to take up a career as a full-time author.

And there was always the compensation that he was absolutely bloody gorgeous. I'd overlook quite a lot of lack of material coordination for that dark gaze, the long legs and the smile.

'Okay, she's on her way. Are you packed and ready?' Max came back through, hands in pockets and shoulders set. 'I need to get back to the icehouse clearing and Jen says she'll sort you a room so you can stay. Although, I warn you, she's just given me thirty seconds of wedding plans and I only rang for a lift – there may be a degree of dashing about with magazines and I fear the words "mood board" may be uttered once or twice.'

'I don't mind,' I said, zipping up my holdall. 'If Jenna wants to distract me from the enviable task of working through several lifetimes' worth of shopping receipts, paint swatches and grass seed sales booklets, I will bear it manfully.'

'I thought you might.' He swung away to watch Mr Next Door Left return, the dog setting a good pace along the far side of the pavement. 'Jen doesn't have all that many close friends,' he said more quietly. 'She may want to offload on you. Her last boyfriend did a real number on her, alienated her from a lot of her old friends, and she's still building up a new base.'

'It's fine,' I said gently. 'I really don't mind.'

'Only I thought, what with her marrying your ex-husband, it might get – awkward? Helping plan a wedding that may be a bit – well, obviously, I don't know how you... but there's going to be bells and whistles brought out here and...'

'Registry office and fish and chip suppers probably won't feature,' I finished for him. 'No, honestly, Max. I am so over Grant that I don't even want to kill him any more. He and Jenna really look happy together, much more made for one another than he and I ever were.' Which made me wonder whether difference of class and upbringing really made *that* much of a difference. If they could do it, then why shouldn't Max and I?

I made more tea and we waited for Jenna without feeling the need to say much of anything. Max sat and flipped through *Prima* whilst I made a desultory attempt at dusting and wished I could have at least invested in a pile of *Cosmopolitan* or some feminist tracts. The *Prima* subscription had been Mum's that I'd not got around to cancelling because it felt too final, but Max knew me and wouldn't judge. He'd have seen that I wasn't really a casual flipper-through of magazines about sex and hair or polemics on the Male Gaze. I was ordinary. Plain, large, sensible Alice. But he genuinely seemed to like that.

There was the descending roar outside of a motorbike pulling in against the kerb. Max and I looked at one another.

'I'm not going to have to piggyback you home, am I?' He got up and looked out of the window. 'No, it's fine. Jenna's on the bike but Grant's driving my car.'

Grant, looking oddly manly in bike leathers, got out of the Range Rover, while Jenna took her helmet off and shook out her hair. They exchanged a few words, then Grant rapped on the front door, dropped the keys into Max's hand, took a helmet from Jen and got on the bike behind her. They'd roared away down the street before I'd even got myself and my bag onto the pavement.

'They're going up to Whitby,' Max said, slightly weakly. 'For a run out. Apparently.'

I watched the two black-leathered figures vanishing into the distance on the shiny black bike. A run out. A motorbike. Whitby. Leathers. Grant really wasn't the man I had known any more.

Maybe he really *had* been hit on the head with something.

* * *

Report via email, unnamed third party, story as told to him by experiencer.

It was 1986 and a bunch of us from college had heard there was a rave up in an old barn on the moors. We got lost on the way and Martin, who'd been on the vodka, got thrown out of the car for being a prick. We were going to let him walk.

We couldn't find the rave and we were all arguing cos some of us wanted to park and have our own party, cos we'd got the booze and the Es and it would be a waste otherwise, and some wanted to head down into town and pick up some girls. And while we were parked at the side of the road, bickering, Martin comes running up.

And, man, he was white! Looked like he'd pissed himself too, and he just ran straight into the car, like, jumped from the road right onto the back seat, where there was about six of us already sitting, and he was ranting. We calmed him down, figured he'd taken some bad stuff and was tripping, but when he could talk, he said that he'd sat down on some rocks out on the moor and, while he was sitting, this hand had come up from between these two boulders. Just the hand, he said, kind of pale and smooth, sticking up and kind of 'patting around' like it was looking for something.

And Mart, he'd taken off running and he hadn't stopped until he saw the car. He said he didn't care who it was, police, game-keeper, he'd have jumped in with a serial killer if it would get him off that moor.

We're all a lot older and wiser now, but, to my knowledge, Martin has not, and will not go back up onto the moors.

13

I didn't see that much of Max for the next couple of days. I did, however, see quite a lot of Jenna, mostly armed with various copies of wedding magazines and accompanied by a cry of 'what do you think about *this* one?' until I had to hide behind the big leather armchair when I heard her coming. I didn't mind talking weddings, but Max had me here to sort the Incredible Paper Mountain, and that was a lot harder to do when having fabric swatches thrust under your nose and being required to have an opinion about purple versus red.

The police removed the bones from beneath what was left of the Fortune House. They were going to perform some tests to see how old the skeleton was, how he or she had died and see if they could figure out why on earth someone would build a house over the top of them, but as there were no reports of anyone disappearing in the area going back as far as they could check, they weren't rushing. 'Probably some nineteenth-century lime kiln worker,' said the Forensic Anthropologist cheerily, when I talked to him on the phone, as I'd apparently become the *de facto* coordinator of all things Hatherleigh Hall. Max was still clearing out the icehouse and Grant was – actually, I wasn't entirely sure *what* Grant was doing, but since he wasn't my problem, it didn't matter.

So my days became all about sorting paper. Tiny slips, so old that the ink was invisible, big, official looking forms from the Ministry of Agriculture which had never been filled in, old newspapers, maps and cards all went into black plastic sacks for burning. The dust was a thing of wonder and I often had to break off to go and stand outside and cough. I had more showers per day than a professional sportsman but at least I wasn't paying for the hot water, and I revelled in bathroom fittings that didn't leak, drip or make peculiar groaning noises for half an hour after the taps were turned off.

I'd just got out of my latest shower and was trying to make my hair do something other than drip languidly, when Max came in and slumped into a chair, looking exhausted.

'Jen's not around, is she?' he asked, making a half-hearted attempt to kick off his work boots but giving up when it involved bending down. 'I've explained and explained why she can't get married in the house, but she's not getting it.' He picked up the tiny pile of paper I'd put to one side as worth keeping, and shuffled through it.

'She's gone into town, but I'm not sure why.' I glanced over at the torrent of paper still left to sort, and my skin itched reflexively.

'Good.'

'And why can't she get married in the house? I would have thought it would be a nice earner, holding weddings here. You don't even need to do anything more than provide the location and maybe some nice décor – the wedding planners do all the rest. I think,' I added, because my wedding planning had consisted of making sure the shop had enough battered cod on the hot plate.

Max leaned back and stuck out his legs. The shorts were once more in evidence and he'd got socks that came halfway up his shins, giving him the look of a hiker who's got lost on their way to a comedy convention. 'Dad put something in the paperwork,' he said tiredly. 'When I inherited, the legal team found it in the small print. It was one of the first things I wanted to do, get the place licensed for weddings and civil partnerships and all that, but no. Dad's terms mean it's not allowed.' A deep sigh. 'He loved Mum a lot,' he said quietly. 'He was never the same after she died. I think the clause was his way of making sure that Hatherleigh was never instrumental in that kind of happiness.'

'Well, that was a bit short-sighted,' I said, without thinking. 'Oh, sorry. Yes, it must have been hard for him.'

There was a long, slightly awkward, pause. The only sound was the hum of the computer fan and the soft chirruping of birds outside. At last, Max said, 'It was hard for all of us, Alice.'

'Yes, I didn't mean—'

'And he shot us all in the foot with it. You're right, weddings are a great money spinner when you've got a place like this, and it would have helped with the finances a lot.'

'Can it be overturned?' I started to look at the overblown desk quite hard, so as not to have to see Max's face, shadowed with loss. For all that he said it was a long time ago, there was still that awful memory, which as he'd explained was overlaid with the wondering whether his mother had returned to say goodbye to her daughter and not her son. I wished that ghosts were a real thing, so I could give them a piece of my mind.

'Not without an awful lot of legal wrangling that we really don't have the money for.' Max stood up. 'Come for a walk with me, Alice. Come and see the icehouse, now I've got it all cleared out.'

'But—' I stared now at the enormous pile of paper, still teetering at the edge of the room, half piled against the wall as though they were keeping one another up. 'I've just washed my hair!'

'You know that whole thing about catching a cold if you go out with wet hair is a myth, don't you?' he said, sounding slightly more cheerful. 'Besides, it's about thirty degrees out there, you're more likely to die of heatstroke.'

I was *actually* worried about the heat and humidity making my hair frizz, but I reasoned that Max didn't seem to worry too much about my physical appearance, and gave in.

We went out through the side door, along the grassy terrace, which was baking brown in the heat. The ground thudded hollowly under our feet, and the edges of the grasses were sharp with dryness, so it was almost a relief to arrive at the dank shadowy dampness of the icehouse.

Rubble bags full of weeds, wilting in the sunlight, rocks, rubbish and bits of old furniture were lined up outside the gate, like servants in a Disney film, waiting to be animated by music. The stones which formed the entrance were cracked, interspersed with ferns and mosses growing at improbable angles, forming little cushions and beckoning fingers.

'It's empty now.' Max ushered me through the gate, which whined plangently as it swung. 'Took me ages, but I've got muscles now that I never had before, lugging that lot up the ladder.'

Once through the gate, we were in a little lobby which led to the steep sided twenty-foot drop to the curved base of the icehouse. Above our heads, the roof arched elegantly away into the side of the hill and the arms of the ladder jutted from the drop, like a person letting go.

'Wow.' I looked down into the shadowy depths. 'You've worked really hard. It looks...' I trailed off. I had been about to say that it looked great, but it looked, mainly, like a brick-lined bucket.

'It looks sinister,' Max finished for me, the sibilants sliding away to echo around our heads. 'But it's done now, and it was quite nice being in here. Jenna couldn't get to me, anyway. Even *she's* not desperate enough to come shinning down a ladder to talk wedding plans.'

I looked again down into the terracotta darkness. Tiny shafts of sunlight, filtered through the wrought iron of the gate, got about a third of the way down and highlighted the depths. The base of the icehouse was a kind of cone shape, I half expected to see a gigantic plughole in the middle, but there was nothing except a muddy circle. It was cool, smelled of damp basements and the acoustics were horrifying, but...

'Could you hold weddings in here?' I turned around, back to the drop, to see Max staring up at the roof. 'You'd need a proper staircase down, some atmospheric lighting, and maybe a proper floor down there, of course. But it's wacky enough that people might like it.'

Max's stare came down to me. He looked as though he was doing very difficult calculations in his head. 'Would it be possible?'

'I'm pretty sure you could get this place licensed. It's an indoor space, after all. I'm presuming your dad's terms don't extend out here?'

Max still looked a bit stunned. 'I'd have to check, but I wouldn't have thought so. The icehouse has been disused for about fifty years, I doubt he would have even thought of it.' He took a deep breath. 'Alice, you are more than a genius, you are quite probably my saviour.'

I gave a half-laugh. 'It's just logic, that's all.'

'No. If it were logic, I would have seen it. You...' he stopped talking and raked both hands through his hair. 'You are bloody amazing.'

The entryway was narrow, a carved stone and brick cavern, so we were standing very close together, I suddenly realised. 'I'm really not,' I said, feeling the pink heat clambering its way up my body.

'I think we've had this discussion.' Max moved to face me. 'I know my own mind, Alice.'

And then he leaned in and kissed me.

Everything in me knew I should protest, but hot damn he was gorgeous, he was here, he seemed to want me, and I was *sick* of sorting papers. I abandoned the coy attitude which I'd held to me like a security blanket and moved closer to him. He shuffled the pair of us back, so that I was pressed against the rough stone wall, the cool sponginess of mossy pillows squeezing water into my shirt and tickling the back of my neck. Suddenly I couldn't smell wet rock and decaying vegetation any more, my head was full of the smell of Max; orange and dust and hot skin and a tiny hint of turpentine. His mouth was on mine, pulling forth all kinds of dreams, and his fingers were holding my chin, curved around my jawline as though the extra inches of flesh were precious and worth touching. *I* felt worth touching.

'Max! Alice! Are you out here?'

Grant's voice was drifting over the lawns, coming closer. Max and I moved apart, straightening clothing and taking deep breaths.

'Max! The forensics people are on the phone, they want a word with you!'

We could hear Grant's footsteps now, clonking over the ground hollow with the lack of rain towards us. I wanted to giggle, but didn't. Max raised his eyebrows at me.

'Are we fit to be seen, do you think?'

I looked him up and down. 'I am. Your shorts aren't leaving much to the imagination.'

'Maybe Grant will just think I get really turned on by caves.'

I gave him a stern look. 'If there's a double entendre in that, please do *not* explain it to me.' Then I moved out, swinging the gate open and meeting Grant under the sun-laden bushes beyond.

'What are you doing in there?' he asked, as though I'd just stepped out of a fairy knoll.

'Looking at the icehouse,' I said briskly. 'Max is in there, tidying up. But I wouldn't go in, if I were you,' I added as he stepped forward. 'There's quite a drop and it's dangerous and slippery.' I almost added, 'a perfect place to fake your own death again, should you need to,' but I bit my tongue because I really *had* to stop remembering that.

'Oh, okay. I just said that I'd let him know the police had rung. About the skeleton up on the moors,' he added, as though there might have been any number of reasons for the police to want to be in touch with Max.

'That's fine.' I started to walk back towards the house. Grant came with me. He'd kept the sharp sideburns and the slightly thinner face, and it was a good look on him. 'Are you really going to marry Jenna?' I asked.

'Yes.' Grant stopped walking. 'It's all right. I really have learned my lesson, Al. She's the woman for me, and I'm not going to tell her about the whole "amnesia" thing. If I do, in the future, don't worry, I'll tell her that it was my idea. I don't want her to think badly of you and Max.'

I stared at him. It hadn't even occurred to me that this might be the case, but, of course, if Jenna ever found out that the memory-loss plot had been mine, well... 'Thank you,' I said humbly.

'I've grown up a bit, Al. Since I blew myself up, I've become a new man, I think.' Grant disproved this by lifting his shirt to scratch at his navel thoughtfully. 'I want to make a go of it with Jen.'

I remembered the hug. The silent tears. 'You're good together,' I said, trying to inject as much honesty into my voice as I could. 'You can do it, Grant.'

'Thank you.' He sounded as though he meant the gratitude. And he was right, he *was* different with Jenna. More lively, more tactile – there wasn't a great increase in his intellect, of course, but she didn't seem to mind that. Added to which he'd already got back many of his IT clients, so he was earning again, too.

We reached the side door and went in. I went back up to the flat to carry on rooting through sheaves of paper, after all, that's what I was here for, and I only had a couple more days... The thought hit me hard. This week spent at Hatherleigh Hall had taken on a kind of charmed feel. I'd got a lovely bedroom, en suite bathroom, a fridge full of food, even if I still didn't know what to do with samphire, and a view that stretched over yellowing fields and trees whose leaves were becoming dusty with incipient autumn. In the evenings, I'd gone through wedding pages with Jenna or played rowdy board games with Max. It had been a long, long way from the little terrace in Pickering.

The thoughts alarmed me. I couldn't get used to this lifestyle. I just couldn't. It wasn't *me*. I was destined to spend the whole of next week trying to find all the files that Malcolm had 'helped' me with by putting away somewhere utterly logical to him and nobody else. Listening to the low-level grousing and sniping that being crammed together in a hot office always leads to. Running out of milk and having to charge across to the Co-op, where I would inevitably end up buying twenty pounds' worth of shopping I didn't really need. While Sheila over-tactfully tried to ascertain whether or not my periods were still regular.

I looked up at the ceiling mouldings, the carved cornices and the full-height windows. Even in here, where the furniture was so masculine I was slightly surprised that it didn't hump my leg whenever I came in, there was an airy, Country House vibe. My house didn't have a vibe, apart from when big lorries went past on the main road. But, I assured myself, shuffling through papers, it was *my* house. It had been Mum and Dad's when they'd married, and they'd bought it outright with part of their insurance payout. It had been the only home I'd ever known. The tiny, cramped rooms, the peculiarities with running water and the ever-present dust were all mine. Hatherleigh Hall was big and part of it was sixteenth century but it took a team of people to keep it clean and Max running about with a screwdriver and paintbrush to keep it maintained.

But you could help him, whispered a tiny voice in the back of my head. Go on, admit it. You're itching to sort this place out and make it earn its keep. Weddings in the icehouse and receptions in a marquee on the lawn. Attractions to bring in the tourists – jousting knights at the front and a cookery school in that huge kitchen... I dropped the pile of papers I had been working my way through and stood, as alarmed as if it had been a ghost muttering all that into my ear. Was that how I was thinking? Really? Making plans for the house that only seconds ago I had been assuring myself wasn't as good as the two-up two-down in a tiny market town?

And then there was Max. Gorgeous, sexy Max. Who genuinely seemed to want me, if that kiss had been anything to go by, and who, if Grant hadn't charged in, might well have had me. I remembered my reaction; the feel of him when I'd run my hands up inside his shirt, the way his fingers had lightly brushed my neck...

'They've got a forensic result.' Max appeared in the doorway. 'You're pink. Did you catch the sun earlier?'

'Must have done.' I carefully, *very* carefully, sat on the edge of the desk with a meaningless pile of paper in my hand and pretended to be scrutinising it. 'So, what did they tell you?'

He bounced into the room and prised off the work boots. 'Well, obviously they couldn't tell me too much, in case I am a murderer who disposed of a corpse under the ruins of the house I'm writing about.'

'Did you?' I put the papers down.

'Of course not. Besides which, they reckon the body had been there for between sixty and eighty years. Give or take a decade.' He peeled off the dreadful half-length socks and balled them up.

'If you're going to do a striptease, I suggest a touch more gyration.' I didn't know why I said it. I was interested in what the forensic examination had shown, but I knew he was taking off dirty footwear before he trampled all over the Exhibition Carpet. They were just the words that sprang into my mouth without my brain's involvement.

Max looked at the wadded socks in his hand. 'Nope. That's your lot.' He placed them on the back of the burnished muscleman of a chair, where they instantly rolled off. 'For now.'

In silence, we both regarded the sock ball as it trickled its way along the floorboards and bumped to a gentle stop against the leg of the desk.

I cleared my throat to let my mouth know I wouldn't be standing for any more of its random pronouncements. 'So, the body's been down there a while?' My voice was slightly high-pitched and I coughed again.

'Yep. It's male, they couldn't see any obvious cause of death but they're going to do more tests.'

'But nobody reported anyone missing, no accidents, nothing, in that time?' I glanced over towards Max's notes on the house. It was quite a thick file. 'What about Alethia's brother? That's about the right time frame, isn't it?'

Max shook his head. 'He went to London. Alethia said that her mother told her he used to write to her occasionally, and I can't see both parents keeping quiet if anything had happened to him in the house, can you? Why would they?'

'Maybe his dad murdered him and threatened his mum to keep quiet?' I wasn't really a detective novel person, but this definitely had overtones of those afternoon programmes that Mum had loved having on. She'd usually fallen asleep halfway through and been baffled by the conclusion, but that, apparently, hadn't really been the point.

'Mr Fortune died before his wife, though. She'd have said something then, wouldn't she? Or told Alethia, at least?' Max pushed his hands through his hair, curling his bare feet into the thick pile of the rug. 'According to Alethia, when we used to chat, her mum was quite a force to be reckoned with. They couldn't tell how old the man was when he died, either. His teeth were good, so dental records are no help, he was well nourished, and an adult under forty. Could be anyone. Oh, but they matched the tooth that they found after the explosion to the body.'

'I'd been wondering about that. I hadn't noticed Grant minus a molar.' I began sheafing the papers back together again. Another pile for the bin bag, which gaped at me from the floor, its shiny blackness already half-filled with random scraps and notes.

'But it's not outside the realms of possibility that the body was already there when the house went up,' Max went on. 'Allowing for a margin of error. Anyway.' He straightened up, dropped his hands. 'I'm off to look into getting the icehouse approved for weddings, thanks to you.'

At the mention of the words 'icehouse' my body had a Pavlovian response and I nearly dropped the papers all over the floor. 'Oh. Yes, that's good.'

He didn't go. I wished he would, because I wanted to wash my face in cold water and possibly change out of these jeans, which felt suddenly very uncomfortable. 'Alice,' he said, after a moment, 'are you all right that we... that I kissed you earlier?'

'Um,' I said. For one definition of 'all right', I was most *definitely* 'all right'. For another, I really, really wasn't.

'You seemed to be into it, but I don't want to cross any boundaries that you may have.'

'I don't have any boundaries,' I said, and then realised how that sounded and sweaty heat shot up my neck again. 'I mean, I do, obviously. Have some, I mean. Just not, well. No.'

He flashed me a look. There it was again, dark and heavy with promise but containing a light of mischief. 'Well, good. I think. Only I'd like to do it again sometime and I don't want to run the risk of you beating me to death with the Elizabethan bed post.'

He didn't give me chance to answer this time, just scuffed his way out of the study and I heard his bare feet padding away down the corridor towards the kitchen. When the kitchen door closed, I let my lungs have a bit more freedom and blew downward to try to cool my chest.

14

Saturday dawned, feeling autumnal. Not only the weather, although that had taken a grey, foggy turn for the worse, but for me too. As though something light and bright was finishing and the future held enclosure, restrictions, layers of clothing and an office slightly too small for the workforce contained within it.

Neither of us mentioned this ending, though it was all I could think about. I sat in the study with Max, who was typing random linking notes whilst referring to his file of papers, and I leafed through more of the loose sheets. Occasionally I'd get distracted – there was a local newspaper from 1973 which had some interesting photographs of the high street, and there was a curious charm in reading old bills and receipts in pre-decimal currency. 'Two tons hay, one pound seven shillings,' I read aloud.

'Mmm?' Max didn't even look up.

'Nothing.' I half looked over his shoulder. He was sorting what looked like random reports from the Fortune House into chronological order. 'Are you still going to write the book about the house?'

He stopped and looked at me. 'I don't know. What do you think? If I write about the Fortune House, then I don't really have a logical ending, other than "destroyed in explosion". It's not very – well, punchy, is it? Unless people keep experiencing the paranormal up at the site, and, since the police have barricaded it off now there's a body, nobody can get close enough to experience anything.'

'I thought you were going to write about the psychology of ghost hunting.' I went back to my pile of papers. The enormous sliding mass had definitely lessened, but I didn't seem to have made significant inroads in my week's sorting. The knowledge that my stay was about to come to an end was a weight in my heart, like the ending of a holiday, which was odd, because I'd worked twice as hard here as I ever did in the office.

'I was thinking I may split the research, like you suggested. Do two books, one on the house itself and another on the whole "who sees ghosts" question. My university may be interested in the second, it could form part of my teaching, but I'm on my own with the first one.'

'Did I suggest that?'

'Oh, yes.' The mischievous smile was there again, lighting his face and making his eyes crease slightly at the corners. 'So it's all your fault.'

'But that will take you twice as long.' Outside, the leaves of a sycamore tree that rattled its branches beyond the windows were getting a definite yellow shading and a few had taken the autumnal hint and see-sawed to the ground to lie face down on the gravel, like drunken party leavers. The fog was weighing everything down.

'Yes.' He paused. 'I'm going to need twice as much organising.' Another pause. I had the feeling that I was supposed to drop something in here, there was an expectancy in the way he was sitting, head half-turned towards me.

'Max, I—' I stopped. I had no idea what I had been going to say.

He carried on not-really-looking at me. 'There's no pressure,

Alice,' he said softly. 'I've already said, you've got all the time you need.'

I snorted. 'To choose between working here with all the coffee I can drink and really nice biscuits and fresh baked scones and nobody telling me to hurry up with that invoice, and no window fitters pressing their bums up against the glass door to make me laugh or being crammed in an office that's either over or under-heated depending on the weather, with Malcolm and Sheila? That's not really a fair kind of "no pressure", is it?'

Max continued to look at a very un-fascinating corner of the room. 'I have to point out the downside of this job is that there is an immense amount of paper-sorting, there will be far more shouting and trying to get me to actually write something once the semester starts and I'm back lecturing, plus Jenna and her one-woman wedding show.' The half of his mouth I could see puckered, so I supposed he was smiling again. 'And this place is also bloody freezing in winter.'

I gazed out over the bucolic acres that were visible from the window. This part of the flat overlooked the back of the house, where parkland scattered with trees stretched down to a lake, ghostly in the mist. Little runs of hedging were nailed into place by the red studs of hawthorn berries, and I imagined it under the brittle glitter of frost, bare and sparse and still belonging to Max.

'You're too good for window fitting, Alice,' Max said softly. 'I hope you're coming to see that now. You don't need to keep doing what you've always done – maybe it's time to stretch your wings, what do you think? Besides...' he nodded towards the slithery mountain range of papers along the floor, 'don't you want to get to the bottom of that lot? Find out if there's anything that will help us give a name to the body under the house?'

'It's the brother,' I said, although, without any evidence, it did sound a bit weak.

'But if it *is*, what the hell happened? Why did his parents say he'd moved out, why did they never say anything, even to his sister? What if it *isn't* him? Get me an ending for my book, please.'

I stomped a small circle, thinking. What the hell did I do? Slough off my old life for something new, when that 'new' was so different? If I'd ever imagined changing jobs, it had always been a vague considering of the admin vacancies in the paper; wondering whether running a team of vets or solicitors would be vastly different to organising a team of window fitters and assuming that there would probably not be much change, apart from fewer buttocks.

'But what if...' I took a deep breath and put into words my *real* concern. 'What if you go off me? What if you decide that I'm just another ordinary girl who's less interesting than you think she is, who makes mistakes and isn't as... as sexy as you imagine. What if, one day, you wake up and want someone else?'

He swivelled his chair all the way around to face me now. He'd slumped down a bit, so his shoulders were resting against the back of the chair and his legs were stretched out, long and ridiculously hairy under the shorts. His bare feet curled against one another, curiously childlike. 'Fair enough. I mean, I don't see it happening, but relationships end all the time, although not always as suddenly and catastrophically as you seem to imagine, but then I suppose you're still shaking off the whole "Grant" thing.' He put his fingers together under his chin. 'What about a six-month contract? To start with.'

'But I'd have to leave my job!' I almost wailed. 'And what if you go off me?'

'There's always the possibility that *you* may find that *I* am not always the unalloyed delight that you see in front of you now.' He took a deep breath. 'You could get another job. Hell, there are other jobs here, on the estate, you wouldn't have to work with me, you wouldn't even have to *see* me. And I cannot believe we are sorting out the arrangements for the ending of a relationship that hasn't even seriously got underway yet. I want to work with you. I want... I want *more*. Right now, I feel as though I'm interviewing you for the position of girlfriend and that is not a feeling I like very much, so I'm going to go outside for a bit.' He stood up. 'Just think about it,' he said softly. 'Please. I like having you around.'

Then he was gone, closing the door gently behind him but still giving rise to a swirl of disturbed air that set my pile of remaining papers whispering behind curled edges, like chaperones at a ball. I continued to stand where Max had left me, by his desk near the window, still not sure how I felt or what I was going to do. Tatters of fog drifted past outside, breaking and reforming, ghostlike. Ghosts. Was that what everything came down to? Me, influenced by the ghost of my past relationship, by the ghosts of my parents wanting me to be settled? Was 'being settled' really going to be the pinnacle of my life? A job and a house until I retired, when I would perhaps acquire a cat, and then die?

I stared down into the fog-filled bowl of the park, where the tops of trees were breaking through as though reaching, gasping for the sky, and I felt an odd kind of tremor run through me. On Max's desk was a piece of paper, notes on how Alethia had left the Fortune House to go into service and from there on into joining the Land Army, coming back on leave to help her mother with her confinement when John was born. She'd left her settled, boring, restricted life on that tiny farm and jumped out into a job she must have been terrified about. But it was that or stay, forever trapped in that house that I'd seen in the photograph, blank windows looking out onto bare hills.

I fumbled my phone out of my pocket, and dialled.

15

The fog didn't lift all day. The flatness of the general surroundings seemed to suck more mist in, until it felt as though the house sat alone in the world; visibility extended only as far as the circle of gravel on which the cars stood. Beyond that, everything might as well have been obliterated. Even sound was muffled and, as darkness drew in early, we closed the curtains in all the rooms in the flat to keep the absence of everything at bay.

The house hadn't been open today. Now the summer was practically over, it only opened two weekends a month – a timetable guaranteed to cause confusion in the minds of potential visitors, and a probable severe drop-off in numbers. I'd written a note to myself to find out whether it would be possible to extend the opening season in line with, say, the National Trust, until the October half term. Then I'd tried to pretend that I'd never thought this; that forward planning for the house and grounds was nothing to do with me. But I did need to mention it to Max, so I waited for him to come back in from whatever prolonged mission had kept him out for the rest of the day. There was also no sign of Jenna or Grant, and, when I went for a brief wander to try to locate another living soul, the house was deserted.

I stood for a moment on the main staircase. It had been left uncarpeted to showcase the broad oak steps with the ornate banister rail and newel posts so carved that they seemed more air than wood, sweeping downwards to the entrance hall. There was no sound, but somehow the house felt 'busy'. As though, out of sight around a corner or behind a door, servants were polishing and sweeping and laying fires and carrying tea trays. In the grand rooms, ladies were receiving guests and gentlemen were planning a game of cards or discussing the day's hunting. As though life carried on simultaneously, with all periods of history running alongside one another, separated by a thin film of reality which sometimes parted to give rise to moments like this.

Somewhere a clock was ticking, a slow, deep tick and an insect buzzed against a window. Below me, on a table in the hall, a bowl of potpourri scented the air with dried orange and rose petals, and occasionally rustled and settled in a draught. And still I had that sense of *things*, that if I were to turn my head sharply enough, I'd catch a glimpse of crinoline, a peek of green satin doublet, whisking away around a corner.

I berated myself. This was the sort of thing that these grand houses demanded. Whimsy. Fancy. I'd never had an inch of fancy in my life, my imagination was limited to strictly practical forethought and planning. You didn't keep twenty sturdy young men heading to the right addresses with vans full of glazing by being whimsical. You needed a spreadsheet, a timetable and lists for that.

'Alice?' Max's voice made me jump. He was above me, on the more workaday and less carved stairway that led up to the flat, looking down over the balustrade. 'Are you all right?'

'Just listening to the ghosts,' I said, my practical tone wiping any trace of fantasy from my words.

'Woodworm, death-watch beetle and rising damp,' Max replied, heading down the steps towards me. 'That's all you can hear,' he added gloomily as he reached me. 'With the added probability of lumps of plaster falling off some of the more neglected walls.'

'How can you live with all this,' I waved a hand at the stairs, the walls; the portraits and the heavy wood, 'and not believe in ghosts?' And then I remembered Jenna and his mother and wanted to bite my tongue off. 'Sorry.'

He'd changed out of the shorts and was wearing jeans and a shirt. His hair was wet as though he'd just got out of the shower, and I tried not to be swayed by the look of him. I was *sensible* and *practical* and him wandering up looking like Lord Byron on his day off was *not helping*.

'It's okay,' he said. 'It's a dichotomy. I *want* to believe – there's *something* in that photo I took of the Fortune House, there's all those stories from travellers across the moors... and then there's this place, as you said.' He looked around where I'd indicated, and his hair flicked a few drops of water onto my skin. 'But if ghosts are real, then I have to believe that my mother didn't love me enough to come back and visit me.' Max put both hands on the banister rail and gazed down over into the hallway. 'So it's easier to think it's all a trick of the light, a mistake rather than spirits.'

'Maybe your mother thought Jenna needed her more,' I said softly.

'Well, she was wrong.' He seemed to be fascinated by the bowl of potpourri on its side table below us. '*I* needed her too.'

I had a sudden vision of the eight-year-old Max, trying to pretend to be grown-up and deal with his mother's death, his father's grief, the lack of real understanding from his little sister. 'Oh, Max,' I said. 'She must have loved you so very much.'

'And maybe that's what I'm still looking for.' He didn't move. Instead, he kept his head bent, looking down. 'Someone to love *me*.

Not all this, not what I seem to be; not the illusion of the man with the estate and the PhD. Me.' He raised his head and looked at me now, and behind his eyes was the scared little boy sent away to school at eight. For a second, the man who'd inherited Hatherleigh Hall, who was doing his best to keep it going, was the illusion and the child was the reality.

There was such a raw honesty in his face that I found I'd reached out and touched his cheek. My heart was scalded by his emotions, particularly since his words were echoing my own dreams, which had begun to feel slightly desperate as I'd inched into my thirties. Someone to love me, for me. Not for my ability to cook a meal or run a spreadsheet. 'We're a right pair, aren't we?' I whispered.

He closed his eyes slowly, then put his hand over my wrist. 'We are.' His voice was as quiet as mine. 'A pair of lonely people, hoping we're doing the right thing.'

A moment of quiet, into which the clock ticked the passing seconds. His cheek was warm from the shower, the pricks of stubble soft against my palm and I could feel the flicker of a muscle working under the skin. Then he dropped his hand away from my wrist. I moved my hand too, and we were just two people standing on a staircase.

'I've handed my notice in at work,' I said. 'I'll have to work another month, but I can come over at weekends to help with sorting the papers.'

He blinked at me. 'Really? That's amazing, Alice, thank you so much.'

'And I can deflect and distract Jenna so you can get on with writing.'

'Again, thank you. There's going to be a lot of organising of my notes too. It's not going to be an easy job.'

I gave him a stern look. 'I can always rescind my notice, you know. According to Mr Welsh, the world is crying out for an admin assistant who knows her way around Crittal fixtures and work ratios.'

Max laughed. 'Would you like to move in here? Or will you commute?'

I thought of my little house, of Mr Next Door Left and Mrs Next Door Right, of the gossip and the dust and the tiny yards and the rumble of passing traffic. 'I'd like to keep my room here, if that's all right. But I'll rent out my house, I'm not quite ready to part with it.' Besides, the steady income from rent would be useful. I could save it up and then if the whole of this 'thing' with Max, whatever it was, fell apart, I'd have money and a home to go to. I wasn't so much burning my bridges as rattling a box of matches in their vicinity.

'I've said it before, but you are my absolute saviour, Alice,' Max said cheerfully. There was no undercurrent of sadness now to his voice and I didn't know whether to be sorry or not. That long moment on the stairs with Max, vulnerable and lost, seemed to have been several years ago now. Then I started to wonder whether I wanted someone to mother, but my midnight musings were most *definitely* not maternal towards Max, and I had to march briskly up the stairs to try to shake the feeling.

Back in the flat, Max gave me a handful of paper. 'These are all the first-person reports of anomalous experiences regarding the Fortune House,' he said. 'Please could you sort them into chronological order for me? Then I can use them as the backbone for the structure of the book itself.'

'I thought you needed me to go through Alethia's papers?' I glanced over at the mound, now flat-topped where I'd worked through the first couple of centimetres of detritus.

'I do. But if I've got these in order, it will help me with the organisation of the book. Alethia's papers are just filler and anything I get from them will be more easily cross-referenced if everything's in date order. Like I said, there are often reports of disturbances in and around houses when there's building work taking place or major disruptions. If we can find receipts from building firms or even a note about wallpaper designs, then we can try to match it to sightings. D'you see?'

I had to remind myself, again, that Max didn't think ghosts were real. But, by the time I'd read my way through some of the eerie tales from observers, and the fog had squeezed the last of the light out of the day, I was about ready to believe in ghosts, the bogeyman and Father Christmas. There was something about sitting alone in a darkening room with this sort of material that knocked the cynic in me on the head and let in someone who jumped at every creak.

Max brought me a cup of tea and I nearly screamed the house down when the door opened to let in nothing but a puff of steam. He followed swiftly afterwards with a quizzical look. 'What's up? Sorry, did I startle you?'

'I've put these in order,' I said, handing him his papers and turning on all the lights. 'And now I need to go and read about muck spreaders and egg-bound hens for a while, if that's all right.'

He looked down at the buff file I'd given him. 'Wow. You've even written on the front how many stories there are inside. You're so organised it hurts.'

'Organised and, now, terrified. That one about the noises in the basement... brrrr...'

'Oh, half of them will be made up. Another third will be misperceptions, misunderstandings and just plain insanity. Only a tiny proportion will have a hint of "What was *that*?" about them. Sadly, it's human nature to embellish stories, which is what makes my job so hard.' He put the file down. 'Well, this part of my job, anyway. Lecturing in psychology to students is hard by definition.'

He perched himself on the back of the sofa, while I decorously drank my tea at the desk. He'd rested the folder on the corner and found it hard to tear my eyes away from it. 'Do you think they believe in ghosts?' I asked, nodding towards it. 'Those people who saw "something"? Some of the reports are so matter of fact, even when there's a huge amount of the inexplicable going on.'

Max sighed. 'It's proven that some people are more prone to seeing "things", whether it's ghosts or whether they have a mindset that turns eye-floaters into beings, and anything they don't understand becomes demons and spirits.' He picked up the file again. 'That's practically the synopsis for the next book,' he said cheerily, tapping my hard work against the desk edge. 'Going into the whys and wherefores of the psychology of belief in the supernatural. But, in the absence of having seen anything definitely spooky at the Fortune House myself, this is all I have to go on for now.'

'Why are you so determined to write about the place?' I leaned back a little in my chair, then felt that this made me look like a Bond villain about to unleash the lasers, and put my elbows back on the desk again. 'Surely writing a book about Haunted York would get more revenue and coverage?'

Max seemed to stiffen slightly. 'I promised Alethia,' he said. 'I mean, after the incident with her chasing me out armed with pans, we became really good friends, and she wanted to get to the bottom of why the house had a reputation for being haunted. She grew up there and it didn't have any kind of reputation then, apart from her father being a persistent late payer of bills and a bit handy with his fists, and her mum making the best parkin in the district.'

His gaze wandered off for a moment, towards the still vast pile of papers. 'I liked Alethia,' he said softly. 'She left home at fifteen, but she came back when she inherited the house, to try to make a go of it in her mum and dad's memory. She'd be horrified to see it now, all ruins and holes. And I hate to think what she'd make of the skeleton under the house. I'm tempted to leave the discovery of the body out, but I can't because it might be the reason for the whole "haunted house" reputation, which is the point of the book. But if I leave it in, it starts to turn what was a simple exploration of the stories linked to the house into some big mystery, which will be impossible to solve. No nice, definite ending for the book, you see.'

'But if there is a secret about the Fortune House, she'd want it to be uncovered, surely?' I put my mug down on the desk, then worried that it might be an antique and nudged a couple of hand-written sheets of paper under the cup in case of tea-rings. 'If the body they found is part of the reason that the house had its haunted reputation, then you're still doing what she wanted, aren't you? She's not around to be upset if it turns out to be her brother, and it's far too late for anyone to be accused of involvement in his death.'

His expression lightened. 'God, I never thought of it like that,' he said. 'How do you do it, Alice?'

'It's easier to see things when you're on the outside.' I was aware that my tone had taken on a slight sarcasm. 'When you're too close to something it's really difficult to work out what's actually going on. At school...' I stopped.

'Go on.'

What the hell. He seemed to like me. Now was the time to see whether he really did, as he'd put it, like *me* for *me*, or for the image I presented. 'I wasn't particularly popular at school.' I could feel my face getting warm at the memory. 'I couldn't hang out, I always had to get home to help Mum and we didn't have a lot of money, so I wasn't trendy, didn't have the latest gadgets. And I was... *am*... not exactly going to be swapping clothes, either. I was... *am*... big and plain and they never let me forget it.'

'Oh, Alice.' Max sounded almost defeated.

'But it meant I was looking in from the outside, and that's not always a bad thing when the inside is a bunch of teenage boys who'll say and do almost anything to get a girl to have sex with them, and girls who regard being the girlfriend of the most popular boy as the pinnacle of educational achievement,' I went on, without reacting to him. 'I worked hard because there wasn't much choice. I could see through what was going on for most of the rest of the pupils, and, even though there was little chance of me ending up married at seventeen with three kids before twenty, I knew that there was more to life than that.'

I took a deep breath. 'I wanted to be a veterinary nurse, you see. I knew I'd never make a vet, not clever enough, but I could assist. So I studied and worked and I was looking at places I could go to college – and then Mum got really ill. I couldn't get any work experience at the vet's because they wanted me during times when Mum needed me. Welsh's Windows offered me a place, and they were more flexible with hours and – well, the rest is history and—' I waved a hand at the scale model of a modest mountain range that was forming against the study wall, 'now, an immense amount of paper-sorting.'

Silence. I couldn't even look at Max and kept my eyes very firmly trained on the far corner of the room, where a cupboard that looked as though the sixteenth century had mated with an IKEA catalogue was lurking with one door ever so slightly open. Everything in me wanted to rush over and close that door.

Eventually Max moved. 'I'm sorry,' he said.

I felt my heart rise into my throat. He sounded sad, as though what I'd just said had changed everything, and the slow sinking of my stomach, in direct counterpoint to my heart, made me realise that I couldn't bear that to be true. Whatever it was in me that had been stopping me from surrendering to emotion and lust and Max's overt admiration of me dissolved, as I realised I wanted him. Hell, I really *liked* him. I wasn't ready to call it love, I'd need more time, more shared experience before I could ever call it that, but I was certainly teetering on the edge of falling in love with Max Allbright.

I opened my mouth, but nothing came out, apart from a stran-gled kind of mew. I had to meet his eye now and so I pushed every-thing back down. I was used to that. Whatever he said now, whatever his reasoning for being sorry – if telling him about my feelings of isolation growing up had made him look at me differ-ently, made him feel differently about me – well, there was still my old job, my house, I could go back to my old life, if this was all over. No harm done, apart from another dent in the bodywork of my self-esteem.

Max's expression was unreadable. He looked as though he were swallowing hard. 'I'm sorry,' he said again, and he sounded a bit choked.

'Why are *you* sorry?' I decided that businesslike and down to earth was the best way to handle this. Hell, I was invested in all this Fortune House research now, the paperwork was perhaps not fasci-nating but it was definitely interesting. If Max had been put off by my outsider status, my lack of experience during my formative years, and had decided that a relationship with me was now out of the question, it didn't matter. I'd got a job to do here, and I'd do it until we found out what the hell the deal was with the body and the ghosts, and then I'd flee for the hills and get a small yappy dog and join the WI and forget this ever happened.

Another moment of quiet. Even the air was quiet, not a rustle or a rattle to be heard anywhere. 'I'm sorry that my life has been so – privileged,' Max said, eventually, very softly. 'I've got a tendency to feel hard done by because I was sent away to school and my sister had a comparatively cushy life and I have to work hard to keep the estate going. But now I say it out loud, it all sounds so "woe is me, boo-hoo", while your life has actually been *hard* and you never really say a word about it. Now I feel slightly stupid and a bit... I don't even know what the word is.'

'Overdramatic?' I suggested. 'Hyperbolic?' I could feel the smile rising to my face. He hadn't been put off. My school days as an outcast hadn't made him think differently about me, it had made him realise how fortunate he had been despite the death of his mother, and that was a lot easier to deal with, especially since all my organs were now dancing the dance of relief.

'Yes, yes, all right, don't rub it in.' There was that light of mischief in his eyes now, as they met mine. 'Whatever it is, I'm sorry, all right?'

'Upper-class? Posh?' I carried on.

He laughed aloud now. 'I refuse to apologise for centuries of lineage, because none of that is my fault. I'm just the one at the sharp end now, trying to keep it all together, with not *quite* enough money and a load of undergraduates who thought psychology would be a nice soft option to study while they worked out what to do with the rest of their lives.'

'What does Jenna do for a living?' A complete change of subject seemed to be in order. I didn't want to tease him too much, I'd learned long ago that there's a fine line between teasing and bullying and, whilst I thought Max would be very hard to bully, I didn't want him to think that I could lapse into being on the wrong side of that line. I'd spent far too long on the other side for that to be a happy thought.

'Jen?' He seemed slightly taken aback by the conversational derail. 'She builds and maintains motorbikes. She's got a workshop down in the old stables.'

'Oh.' That seemed to be the end of that. 'I just wondered.'

'She's more practical than I am. Good with her hands. That whole family trait seems to have passed me by and left me with not much more than knowing my way around debunking Maslow's Hierarchy of Needs.'

'You're painting that fence,' I reminded him. 'For the last several months.'

'Painting fences doesn't require much actual skill, though. Just the ability to keep upright, not die of boredom and put the paint on the right end of the brush.' Max still had that mischievous look in his eye. As though he were also relieved, somehow. 'Even a posh git can manage that. It's hardly assembling the space shuttle.' Then he straightened his face. 'And I really am sorry, Alice. I didn't know. About your life, I mean. I wondered why you were stuck in that job that you were clearly much too intelligent for, why you didn't look for something a bit more challenging, but I can understand it now.'

'Can you?' I asked, a bit stiffly. I wasn't quite sure I could really understand it myself, other than being too lazy to be bothered to move and there not exactly being a plethora of jobs for someone who never got as far as A levels.

'You value consistency. An unsettled upbringing as a young carer has given you a fear of the unknown, probably instilled by your parents. And your schoolmates' lack of understanding of your circumstances has made you crave stability and a close social connection.'

'All right, spare me the psychology lecture,' I said sharply. 'My upbringing wasn't *that* tragic. I was fed, I was warm and I was loved, and a lot of other people had it worse.'

'You're right, and that's what links us all here, isn't it?' Max got up off the arm of the sofa and came to stand by the desk. 'You, me, Alethia. We all had "duty" fitted as standard. You caring for your parents, me with this bloody great house and the estate, and Alethia came back to take on her parents' place out of duty.'

'There doesn't have to be a "theme", Max.' I tried to sound gentle. 'This really *isn't* a psychology lecture. You don't have to strain to give us all something in common – we're just people doing what we think is best and right.'

He laughed, a ringing laugh that felt out of place amid all this solemn furniture. 'Oh, Alice, you are wonderful! I know you can' see it, but you really and truly are. You've always got the right words to puncture my pomposity and sense of over-importance.'

'I just think,' I said carefully, 'that having all this – the house, the estate, all the responsibility – it's made you lose your sense of wonder at the world a bit.'

'You mean I've got no sense of fun?' He frowned. 'I showed you the Boobie Room, right?'

'That wasn't fun, that was four hundred years of tits and minge.' I surprised myself with this. 'Do you know how to have proper fun?' I wasn't even sure what constituted 'proper fun' myself. I'd tried to persuade Grant into it, until it turned out that his idea of fun was weekend-long gaming sessions while I'd been thinking more of city breaks and cocktail bars.

Max looked as though he were thinking deeply. Finally, he stood up dramatically. The lamps which lit the study illuminated him from one side, his other side was turned to the night outside the window and the resulting shadows made him look taller. Darker. And, I hated to admit it, more handsome. 'Right,' he said, 'right. You want fun? There's limited fun to be had in a house this old in the middle of the night, but I'll see what I can do. Give me ten minutes and then come down the main staircase.'

'What?' All my internal organs rattled. I wasn't sure if it was anticipation, anxiety or just hunger, but he was already on his way out, closing the door so firmly that the draught scuttled through the paper pile like a mouse. 'Oh, hell,' I said to the desk. 'I've provoked him into spontaneity. This isn't going to be pretty.' As long as it wasn't going to consist of him prancing about with his trousers round his ankles, trying to get his willy to 'helicopter'... and then I mentally kicked myself. This was Max, not Grant.

I tidied up the desk. I tried to impose some order on the heap of papers on the floor, but couldn't do more than kick at the edges until it looked a bit straighter. Postcards slithered from between layers and I picked them up absent-mindedly, putting them down on the desk with only the most cursory of glances. One was a picture of Piccadilly Circus, featuring an old-style London bus, the other showed Buckingham Palace looking austere. They reminded me of something, but I wasn't quite sure what, and anyway, it had to have been more than ten minutes now.

I crept out of the study, along the corridor and down the servants' staircase to the top of the main stairs. There was no sign of Max and only the faintest glimmer of illumination from the emergency lighting along the long hallway on the lower floor, but a faint drift of music, half-heard like fairy pipes, came to meet me.

I followed it. Past the huge windows, outside of which the darkness pressed, I moved as though in some kind of enchantment, or that's what I told myself anyway. This wasn't me, sensible Alice, trundling along through the bland, visitor-friendly passageways of Hatherleigh Hall, it was someone else, my inner me. The slim, ethereal person I'd always been assured lived inside me, who skipped and trod lithely through life, distracted by butterflies and colours and phrases from fiction. Called by the music to the land of my faery origin.

I tried a little skip, but my bust slumped heavily and it hurt, despite my scaffolding of a bra, so I stopped. Nope, it was definitely me. Nothing otherworldly going on here, and I was responsible for everything that happened from here on in. The thought made me nervous at the same time as sending a stinging pulse of excited adrenaline through my blood.

Fun. Max said he could be fun. Was that what I wanted?

The heat in my heart said *yes*.

16

The increasing volume of the music led me to double doors at the end of the house. A thin, flickering light showed in the gap between the doors, and I took a deep breath. Any hint of helicopter-willy and I was fully prepared to go and wrench that Elizabethan bedpost off, just for continuity's sake. Then I opened the doors.

It was the ballroom. Or, at least, a room that had a long, polished wooden floor and a moulded ceiling that gave the place the feel of a huge secular cathedral. Alcoves in the wall had built-in seating, for that 'chaperone-free canoodle' experience, and mirrors reflected the light from candles along the walls.

In a decidedly less historic move, Dua Lipa was playing from a device plugged in at the far end. I stood, amazed.

'Come and dance.' Max appeared out of the flickering darkness. 'Come on, Alice. Let's have this "fun" you talked about.'

I *wanted* to say that I couldn't dance. That I didn't. That the candles were probably dangerous. That there wasn't enough light and we might twist our ankles. But I didn't. I let Imaginary Alice, slender and supple, have her fairy wings.

'Yes, please,' I said. I took his hand and stepped out onto the dance floor.

Max could dance. He actually had the long, lithe body that I was trying to imagine for myself. He had long legs and slim hips, and he moved to the beat, even as Dua Lipa segued into The Weeknd, and I stepped into it alongside him.

I loved dancing. It was one of those secrets I kept, because nobody wanted to see plump, shapeless me on a dance floor and the only times I'd dared, people had stopped dancing to watch and tease, after which I'd only danced alone in my room. But that had been school, and things were different now. *Now* there were no spotty fifteen-year-old boys thinking they'd 'get a go' because I'd be so afraid nobody would want me. No girls in carefully drawn-on make-up covering their acne, skin-tight jeans covering their uncertainty. Nobody except Max, who took my hand and led me into dance after dance, with the candlelight shining in his eyes and his hair electrified by the motion. Nothing except Max. Even with the music, he was all I could focus on. He kept those flame-filled eyes on me as we spun and twirled on the slippery floor, dancing out of the light and into the dark and then back again.

Then, with the Jonas Brothers trying to up the pace, we moved in close. Slowly, together, dancing as though they were playing 'The Last Waltz', we circled, arms around one another. Max felt hot through his shirt. I couldn't see his face now as I had my head tucked into the crook of his shoulder, my own skin sticky with the exertion, but I didn't care. All there was now was the music, the light, and Max, holding me as though this was all he wanted, and I remembered the way he'd held me when I'd cried back in my dusty little living room. As though I *mattered*.

'Max?' I moved my head and looked up at him.

As though he'd been waiting for this, he looked down, smiled slowly, and cocked his head to one side, moving in and down as I moved up and out and our mouths met in the middle in one huge explosion of heat and light that even the Jonas Brothers couldn't have predicted. Vaguely I noted that they were singing about 'What a Man Gotta Do', as we moved backwards into one of the cushioned alcoves, but, as we passed, Max gave the device a swift kick and the machine fell backwards, muffling the music to a background beat.

We managed to fill the space where the music had been. Max treated my body as though it was something to worship, and there wasn't an inch of me that didn't go unappreciated, either by fingers, eyes or tongue. I like to think that I returned the favour, at least, he seemed to find everything satisfactory, with his head thrown back and his skin flushing as we crushed the velvet-covered seating into waves and troughs with our vigour and enthusiasm. I didn't even think twice about how I looked naked, I was too busy taking in the sight of Max's body, lean and spare, saving up all the memories in case this was a one-off. Trying to lock away the feel of his mouth, the graze of his stubble, the taste of him and the wonderful, amazing way he made me feel as I arched above or beneath him, whispering his name.

When we were an overheated huddled heap at last, slumped together on the floor of the alcove with the cold seating against our backs and our hair tangled over sweaty faces, Max put his arms around me. 'Told you I knew how to have fun,' he murmured. 'And that I'm nicer to my women than Heathcliff. Bet he never made a woman scream.'

'Not in a good way, anyway,' I agreed. My head was comfortable against his shoulder and I felt the drowsiness of good sex beginning to drag me into sleep. 'He was a "one up against the stable wall" man, if ever there was one.'

'"Lift your skirts, wench, for you are merely a servant and must obey me," kind of thing?'

There was a moment of silence. 'You sound like you practise that sentence a lot,' I said.

'Oh, yes. I regularly exercise my *droit de seigneur* on Daisy, when she's not hoovering. And Mrs Plumstead, who comes in to do for us in the flat, she's not safe either.' Max sounded as sleepy as I felt. 'And if you believe that's true, then I'm glad, because it will let me know that this didn't feel as though I've not had sex for a year.'

'Wow. A year,' I said, forgetting that I'd not had anything but solo sex for six years.

'Yep. And every time I looked at you, I wanted to get my *droit* out and give it a good gallop, so I hope I get points for restraint tonight. It could all have been over before the end of Post Malone, if I hadn't thought very hard about fence painting. Oh, and the music is Jenna's, before you criticise my Spotify playlist.'

I barely heard him. I'd drifted off into a dazed doze, to half-dreams of postcards and waltzes. I think Max may have slept too, because he shook me awake. Enough time had passed for the candles to have dribbled down into stubs and the lighting to have become sinister. 'Come on, let's go to bed,' he said. 'And I'm not expecting you to finish the night with me if you don't want to.'

But I did want to. Max's room was pleasingly ordinary, without a four-poster or an armoire to be seen, just a comfortable, large bed, into which we fell in a tangle of arms and legs, to check that the ballroom hadn't been an aberration and things could be as good the second time around. Which they were.

They were pretty bloody amazing the third time too, but now it was morning and yesterday's grey skies had given way to blazing blue. The sun shone into Max's room at dawn, but was nowhere near as bright as Max himself, bursting through the door with a large jug of coffee and some toast and the air of a man who has achieved a Personal Best.

'Wow,' he said. 'You're still here. I thought it might have been a dream.'

'I was here when you went off to make the coffee. Unless you sleepwalk, that must have been a bit of a clue.' Embarrassed, for some reason, suddenly, I sat up with the covers pulled to my chin like a 1970s sitcom. 'But thank you for the coffee. I need it.'

Max gave me the grin again. It was an open, happy grin which contained a bit of naughtiness and a lot of relief. 'I'm so glad I've got you here,' he said, pouring gigantic mugs full of fragrant coffee. 'That we've finally got round to... err... having all the fun. I didn't want to rush you into anything but, my God, I've been trying to plan for this for weeks.' The grin stuttered uncertainly. 'Alice, please, tell me you've been wanting to do this too. That it's not going to be a "thanks for the memories" type of thing?'

He sounded genuinely uncertain. This man, who had stalked with variations through my dreams since I hit puberty, who was the very embodiment of the men that I'd read about in Sheila's books with swooning heroines on the covers, was uncertain as to whether *I*, with my wobbly thighs and stomach and lack of waistline, would want *him*.

'Well.' I chewed a piece of toast thoughtfully. 'I think I can probably lower my standards. In your case.'

A pause. Then the relief flooded back onto his face, and he was laughing until the coffee in his mug began to slop onto the bed. 'Oh, Alice,' he said. 'Oh, Alice. I do l... need you.'

'Quite right too,' I nodded, but I'd heard it. That little slip. It was too soon for the L word, for me anyway. Grant and I had said it, but now I realised that what we'd had wasn't love. Not really. We'd said it because it was expected of us. Now, with Max, nothing was expected. We could take our time and he seemed to feel that too.

I went home later that afternoon. I had four weeks of facing Sheila's questions about whether or not I'd started wetting myself yet to get through, and I didn't want to run the risk of Grant and Jenna walking in on Max and me pretending to work whilst touching one another at every opportunity.

We hadn't seen them all weekend, in fact. They were probably off having fun, I thought, and then the memories of the fun I'd had with Max came sweeping back, and I had to put the car windows down and drive with the cool of the darkening air on my cheeks for a while. Max had got lectures to prepare and give, I had windows to plan. We were old enough and wise enough to know that real life continued outside Hatherleigh Hall, and we couldn't spend days in bed, however much we wanted to.

To tide me over, I'd brought a bag full of papers from the stack with me. It bulged complacently on the back seat of the car, and then in the armchair, where I dropped it as I came in. I could sort here as well as at the Hall, and I might as well spend my evenings doing something useful, rather than reliving Saturday night and wondering whether Max would have changed his mind about me before Friday night.

He wouldn't, if the messages I'd had from him during my drive home were anything to go by. They were light-hearted messages, not blow-by-blow accounts of what he'd like to do to me next time we met – although I wouldn't have turned my nose up at those either, but they might have indicated that this whatever-we-had was purely sexual. These messages were funny, observational, little updates of how his life was going, to which I replied in kind from lay-bys and viewpoints, where I'd stopped whenever I'd heard the buzz of his incoming messages. I might have cast caution to the winds in the ballroom, but here I was Sensible Alice again, and being prosecuted for using my phone whilst driving was Just Not Me.

My house felt different, now I was in it with a different mindset. The clonks and yells from Next Door Right were family life I could smile at, rather than annoyances. Mr Next Door Left's jaunty wave as the dog dragged him past my window was a friendly observation of me standing there pensively rather than a sarcastic note on my lack of a life.

I couldn't settle. The house felt chafingly tight around me, like a slightly-too-small bra. I reasoned that it was because I'd been wafting around in the huge, high-ceilinged space of Hatherleigh Hall for the best part of a week, and that the contrast between all that air and the cramped little space of my nineteenth-century cottage was giving me claustrophobia, until I found a mug out of place in the kitchen. I had a 'favourite' mug and always used that one. The 'visitor' mugs lived in the cupboard over the hob, but when I opened the cupboard where the biscuits were kept, there was a mug. A nondescript, inoffensive mug, one of the Secret Santa gifts that circled the office every year, occasionally containing a selection of cheap chocolates or a mini bottle of Prosecco. But, more to the point, a mug which was never used.

I stood back and stared at it. Its logo, a picture of the North York Moors, stared back. Carefully, considering every move, I picked it up and weighed it in my hand. A normal mug, of normal mug weight, it couldn't have fallen or flown through a closed cupboard door. Could it? I had a flashback to some of the stories I'd put in chronological order for Max. A dark night. *Things that moved.* I almost dropped the mug onto the work surface.

Then I began to notice other things. The chair, which I only moved to hoover under, and that only once a year, was slightly out of alignment. I pounded up the stairs and found that the soap in the bathroom had been put back in the dish upside down. A towel hung off centre.

I knew I wasn't the most diligent person in the world regarding housework; dusting and cobweb removal and tidying away of plates and clothing weren't top of the agenda while I lived alone. After all, who cared, apart from me, if there were socks in the living room and a plate beside the bed? But these out of place things didn't come under housework, they came under *someone has been here*.

I rang Max. This was the first time I'd ever been able to call someone who might have had the slightest interest in my life, and I felt it as I dialled. Besides, I wanted to talk to him, to hear his voice. To know that what we'd shared last night had been real.

'Hey, Alice.' He sounded pleased to hear from me too. 'Can't keep away, eh?'

'Someone's been in my house,' I said, keeping my voice low, although I wasn't sure why. They definitely weren't still here, unless they were standing sideways in the wardrobe.

'Oh, yes, Jen just got back and she mentioned something about Grant taking her there? Just for a quick coffee, breaking their journey on their way back from... actually, I'm not sure where they went. But they're back now.'

'They... Grant brought her *here*? To *my house*? How did he get in? He didn't shove her through the upstairs window, did he?' The bathroom window didn't quite lock. It was only accessible by climbing up on the kitchen roof, though, and you'd have to be very skinny to get through.

Max sounded cautious now. 'I *think* he's got a key?'

I put the phone down and dashed to the fruit bowl. It almost never contained actual fruit, being used as a receptacle for all the loose bits and pieces that may or may not come in useful at some future date. My spare keys lived there. *Used* to live there, anyway.

'He promised he'd put it back when he was here on Monday. The absolute...' I ran out of words. 'And I thought he was improving.'

Now I was angry. Max and I ended the call, and I went through to the living room, where the complacency of the bag of papers made me even angrier. What kind of family kept *everything* like this? When Mum had died, I'd gone through all her paperwork and thrown away anything that wasn't relevant, in those first weeks of baffled grief and confusion. Grant hadn't helped at all, of course, he'd pleaded work, but I'd often come into the spare room to find him LionLording it with his cohort. The utter turd.

I dropped the bag onto the floor, where the insufficient carrier bag seams split and the papers toppled out onto the carpet. On top were the two postcards I'd picked out last night. Old pictures of a long ago London. London. Wasn't that where Alethia's brother was meant to have gone?

I turned them over. The first one bore the message 'I AM HERE'. Carefully printed in capital letters and signed with a firm J. Just the initial, carved so deeply into the postcard that it had embossed its way through to appear in reverse on the side of the double decker in the picture. Addressed to 'Fortune House Farm, Great Riccalldale, North Yorkshire'. No postcode, but then they didn't have postcodes then, did they?

The postcard of Buckingham Palace had the same writing: 'DOING WELL. I AM HAPPY NOW. J'. John had clearly been a man of few words. But these were proof that he had gone to London, anyway. Which meant he wasn't the body under the house. Damn. I'd been so sure.

But now I needed to know who it was, what *had* happened to someone in that house, to give Max the closure he wanted, the end of his book and a proper conclusion to the story of a house which had frightened so many people through the years. As Max had said, some of those stories could have been over-imagination; the dark of the moors and the austere bulk of the house would have lent themselves to that sort of thing. Some of the stories would have been pure invention for a warped kind of fame or self-aggrandisement of the teller, those who had always wanted to write a book but lacked the wherewithal, perhaps. But *some* were so inexplicably mundane

that imagination surely couldn't play a part and the sheer pointless-
ness gave them a forgettability that anyone in search of making
themselves a name would have at least given a layer of creeping
horror; fog, a dog howling, a mysterious cry.

We had ghost stories. We had a body, mysteriously buried. I had
a pile of paperwork which might or might not hold the key. And,
talking of keys, I also had an ex-husband who still had my front
door key. I went and put the chain on the door, in case. Then,
putting the postcards aside on their own separate pile, which I
mentally labelled 'possibly of interest', I started sifting through the
papers.

* * *

Extract from *Walking Holidays on the North York Moors* by
Norah-Jane Garfield, privately published in 2017.

We had taken a walking holiday, following part of the Coast-
to-Coast path, and on this day we were crossing the bit of the
moor from where the path joins the Lyke Wake Walk near to
where the Fortune House stands. We had been warned by the
walk leader not to stray from the path as the landowner did not
like walkers, so we were all carefully keeping to a fairly well-
trodden way through heather and bracken, and were climbing a
long slope of maybe 1 in 12 towards our lunch stop at the crest
of the hill.

It was a gloomy day and there were seven of us on the walk,
including my husband and myself, all of us fit and keen walkers,
suitably attired. I was walking at the front of the group, following
the guide and talking about the local landscape. He had pointed
out some feature or other and, as we were well ahead of the
main group, we stopped on a convenient ridge to turn and look
out over the dale. As such, we could see the rest of the group

straggling behind us up the hill, which was steep and a difficult climb.

All of a sudden, my guide exclaimed, 'Who on earth is that?' and pointed. At the back of the group, and climbing the gradient in a smooth, untroubled way as though it were flat ground, was a young man we didn't recognise. As I say, all our group were suitably dressed for a long walk through moorland, with good all-weather jackets and trousers and heavy walking boots and gaiters. The young man following us wore a flat cap and tweed jacket. I did not see his lower half, the undergrowth being sufficient to obscure it. Momentarily I believed him to be a local, or another walker who had simply attached himself to the back of our group, but his movement soon disabused me of that belief. He was not bending forward to accommodate the slope, nor showing any sign of physical effort, but rather was moving almost as though pulled on a trolley in a kind of 'gliding' movement.

There was something unnatural about his motion. The track was steep, broken by rocks and roots, and even the more experienced walkers in our group were finding it hard going to reach the top. This man seemed almost to be floating up the hillside. As we watched, one of the walkers towards the front of the group stumbled and our attention was diverted for a second, and when we looked back at the rear of the group, the stranger was gone.

I should point out that we were on bare hillside, with nothing but undergrowth. There was nowhere for the man to have gone, apart from collapsing to lie completely flat, whereupon the heather may have concealed him. He could not have left the dale without us seeing him.

After a moment, the guide, who had up until now been a stalwart and phlegmatic man, collapsed onto the turf, white and shaking. I was worried by his appearance, he looked most unwell, and he was muttering something about not believing it until he saw it, and how it was the ghost of the Fortune House, or some such. I, still thinking that the man had been flesh and blood and perhaps playing a trick or joke on walkers, went back down the slope to search the ground where the man had vanished, expecting to find him hiding among the bracken and laughing to himself. There was nobody. I investigated the path we had followed for any signs of apparatus which could have produced the 'smooth gliding' effect, such as tracks of wheels or any kind of pulley, and there were none. On questioning the rest of the group, nobody else had seen our mysterious follower, even my husband, who had been the rear guard and, as such, within only a couple of feet of the man as we had watched from above. Even to this day, my husband swears that there was nobody else in our group, and only the fact that both the guide and I had seen him and described him in a similar way prevented him from thinking that I had had a touch of the sun on that day!

17

The week went surprisingly quickly. Work were obviously having a whip round for me, and Sheila would have organised a card, because they all went very quiet whenever I walked in on more than two people. Malcolm had become rather sullen and Sheila was full of questions, but apart from that, we worked on normally. The onset of an early autumn had concentrated people's minds on their blown double glazing or that draught from upstairs, and enquiries were coming in thick and fast. I fielded calls, organised appointments, sent out brochures both in PDF and paper form, and felt a daily poke in the ribs of regret that this job I could do so easily would no longer be mine.

The shiver of anticipation about moving on to something new and different had mutated to a grim fear that I'd be no good at it. That Max would get bored with me after a fortnight, that the organising that he seemed to think he needed would turn out to be two phone calls and an alphabetical ordering of his filing system, and I'd be out on my ear, back at Mr Welsh's door, pleading to come back. Sheila had mentioned something about them getting in a series of temps from the agency to fill my role 'for the time being', so everyone clearly expected the same result, me back in my chair before the year was out.

But Max seemed decent. Kind. He'd accepted Grant back, even after the furore he'd caused, when he could have refused to let him set foot on the Hatherleigh Estate. He'd repeatedly reassured me that, should things fall apart between us, there would be other jobs for me. The estate seemed to need workers, I'd still have my home, although renting it out was going to be a bit of a problem as who would want to live in the middle of Pickering amid my furniture and rattling windows? I'd made approaches to a rental agent, who'd made, 'Weeeeelllll, possibly, if you price it low enough...' noises, which hadn't filled me with hope, and I was starting to resign myself to leaving it empty and dashing back every weekend to check that Mr Next Door Left hadn't knocked through to give the dog a room to itself. But that wouldn't work, there would still be bills to pay and I was relying on the house to pay for itself and perhaps give me a little bit for savings, not actually cost me money.

So, all in all, I didn't know whether to regret my decision or celebrate it.

Then it was Friday evening and I was heading back to the Hall, the much smaller pile of papers, now reduced only to those I thought would be of interest, tightly bound with string on the back seat.

Darkness was drawing in early these days, with the frost-crisping of the leaves, and the distant lights at the top of the Hall beckoned me down the drive, with the gravel cracking and spitting under my wheels. The black-railed fencing that Max was evidently still painting outlined the rutted shadows of ploughed fields and I kept my eyes strictly to the front so as not to catch sight of a ghostly horse and rider plunging to their deaths over the distant hedge-line. I was still a little hazy over exactly how Max's mother had died, but I didn't want to see a spectral replay when I had a full bladder and the need to stay in her home for the rest of the weekend.

My worries about my now-uncertain future had crystallised into a grim determination to get to the bottom of the Fortune House papers. Once they had been sorted and sifted down to only those of importance to Max's book, then we would see. Either more organisation would be necessary, or I would be out of a job, but the faster I got to that point, the faster it would all become apparent. If I found something amid all the scraps and torn-out pages that could give Max his definitive ending, then so much the better. If not, well, if it all fell apart, then I'd move back to Pickering and spend my remaining years knitting hot water bottle covers and running jumble sales.

As I pulled up at the front door, I could see Jenna's motorbike slewed at an angle beyond the steps. This reminded me that Grant was in line for a tongue-lashing, and I readied myself for his crouched contrition, his promises that he'd never do it again, all to be instantly forgotten when expedient. I knew Grant only too well.

Max was there. Lovely, lovely Max, outlined in shadow by my headlights, coming down the steps like a game show host to greet me. The second he opened my door and threw his arms around me to envelop me in that orangey scent and the drift of his hair, I knew I was doing the right thing, and revelled in that feeling because I knew it would vanish like the frost in the sun come Monday morning.

'Oh, I have missed you,' he breathed against me.

'We video-called this morning,' I pointed out. 'And last night.'

'Well, yes, but it's not the same, is it? For a start, your Wi-Fi is dreadful and you kept dropping out and freezing. I'm not sure we managed more than half a sentence without having to stop and apologise.' He stood back so he could see my face. 'I really have missed you,' he repeated.

'Then lead me to your centre of disorganisation and I will make a start.' I hefted the pile of newly sorted papers from the back of my car by their string tie.

Max widened his eyes at me. 'Hold on, it's Friday night, let's wind down a bit first. There's plenty of time for all that.'

This jolted me a bit. He was right, there was plenty of time. Why was I going about this as though it were some kind of temporary job, to be got through as fast as possible? Because I wanted to see what would happen after it was over? That seemed a bit counter-productive.

'All right.' I put the papers back in the car. 'But I do have to kill Grant first, for letting himself and Jenna into my house last week-end. And use the loo.'

'They're inside.' Max waved an arm at the open door, which was letting a tempting slice of bright yellow light out to illuminate the gravel. 'If you can get a word in edgewise past Jenna's favour samples and chair dressings.'

We went into the main hall, where it struck me again how odd it was that this whole huge house could be so empty, yet so full of shadows, but it no longer felt sinister. Now it was just the Hall, and I knew what all the rooms were and could find my way along most of the corridors with only the occasional wrong turning. The Visitors' Toilet, which had the grace to be signposted in quite large lettering, was just off the hallway, and while I availed myself of its facilities, I primed my anger towards Grant for making free with my house particularly when he hadn't given me chance to hang clean towels or – I sniffed at the luxury brand handwash that filled the dispensers by the sinks – put out my best soap.

Grant was sitting in the old kitchen, on one of the stools, whilst

Jenna talked over several piles of coloured material. He looked rapt, I thought, as I went in and caught them not knowing they were observed. As though he were genuinely *interested* in purple velvet versus fuchsia satin. I'd never seen him look as engaged in anything I'd tried to tell him, and I felt another one of those pangs, below the heart but above the lungs, that told me again how wrong I'd got it by marrying Grant.

'Hey, Al.' He looked up and saw me standing in the doorway.

'My key.' I held out my hand. 'Right. Now.'

'Oh yes, we went to the house last week,' Jenna said, without a trace of shame. 'I love your house, Alice.'

'If you could love it in future only when I'm actually, you know, there inside it, I'd appreciate it,' I said, watching Grant search his pockets.

'But we want to rent it from you.' Jenna was collecting up her samples, so she didn't see the utter gape of disbelief that came onto my face. Grant dropped the key into my hand and it slithered straight off my palm and onto the floor.

'You... want...?' I looked around the high ceilings, the solid wood units, the vast acres of historic storage and the sheer Big Housedness of the kitchen. There was not one single point of reference that aligned with the kitchen in my house, other than that they both had some form of cooking apparatus in them. Here there was a range big enough to cook a ten-year-old on. In my house, you could barely get a small chicken in the oven, and that had to go sideways.

'Yeah, Max said you want to let the house out rather than sell. It's in the perfect place, because I want to move the bike business somewhere nearer town, and Grant can work from anywhere,' Jenna went on, obviously not seeing my sheer disbelief. 'There's more passing trade near a main road, down here people have to make a special journey, which is a pain if your bike's broken down. I've been looking at premises on the little trading estate on the Scarborough road, and it looks brilliant.'

Right next to Welsh's Windows, I thought. It was as though Jenna and I were swapping lives. But it would solve a lot of problems; the house rental would be straightforward, and Grant already knew about the peculiarities of the hot water system and the strange floor arrangements.

'Oh. Well.' I was winded for a second. 'That sounds... are you sure?'

'I mean, obviously we'll buy a place soon, but it would be great to start out, make sure the move works and everything,' she went on with the blithe lack of concern for actual financials that would be involved for anyone without an upbringing that contained a carriage house. 'We only popped by the other day so Grant could have a wee – you know how he is with public toilets,' she rattled on, still not the least abashed. 'And your little house feels so... so...' She groped for the word.

I could have supplied her with half a dozen, but they were all prejudicial, and she did seem enthusiastic, so I picked up the key from the polished oak floor, marvelling again at the contrast between how Jenna lived now and how she seemed to want to live.

'And what do you think of these?' Well, I couldn't say I hadn't been warned, I thought, as she thrust a pile of photographs under my nose when I stood up again. 'Samples from photographers. *I* like the guy who does the black and white arty shots, but Grant says it looks like we'd be getting married in 1956.'

The photographs were all watermarked with the name of the photographer, presumably so you couldn't forget who had taken which photo. The arty shots had the watermark over the face of the bride, which I thought was a bit tasteless, but I agreed with Jenna that they looked pretty, and then wandered off to find Max. My intention to berate Grant had dissipated under Jenna's sheer excitement and anticipation, and as his desire for a private toilet stop had been instrumental in their decision to rent the house, I could hardly yell at him about it now. Actually, no, I *could* yell at him, but it had never done any good before. I couldn't see him suddenly having an epiphany about his behaviour towards me, which, I was increasingly realising, was very sibling-like.

Max was standing by the front door. 'Shall we go for a walk?'

'A *walk*?' The question came out as though this was the most outrageous suggestion I had ever heard.

'Yes, walk. Transfer weight from one leg to the other whilst swinging your body forward – it's the new craze, you'll love it.'

I raised my eyebrows.

'I know it's dark. I know it's probably going to be frosty. But there's something I want to show you. And I want to be with you, on our own, without Bonnie and Clyde rustling around and producing sample invitations like a magic trick.'

I fell into step alongside him and he led the way out of the main door, across the gravel and onto the lawn. 'You're taking me to the icehouse?'

'Well spotted.'

There were fairy lights up now, around the entrance, which gave it the inviting look of a grotto, until we got through the gate, where it still had the look of a brick-lined bucket and a smell of damp stonework. With half my brain, I could see it as it could be. A wooden floor to level off the worst of the 'bucketness', a rail around the platform which circled the sides, so that a congregation could watch the ceremony. Bride and groom and officiant in the middle, lights and acoustics and music – it could be beautiful and quirky.

The other half of my brain saw moss and mould. I tried to ignore the, probably expensive, 'plink' of water dripping somewhere.

'You don't seem to believe that I could possibly find you attractive,' Max said, out of the blue, as we stood under the arch of fairy lights. They had obviously been stolen from a Christmas tree somewhere, because one or two of the lights were elf-shaped.

I looked at him. 'I'm trying to,' I said honestly. 'I really am. I mean, I've seen the Boobie Room. But *that* was your however-many-times-great grandfather, it's not as though you had it done to demonstrate your tastes. It's just that a part of me won't *let* me think you could...' I breathed deeply and forced out the word, '...that you could... *love* me.'

'And you don't think that's more down to you and your self-esteem than me and my preferences?' Max asked gently.

'Probably. But why I think it doesn't matter so much as the fact that I *do*.' I stared up at the curve of the lights. 'Why are we having this conversation, Max?'

'Because I wanted you to see these. They may help.' He pulled a small case out of his pocket. 'They took a bit of hunting down, and Grant had to help me with the recovery of some of the more prejudicially deleted items.'

They were photographs. Some of Max with a girl, some of a girl on her own, laughing at the camera or performing various activities; punting down a river, sitting in front of a picnic basket. The ones with Max had him with his arms wrapped around her, or with the two of them standing facing one another. Some looked posed and very *Country Life*, others more spontaneous. The girls were all different. Two were shorter than Max, one topped him by half a head; two were black, one wore glasses and not one of them was the skinny model-type I'd always imagined him with. They were all very attractive in their own unique ways, but there wasn't a size ten or even twelve amongst them.

'This,' Max flipped the photos, 'is my dating history. Well, most of it, there's a couple of one-nighters when I was at uni and Sophia, who hated having her photo taken, but, yeah, that's pretty much my past, right there.' He looked at my face and added quickly, 'Not all of it, obviously, there was studying and essay writing and an appalling amount of drinking too. But this is the part I thought you'd find most interesting.'

I shuffled through the pictures. Curvy, wonderful women. *Beautiful* women. I felt a little part of myself shift. I *was* Max's type. He wasn't slumming it or doing me a favour or lowering his standards. One of those women, in fact, looked a little bit like me. I held up her picture.

Max took a deep breath. 'That,' he said, and his voice was slightly hoarse, 'was Rebecca. She was the one who didn't want children.' He looked down at the picture, sparking and twinkling in the little lights. 'I loved her,' he said, simply. 'But – well. What we wanted was just too different. She's working for NATO now, apparently.'

I frowned. 'I hope I'm not a do-over.'

He tore his gaze away from the picture and looked at my face. 'Good Lord, no!' He sounded horrified. 'That was years ago, I'm over it now. Well, mostly.' A cheeky grin. 'Apart from the nights I wake in a sweat screaming, "Rebecca, Rebecca, please don't leave me."'

I gave him a stern look and then laughed. There was a bubbling of something in my chest, an uplifting of spirit that was almost joy. 'You are an awful boyfriend,' I said.

'I know, but I try really hard.' He came in close and kissed me. 'You've got to give me points for that.'

What happened next was probably inevitable. After all, we hadn't seen one another for a week, but it was enough to give me fond feelings towards the icehouse for quite a while afterwards. We tested those acoustics to destruction. I felt more able to be abandoned now I'd seen those pictures, more secure that Max really did want *me*, the way I was. I wasn't some stand-in for a thin girl called Arabella, he wasn't making love to me because I was the only woman around to whom he wasn't related. Me. Max wanted me. And, I have to say, he had me, quite definitively, in that icehouse.

Sweaty, despite the chilly air, red-faced and with our clothing dishevelled, we walked back towards the house hand in hand. The sky mimicked the fairy lights we'd just left, an arch overhead of bright pinpricks twinkling and winking at us, and the grass had the slight crispness of an incipient frost. The air was very still.

We'd reached the gravel of the drive when a thought struck me. *Jenna. Those watermarked photographs. Postcards. The strangeness of them.* I dodged into my car and retrieved the bundle of papers I'd deemed 'interesting'.

'Thank goodness.' Max watched me emerge with the package. 'I thought you were going for a reprise on the back seat of your car. I might need a moment longer, I'm not twenty any more.'

'Look.' I pulled loose the two postcards from the top. 'Postcards, from John.'

'Yes.' Max turned them over to catch the light coming from the two long windows beside the front door. Hatherleigh Hall looked like a music box, some windows illuminated and a faint glow from others, as though it were waiting for a giant key to turn so it could play 'Für Elise'.

'But look at the postmark. I noticed it before but I've only just remembered, thanks to Jenna and her bride with the written-on face.' I moved the cards to show him. 'Look.'

He held the squares of card up, and then went closer to the house to throw more light on them. 'The postmarks are fuzzy? Is that what you mean?'

'Neither one is readable. They both look as though they've been obscured, maybe deliberately. You can't tell if these were posted in London or Luton. Or,' I said, meaningfully, 'York.'

'You think,' Max said slowly as though he were piecing things together in his head, 'that Mrs Fortune wrote these and posted them *to herself* to make everyone think John was still alive?'

'Or Mr Fortune.' I took the postcards back from him. 'Or even Alethia. It makes sense. If John was killed in the house and they buried him under the basement floor, then put about the story that he'd "gone to London" with occasional bits of proof...'

'It wouldn't be Alethia.' Max was still speaking slowly. 'She would know and she'd have thrown these away. Well, I say that, given the amount of trash she held on to, she may not have done.'

'My money is still on the father.' I lifted the rest of the bundle from the floor and Max, in a very gentlemanly way, took it from me as we walked towards the house. 'Handy with his fists, didn't you say he'd been? Keen to keep people away, and armed with a shotgun? So he could have killed his son, and the mother is covering up for him. Alethia knew nothing and was told her brother left home, never to be seen again.'

'Yes, and her mother, old Mrs Fortune, told Alethia what she wanted to hear, maybe to let her keep her memories of her father as good ones.' Max looked down at the pile of papers. 'Is there any more corroborating evidence?'

'I'm not sure. This is the stuff that looked most interesting, once I'd whittled out the worst of the junk and the dead spiders. The rest is still taking over my living room back in Pickering.'

Max draped his arm around me. Not in the half-hearted, siblingesque way that Grant had used to, though, this was a drape that pulled me in close against him as we walked. It was a cosy, accepting sort of drape. 'I know I keep saying this,' he gave me a little squeeze, 'but you really are the most amazing person I have ever met.'

Stifling the feelings that kept rising of being far more on the

Clouseau end of the spectrum than the Poirot, I went with him into
Hatherleigh Hall.

* * *

Interview with a retired nurse, who asked not to be named (information available upon contact with the author). Transcribed via
recording.

I was a nurse for many years, and, as such, saw a fair few
things that I couldn't explain, but your letter in the *Yorkshire Post*
asked for anything in or around the old Fortune House up on the
moors, so I thought I'd send you my 'strange tale'.

Old Mrs Fortune was very ill and presumed dying. Her
daughter had been sent for and was making her way from somewhere in the Home Counties, so I had been employed to stay
with Mrs Fortune and help keep her comfortable until her
daughter could arrive and take over the duties. So it was that I
came to be spending nights in the house.

This particular night, Mrs Fortune had had an unsettled day
and looked to be in a good deal of pain. I'd given her her
medication and was waiting for her to fall asleep, when we both
heard a noise downstairs (Mrs Fortune's bedroom being the old
marital bed in a room on the first floor). I said, 'Sounds like rats.'
Mrs Fortune replied that it wasn't rats, they didn't have rats.

Bearing in mind she'd been confined to her bed for nearly a
month, I still suspected vermin of some kind. It was that sort of
noise, that shifty shuffling, if you know what I mean. So I said I'd
go down and look, but Mrs Fortune became very distressed by
the suggestion, and so I stayed up with her until her medication
took effect and she fell asleep.

At this point, the noise became more insistent. I took up the
lantern (there's no electricity up to the house, so we were using

oil lamps) and went downstairs. The noise sounded as though it was coming from the old basement, so I went down to try to determine the source of the sound, as I was concerned that an infestation of rats might mean that my patient needed immediate removal to a more sanitary environment. As I approached the basement stairs, which ran from inside a cupboard in the kitchen, the noise was a definite scuffling, as though something was being dragged along the floor down there, but the second I set foot on the staircase, it all went silent.

I believed that the vermin must have seen the light, and frozen to avoid detection, so I went down a few steps and held the light up, so that the flame illuminated as much of the basement area as possible. The floor area, of approximately twelve feet by twelve, was devoid of any items, and the entire room was empty. There was no sign of any rats or mice, nor of anything which could have caused the dragging, shuffling sound. I went right to the bottom of the stairs at that point and began an investigation of the four corners of the room, to try to ascertain whether or not rodents had either gained entry or formed a nest. As I reached the far side of the room away from the staircase, and bent to hold the lamp close to the wall, the noise started again, behind me. It had the distinct hallmarks of footsteps now, but the footsteps of someone afflicted or dragging some heavy weight; they lingered between each step.

I turned and once more held the lamp up, but there was nothing in that cellar besides me and dust. My flesh had begun to creep now, there was something very purposeful about the sound of those invisible steps, and I made my way at haste back up the staircase to the main house, where I remained the rest of the night in the room with Mrs Fortune.

Her daughter arrived the next day to take over the nursing of her mother. I never mentioned the strange sounds to her, as I believed that I could have been mistaken and the sounds could have been due to floorboards creaking above my head in the farmhouse parlour. That is the only explanation for the noises, but, in my heart, I believe that there was someone walking with me in that basement, someone that I couldn't see.

18

My four-week notice period seemed to last no time at all. In a 'blink and you'd miss it' moment, I'd had my leaving party, opened the cards and presents from my team – only one vibrator, I noted, the fitters were losing their touch – and had packed up everything I wanted to take from my little house.

Grant and Jenna were standing on the doorstep, practically with their faces pressed against the window, waiting for the keys the day I moved out.

'Our first proper home together,' Jenna said. They'd come over on the motorbike – 'the van's coming later' – so she was turning a few heads in her leathers. I could see Mrs Next Door Right already preparing the indignation that a pair of Hell's Angels were moving in to lower the neighbourhood. 'I can't wait.'

Grant had taken her hand. 'I should carry you over the threshold,' he said, and, laughing, did so. I tried not to remember him refusing to even attempt to lift me over the doorstep on our wedding day, despite Mum trying to encourage him. Even now, I still felt little pricks of resentment about the way he was so different with Jenna, but I stifled them. Jenna was lovely and bubbly and kind and she loved him, and her mental health seemed so much better now. Even Max remarked on the fact that she had recovered more since reuniting with Grant than she had during the months of therapy after the split with her abusive boyfriend. Grant was maintaining the 'amnesia' story and the wedding planning was going as well as could be expected, with Jenna's ability to change her mind about the entire colour scheme every half hour. He was good for her. The fact that his redeeming factors hadn't been enough for me shouldn't enter into it. This wasn't my relationship.

For appearances' sake and because I didn't want to seem a pushover, I moved all my stuff into my bedroom at Hatherleigh Hall. The fact that I never slept in it, because I spent every night with Max, was neither here nor there. But it did provide the perfect place for the piles of paper and my less-flattering clothes, plus many of the photographs of Mum and Dad, although I took advantage of Max's offer to put some of them in the Piano Room and displayed their wedding photograph on the piano, along with Max's parents.

Winter arrived. Max had been right, it was cold in the house. I could see my breath in most of the hallways. To try to preserve the fabric of the house, Max had to run heating, but Queen Anne windows didn't keep much heat in, and Elizabethan walls didn't provide as much protection against the weather as they probably had done when they were built. So we spent a lot of time in the study with a radiator, Max writing whilst I sorted, made notes, tried to keep him going with frequent cups of tea and coffee and carried on sifting through the paperwork Alethia had left. Our forays into the main house were usually limited to dashing along corridors in search of the source of mystery noises which Max suspected to be rats in the walls or things falling off other things, usually plaster of walls.

I began to learn that a house like Hatherleigh Hall wasn't just a spread in a lifestyle magazine. It was a whole way of life, even if part of that way was rodent-repelling or attempts to restick eighteenth-century wallcoverings. It was nerve-shredding and expensive, but there was a huge amount of fun to be had too.

Only a skeleton staff came in over winter. I got used to coming across Daisy and her hoover in random rooms, and we hid from Mrs P twice a week when she came in to tidy the flat. She was, according to Max, very prone to telling long stories laden with doom and gloom which prophesied every kind of bad end you could imagine and could, apparently, have provoked a case of depression in Mr Tumble. So we kept out of her way, whilst I quietly speculated as to whether she could be related to Sheila. When Max was at the university, I dealt with various admin tasks, either generated by the house itself or by Max's increasingly frantic attempts to write the Fortune House book whilst planning his psychology book and sorting out lectures. I got used to switching from filling in forms for Public Liability Insurance for the icehouse to searching online for a copy of Harry Price's biography.

'Well.' Max pushed his chair away from the desk. 'That's the main body of the book about done. All I need now is a cracking ending to wrap it all up, and to sort the illustrations out.' *The Haunting of Fortune House* was being published by his university, who were hoping he'd write what they called a 'proper book' next. *The Psychology of Ghost Hunting* was in the 'preparation' stages, apparently, which seemed to mean that Max had written the title down somewhere.

'What sort of cracking ending do you have in mind?' I turned away from the papers I was still sorting through. Alethia had kept some interesting recipes and I'd been extracting them in the hope that we could use a few in the café next year. The more acceptable ones, obviously, I didn't think the visitors to Hatherleigh Hall would be particularly entranced by Tripe and Parsley Stew. I was still searching for the recipe for the famed parkin.

'I've worked in chronological order.' Max swung the chair back on its two rear legs and, somewhere, Sheraton whirled in his grave. 'First stories of ghost sightings or experiences through to present-day explosions and body finding. I thought I'd finish off with what we've got so far on the identification of the body – that it *could* be John, from all the evidence we've got. I'll leave the cause of death as an accident, though, no need to drag the family name through the mud when we have no proof. And now the site is cleared, I thought we could take a run out to get some final photos, give the place the once over.'

'That sounds nice,' I said, looking out of the window at the leaden sky and outlines of trees reduced to dark silhouettes. 'Can we wait until July?'

'I was thinking tomorrow?' He grinned. 'We could take a picnic? Jenna said she and Grant may come over, we could all go up there together. She's still trying to help him recover his memories, you know.'

'If they start to surface, I volunteer to be the one to bash them straight back in again.' I removed another envelope that had had illegible notes scrawled on it in pencil. 'Actually, a picnic on the moors sounds rather good. As long as it doesn't snow and trap us all up there. I've seen those films. We'd end up eating each other, or there'd be a werewolf. Or a serial killer.'

'Alice, has anyone ever told you that you have an overactive imagination?'

'I think you mentioned it, last night.' I wiggled my eyebrows at him.

'Oh yes, so I did.' He waggled right back. The chair legs creaked, and I had a moment of wondering whether you were allowed to fix antiques with a couple of screws and some superglue. Nothing expressed the divide in our upbringing like the casual way Max treated things that I dared not even dust. 'Anyway, Mrs P will do us a hamper and Jen said she'd bake some bits and bring them over.'

I hoped she'd got to grips with my oven. We'd had the occasional midnight phone call from either a panic-stricken Jenna or a laconically unconcerned Grant about the randomness of my little house. The inability to fully shut the bathroom window and the tendency of the electricity to trip out on windy days had prompted them to ask if I'd mind if they called in some professional builders at their own expense. Strangely, I had not minded at all.

'I will wear all my jumpers,' I promised.

'And...' Max stood up now, for which both I and, presumably the chair, were grateful. 'I've been thinking. About the Fortune House. More exactly, about that site up there, on the moor.'

'Mmmm?' I began tidying the papers I'd been sorting through back into their usual uneven lumps.

'I was thinking, of, maybe, rebuilding? But not the house as it was, more a proper traditional moorland cottage. There's a fair bit of land with it. I could turn it into some kind of central location for taking groups of researchers up onto the moors. And then, when it's not in use, we could have it as a weekend place. What do you think?'

'A weekend place? When we've got—' I waved a hand at the Hall, where we could have occupied a different room every day of the week and saved an entire floor for 'the weekend'.

'Well, yes, but this house is work, isn't it? At least, that's how it feels to me. It's like living above the shop. I thought it might be nice to have somewhere else to go. Somewhere a bit less—' he copied me and waved a hand, 'flamboyant.'

'Well, I...'

'And I thought you might like somewhere to be able to get away. And study.'

It felt as though ice had now begun to form down my spine. Part of me wondered if this was shock of some kind, or just the cold draught that tended to creep in under the door as the house cooled. 'Study?'

'You still want to be a veterinary nurse, don't you?'

Now I nearly fell over, as though the draught contained some kind of paralysing agent. I'd mentioned it to him once. Once. And he'd remembered. 'Veterinary nurse?' The words tumbled out of my open mouth.

Max came over and put both hands on my shoulders. 'If you repeat everything I say, this conversation is going to take a lifetime.' He kissed my hair. 'But, since we've actually and hopefully *got* a lifetime, I'll finish my bit and then you can repeat as much as you need to. Yes. I want to build a cottage on the site of the Fortune House, and we can do what we want with it. Rent it as a holiday cottage, crayon all over the outside, blow it up, whatever. Only, no, not the blowing up thing, I don't think the police can stand another detonation up there. Okay, it's your turn now. Oh no, one thing more, I nearly forgot. I picked up some of the information from Askham Bryan college on their Foundation Degree in Veterinary Nursing the other day. It's not that far from here,' he added.

'Max, I...'

'Well, I'm not going to be writing books forever, am I? It just *feels* like it at the moment,' he finished, with a decidedly glum note to his voice. 'You can't always be my attractive assistant, you need to do something for you.'

'Oh.' I had to step back away from him now. This was... actually, I didn't know *what* it was. Too much. It felt like too much. 'Max, I don't know.' I turned away and started tapping the edges of the papers, trying to make some kind of neatness out of chaos. Did I still want to be a veterinary nurse? I mean, yes, on the one hand, I did. On the other – I was no longer the sixteen-year-old ingenue with the world just opening up to her. Maybe I should know my limitations and stick to admin. Admin stayed where you put it. Apart from this pile of paper, which kept trying to demonstrate that gravity was omnipotent.

'You can do anything you want, Alice.' Max sounded very serious now. All the laughter and teasing had gone from his voice. '*Be* anything.'

'Except that I've had thirty-four years of being me and half of that has been spent on spreadsheets, timetables and window fitters. It's a bit late to be an astronaut.'

'You'd had a lot of years working for the window people. You threw all that over to come here.' He was looking at me with a very direct, dark look. Challenging me. I was quite unused to the feeling, normally everyone did what I said. 'I know this place is hardly the space shuttle, but it's still a change. You did it once, you can do it again.' He picked up a massive magazine-like sheaf of paper and added it to my current pile. 'I'll put this here. It's up to you what you do with it.'

'I came here because you needed me. And you promised me an attractive remuneration package.' I carefully kept my eyes away from the brochure.

'Perhaps, but I am sure that there are fluffy animals out there who need you too.' Max walked to the door. 'Plus, and I hate to say this, attractive as my package is, you need to earn your own money.' Then he went out, quietly closing the door and sending all the single sheets of paper from my pile dancing and flirting.

The horrifying heat and redness hadn't been in evidence quite so much in recent days. Not only because it was cold and my body kept all its heat for necessary functions, but also because having Max around a lot of the time meant that my initial crush on him had died down to something more manageable. It's hard to have a crush on someone you've seen fleeing down a corridor in the middle of the night towards the toilet, or peeling off his socks to stare morosely at feet that had been in soggy boots all day. But now the heat came back. It prickled my armpits and the back of my neck, then made its way round to fry my cheeks.

I hadn't thought of needing to bring money in. Me, Alice, who usually thought of everything! I'd been seduced by, well, yes, by Max, but by the whole lifestyle of the big house. Even though I knew he worked hard to keep the fabric of the place going, I'd been happily tootling about being his 'assistant'. Working on ideas for making the house earn its own keep more profitably to be sure, but still. Max loved teaching psychology and it gave him a wonderful excuse to indulge in his ghost-hunting passions, but even so, it hardly brought in enough to keep us in wall plaster and damp proofing.

The door opened again. Max and I looked at one another and then we both said 'sorry' at the same time.

'Why are you sorry?' He was balancing two mugs of coffee, one in each fist and trying to sidle past the spreading paper pile without spillage.

I explained my thinking. 'I never intended to just sit here and take money from the estate,' I said, with my cheeks still pulsing with blood. 'Of course I didn't.'

'And I didn't mean that you had to go out and earn money to support this place.' He put a mug down in front of me, where it formed a small brown puddle on the 'tripe and parsley' recipe, which was probably the best use for it. 'I only realised how it may have come across when I got into the kitchen. I meant that you should have money that isn't dependent on me. Obviously you'll be getting a salary for all the work you're doing on the books, and helping me and everything, but I thought–' Max stared down at where the ink was running into the spilled coffee. 'I thought i might be nice for you to have a chance at doing what you've always wanted.'

'I've always done admin,' I said, slightly weakly.

'But you haven't always *wanted* to do admin, have you? And – and I know that you'd hate to feel dependent on me, well, on the estate, for money. You want your own career. So you feel secure.'

'I've got the rent from my house.' I realised, as I said it, that this was *also* slightly contingent upon Max, with it being his sister renting it, and how hard it may be to re-let if they left.

'What I really thought was it's what you've always wanted to do, be a veterinary nurse.' Max propped himself against the side of the desk. 'Why not train now? Then you'll always have that qualification. Once you've got to the bottom of Alethia's pile, obviously. There's a vet on the estate who will take you on for your training, I'm sure, and running this place—' he jerked his chin at the walls, 'isn't really a full-time job, it ticks over nicely. Maybe, in a few years, we could start thinking about opening more than weekends and for weddings, but that might be something for the next generation...' He stopped talking, swallowed coffee and then coughed most of it back up over his shirt, whilst going purple.

I watched, dispassionately, for a moment until he regained his breath and stopped gasping. 'Or...' he finally managed, 'it can go to the National Trust. I'm not forcing any child of mine to take it on.'

He was thinking of the future. A future with me. And our possible children. It came as something of a shock, even though I'd had no reason to doubt him. Hatherleigh Hall could be my future. That was a big thing. 'Coffee is still coming out of your nose,' I observed.

'I know. I think I must have leaky valves or something. But you don't object, in principle?' He wiped his nose on a piece of rag that he dragged out of his pocket. It looked as though it had previously been used to clean paintbrushes.

'To the idea of making this place profitable? No, I think it's a great idea.' I managed to drink coffee whilst keeping my eye on him. If he was going to backtrack, I wanted a clear and cogent plan for no misunderstandings.

'That, and there being another generation,' said Max. 'Only, I'd really like children. They don't have to inherit all this, and they most *certainly* do not have to go to boarding bloody school. But I thought I'd run the general idea past you, in case you need to do a Rebecca and bow out gracefully.'

I sipped again. Grant's refusal to try for a baby had made me cautious. Whilst I had known that Max wanted children, I wasn't quite as sure of my own position nowadays. But then I looked at him, and wilted crush notwithstanding, and ignoring the streaming eyes and nose, he had the bone structure and leggy elegance of aristocratic genes. He had kindness and concern for others, patience and tolerance, and he hadn't been lying about being sensational in bed either. 'Well,' I said, mouth sideways on my mug. 'We could give it a try, I suppose.'

'I'll get you a ring and everything. We'll do it properly.' He was still trying to mop coffee from his shirt. 'It's sort of expected, you see.'

'Are you proposing to me? Or are we planning some kind of business merger?' I still wasn't quite sure what to feel. Amusement was winning out at the moment.

'I can't – I mean, I'm not really sure how one does this sort of thing. No practice, you see.' Max finally stopped snorting and blowing. 'If you'd like a bit more romance, then I could go and fill the Blue Room with petals and borrow Jen's music again.'

'No, no.' I was laughing now. Properly laughing. It was a laugh that let go of a lot of the past. 'No, this is fine. Practicality is far more my sort of thing, Max. All the romance in the world won't make a dodgy proposition any less odd. This is the best way, for both of us, I think.'

'*Is* it dodgy?' He stuffed the handkerchief back into his pocket and looked at me directly now. His eyes were red and streaming and yet he had never looked more gorgeous.

'No.' I kissed him. 'Absolutely not. And I will look at the veterinary nurse training information, thank you. I just need to sort out the rest of these papers so you've got an end to your book first. One challenge at a time, that's what I used to tell the window boys. Worry about number fifteen after you've got number twelve sorted.'

'Weirdly specific, but I get your meaning.' Max kissed me back. 'By the way, I will propose properly, one day. Flowers, ring, champagne, all that. I just wanted you to have advance warning. So you know that I see this, us, as being something real. Before I embarrassed myself totally, you see.'

'And coughing up coffee whilst trying to ascertain my position on marriage wasn't embarrassing?' I rested my forehead against his and tried not to look at the stains.

'Mortally. But it's you, Alice. I don't have to be something I'm not, with you. You understand. You *see* somehow, what, and I hesitate to say this because it does make my dating history sound far more extensive than it was, what my previous girlfriends didn't. That Hatherleigh Hall isn't just somewhere stylish to live, it's a duty and obligation. It's a bit like...' He trailed off and stared around the room, obviously searching for a suitable metaphor.

'It's like an old faithful pet.' I helped him out. 'That you owe it to, to keep in as good condition as you can, for as long as you can.' Then I gave him a stern look. 'Just don't start comparing it with mating dogs, because I already know about your tendency to fall back several hundred years in your ancestry whenever animals are mentioned.'

I picked up the papers to try to shove another armful back, and an envelope fell out. It was very thin, but of the thick kind of parchment that speaks of Importance and Solicitors. I opened it without really thinking.

'Yes, I think we've rather covered that one.' Max looked down at the envelope. 'What's that?'

'I *think* it's Mrs Fortune's will. A copy of it, anyway.' I unfolded the paper. 'Yes. Look. It's her leaving everything to Alethia. "To my daughter, Alethia Ermintrude Fortune, I leave and bequeath my entire estate." That's all straightforward, anyway.'

Max read over my shoulder. 'No mention of John. Not even a token bequest.'

Now we both glanced up and met one another's eye. 'That's reasonably conclusive,' I said. 'Nothing left in trust in case he came back from London? No money put aside for him?'

'She knew he was dead, didn't she?' Max went over to the window and looked out over the dark acres. The night was so still and cold, I could almost hear the ice forming on the lake. 'It sounds definite.'

'Ghosts.' I went and stood next to him, and he curved his arm around me as though he'd been doing it forever. 'Maybe whatever was left of him haunted that house?' I put my head on Max's shoulder. There was a lovely feeling of permanence coming from him, but it was largely overpowered by the smell of coffee from his shirt.

'What really happened?' Max's eyes were raking the tree-dotted fields. I wondered whether he was still looking for the shade of his mother out there.

'Short of finding a written confession amongst all that lot, I don't suppose we'll ever know.' I bumped my head against him gently, to let him know that I'd noticed his introspection. 'But it wasn't ghosts. You know that really, don't you? Just weird stuff and brain farts and misperceptions. There are no ghosts, Max.'

He sighed and gave me a little squeeze. 'I know. At least, I *think* I know. Jenna talking about our mother was just a small child not being able to separate dream and memory from reality. The dead don't come back, do they, Alice?'

I thought of my mum and dad. Of all the hospital appointments, the treatments which made them feel worse, the scheduling of drugs and doctors, and the pain. 'I think, maybe, they deserve a rest,' I said. 'Not to be wandering about after they've gone. If they know they did a good job while they were alive, then that's it. And I'm sure your mother knew she'd done a good job with you and Jenna – it may have been cut a bit short by the accident, but she'd made you resilient and healthy and able to go on without her.' I put my hand on his cheek. 'We have to let them go,' I whispered.

Max's head slumped forward for a moment. Then he took a deep breath. 'Yes. You're right, of course you are.' He turned round. 'My wonderful, wonderful Alice. Sensible and gorgeous and practical and *mine*.' He paused for a minute, looking into my eyes. 'Sorry. Did that sound a bit possessive and weird?'

His eyes were amazing. Huge and even darker than the night encroaching against the windows, with little tips of reflections from the light. 'Perhaps a little bit.' I stretched myself against him. 'But not necessarily in a bad way.'

19

———

There was a powdery residue of snow up in the bowl on the moors. It had largely melted away from the grassier stretches, but lingered at the roots of the feathery whin bushes and the dormant heather clumps, and filled holes and dips to smooth whiteness. The Fortune House was nothing but a crater, fenced off with incongruous orange plastic wattles and the remains of police tape. Snow had pillowed inside the depression, looking as though someone had dropped a pristine white duvet to soften the edges.

We stared into the hole. A thin skin of frosted ice stared back from the bottom.

'Maybe there was an argument,' Jenna said thoughtfully. She'd got a scarf wound round her head and she and Grant had evidently come in the car because she wasn't wearing leathers. Instead, she'd got on a baggy pair of dungarees that made her look as though she were playing dress-up in her dad's clothes, and a pair of Dr Marten boots. She still looked slender, but her face had filled out of the sunken misery and there were no bags under her eyes. Grant was good for her. 'And it ended up with John being killed.'

'Or he could have died out on the farm,' Max said, snuggling himself against me. 'And for some reason, they didn't want to tell anyone. Maybe some kind of accident and Mr and Mrs Fortune were worried that they could be prosecuted?'

I bumped gently against him. 'No. He died in the house. Whatever happened, it happened in the house,' I said.

Max looked down at me. Chilly fingers of wind were making his hair twist into curls against his cheek. 'You sound very certain,' he said. 'Want to explain?'

'The tooth.' I jiggled a bit. That breeze that was making him look picturesque and more than a little Heathcliff against the barren landscape and the background snow was getting down the back of my neck and chilling my spine. 'The police found the tooth in the house when they thought it was Grant.' I spoke slowly, policing my words so that no hint of 'pretending to be dead' leaked out. 'So whatever happened that knocked that tooth out was violent and happened in the house itself. The body was in the basement, after all, buried under concrete.'

I'd found a receipt, in among the papers. Not completely damning, of course, there were a million reasons why a farming family would need a ton of cement, from building a wall to patching up a cow byre. But in 1965, they had taken delivery of twenty-five sacks of cement mix and a lorry load of sand. Circumstantial, not *absolute* proof, but putting it all together made it look obvious.

Max nodded a sideways nod of acknowledgement, then dug into the pocket of his big black coat. I smiled to myself. I had a fond attachment to that coat. When he'd finished fishing about, he came up with the photograph he'd taken of the Fortune House, before Alethia and the pursuit with the saucepans. He held it up, aligning it to fill the space where the house no longer was.

'There was something in that room,' he said. 'I know I saw *something*. An empty room, possibly John's old bedroom, with *something* at the window. And then there are all those stories.'

Jenna and Grant had moved off and were laying out a picnic under the spindly shelter afforded by the trees. Mrs P had, as promised, packed us up supplies and Jenna smelled of fresh baking. I had high hopes of the provender. I hoped that the wind would let us eat it.

'It's like all ghost stories ever.' I took the picture from him and scrutinised it. 'A mysteriously empty room, something half seen.'

'Well, it got me started on the book, which kind of brought us together in a roundabout way.' Max smiled at me. The wind had another go at his hair. 'And I've come to terms with the not knowing now.'

'To be fair, it was your obsession with the house that got Grant up here to blow himself up, which was what *really* brought us together.' I was still looking at the picture. 'And that shape at the window could be a reflection, you know.'

I thought of Max, lonely and dark, stalking across the moors, obsessed with the idea of ghosts, and then I looked at the Max in front of me. Still dark, hopefully less lonely and with the whole ghost fascination now mutated into a more pragmatic view of 'most of it is explicable, but there will always be things we don't understand'.

'I know.' He took the photograph back from me. 'I just wanted it to be a ghost. At least, I thought I did, but now it doesn't matter. Like you said, I know Mum loved me. I didn't need her to come back and tell me so.'

We both looked over to where Jenna was carefully fetching plates from a wicker hamper and directing Grant's attempts to spread a rug over the tree roots. The breeze was flipping the blanket back to hinder him, and they were both laughing.

'Life is strange enough,' I said. 'Who would ever have thought of those two being together? Or us, come to that, a window fitters' admin girl and a posh git. And if life can be that weird, we don't really need ghosts to make it any weirder, do we?'

'Oh, I don't know.' Max put his arms around me. 'I actually like a bit of weird, here and there.'

* * *

My new life was surprisingly busy, and I found that I didn't miss window fitting at all. As summer came in, carried on warm breezes that smelled of heather, we had to face all the new challenges of reopening Hatherleigh Hall to the public, and I had to cope with learning to make a variety of scones for the tea shop. Not quite the same as booking sets of double-glazed windows and making sure they arrived at the right address, but involving nearly as much administration. I also had to make sure that Max finished his book, which wasn't easy. With the coming of the nice weather, he showed a disturbing preference for painting fences and repairing walls which was, he said, a lot easier than making words work.

But he wrote, and rewrote, and I organised and baked. And in the short, hot, summer nights I truly came to believe that he loved me utterly.

Eventually, we reached the day when Max's book was due to be published and we were holding the launch party up at the site of the Fortune House. Minibuses had been laid on for attendees, so the place was swarming with Max's students, both current and past, and friends and family. Ghost-hunting groups had come out in force – 'Free booze,' Max had said – and the *Fortean Times* had got up a party. Max had written a long and learned article for them about the history of the site and they'd all come to look.

Everyone was chatting happily, some were staring moodily out over the heather, scarified by the effects of the sunlight. It was almost impossible to imagine this place as haunted. Even the birch trees had gained leaves and now looked properly arboreal instead of resembling dark dead arms reaching for the sky. The atmosphere was completely different to that of the oppressive isolation that had hung over it before. The filling in of the big hole had helped too, of course; the place was one smooth ribbon of sward now, surrounded by perky tufts of flowering heather and sheltering hedges of gorse. Everything was flowering like crazy in tasteful shades of purple and yellow and even the birdsong was limiting itself to some high lark song from above.

It could not have looked less ghostly if it had had a McDonald's in the middle of it.

Max had refused to hold the launch party at Hatherleigh Hall. 'I want to keep the book separate to where we live,' he said, when we'd been drawing up lists of potential venues. 'I'm not having a bunch of despondent critics wandering around my home. If they want to do that, they can come at a weekend and pay admission fees like everyone else.' He'd also turned down famous 'haunted' sites around York on the grounds that this book was less about ghosts and more about his own personal experience, and, as that was limited to seeing 'something' in an empty window, it had seemed somewhat egregious to hold a party in a location mostly known for its ghosts.

'This is the "taster" book for the follow up,' Max was explaining over glasses of free wine to the book reviewer from the local paper. 'The Haunting of Fortune House is about the "what" of ghosts, where I explore the history of the house and its ghost sightings. My next book will be more about the "why" of ghosts; *why* we think we see what we do.'

'Plus this book is full of scary local ghost stories,' Jenna added, hovering by Max's elbow and looking incredibly pretty in a floaty white frock. She was carrying a copy of The Haunting of Fortune House and looked like a girl in a TV ad. 'So it's got that too.'

I was staying under the trees. Max had introduced me as his partner and assistant on the book when he'd made his introductory speech, which made me feel a bit of a fraud. All I'd really done was try to beat Alethia's papers into order to give him the proof he'd needed to round the book off with the supposition of John's death and a reason for the haunting. There was nothing of the Fortune family remaining to be harmed by this rationalisation of the stories or the atmosphere that had been said to hang over the house. I'd dug into records and double checked, because we hadn't wanted a second cousin to burst out of the woodwork declaring that we had besmirched the Fortune name and demanding a cut of the profit in recompense. Although, at the thought of the word 'profit', Max had laughed for a very long time and in rather a sardonic way.

Now, with the shadows of the trees lengthening towards dusk, the tone of the place began to edge towards 'slightly spooky'. The cluster of guests gathered closer together in an atavistic, safety in numbers way, apart from little knots of students who were using the opportunity to improve their 'lone windswept poetic' look. From the amount of coupling-up that was going on, it was proving quite successful too.

Max came over to me, holding out a glass of something fizzy. 'Are you all right?' he asked. 'You've been a bit quiet the last couple of days.'

I gave him a stern look. 'Max, I've been organising this party, sorting out the architect's drawings for the cottage, helping Jen with her wedding invitation list and trying to track down seemingly the only person in the entire known universe who can sign off on the permissions for the icehouse. Believe me, I've not been quiet, it's just that, by the time you've got back from lecturing and we've managed a moment together, I've run out of words.'

'Sorry. Yes, of course. I didn't mean to sound as though I were overlooking how busy you've been. You've been working absolute wonders.' He came in close and kissed my neck. 'You're a wonder in all forms, my Alice.'

We drank our champagne in a companionable silence. Over at the far side of the site, Grant was chatting happily to a couple of Jenna's biker friends, invited to bump up the numbers just in case. Jen was hostessing admirably, tidying the display of books which we'd cunningly arranged next to the booze. 'The danger of spillage is outweighed by the fact that it takes a really miserly person to take free wine and not buy a book,' she pointed out.

'You're happy with the book?' I asked Max eventually, when the bubbles had carried sufficient alcohol into my system. 'Even the end?'

The dusk tangled in his hair and made his eyes look deep and mysterious. I still couldn't really believe that this gorgeous man was planning to marry me, and it was times like this, when alcohol came into the picture, that I nearly chickened out and ran back to a life of knitting patterns and cats.

He sighed and casually looped his arm around me. 'Pretty happy,' he said. 'I mean, no author is ever completely happy with their book. There's always *something* that you want to change, but only once the entire thing is in print, with a cover, and on sale somewhere.' He took another mouthful. 'Funny, that. You think it's perfect until the day it comes out and then you realise all the mistakes you made.'

'I think that's called being human.' I stared out at where Grant and Jenna had drifted together. She was explaining something to him, probably wedding-orientated. There were only two months to go before their nuptials, and most of her conversations were centred around whether the icehouse floor would be in on time. I hadn't done my stress levels any good. 'But everyone seems to think the ending is good.'

'The supposition that it's John Fortune haunting the house and his body that was hidden under the floor? Yes, they do.' Max looked at me thoughtfully. 'Why?'

'Oh, no reason.' I leaned into him. 'Whoever died here, I shall forever be grateful to them for bringing us together.'

'And that's an epitaph that anyone could be proud of.' He gave me a quick squeeze. 'Are you sure you're all right?'

'Positive,' I said firmly.

'Then I'm going to go over and try to persuade a few more sales out of the ghost-hunting bunch. Might as well make use of the fact that they're all getting legless.' With a cheerful grin, Max headed off over the springy turf towards the drinks table.

I gave a sigh of relief. He was happy with the book and had no qualms about having to end it with a whole raft of assumptions and hypotheses. The absence of anyone to cross-match DNA with meant that the bones from the cellar had been sampled by the police and then buried. We'd laid on a small funeral in the Hatherleigh Hall estate chapel, and interred the skeleton in the family burial plot, with a small stone denoting where it had been found and the belief that it was John Fortune. 'It's all we can do,' Max had said. It had given him a good rounding off and summing up for his final chapter, making sure that the book finished with the hint of doubt that would keep the reader hooked, yet enough of a conclusion to be satisfying. He had redrafted and rewritten that ending so often that I'd been able to recite most of the last five thousand words of the book by heart, having had it read to me most evenings. If he'd had to rewrite it once more, I feared that I might have been tempted to beat Max over the head with the manuscript until he stopped.

Which was why I hadn't said anything when, just as the final, absolutely totally finished, no-more-editing-allowed copy had gone to the printers, I'd found a letter.

It had been folded and refolded, scrunched up into the corner of the pile of papers. A tiny hump under a selection of Yorkshire Show catalogues had drawn me to actually flip through, when I'd been going to carry the entire armful down to the paper recycling bin, and I'd found it and smoothed it out.

It was dated October 1966, and written in a scrawled and childish hand.

Mam

    I wants to let you know, I is safe and happy now. I is living in London where I can be who I wants to with other people like me. Don't tell Da, he will only be angry and take it out on you and Alley. Don't tell Alley neither that you has heard from me because I won't be writing again. I has changed my name so it's no good looking for me. I don't want no more to do with the family. After what Da said when he found me and Bernard was still meeting, I knows he wont change. I loves you, Mam, and Alley, but I has got to live my own life the way I wants.

    Bernard said he'd come to me when he could, but hes not come yet. If you sees him tell him Im still waiting for him in London and I miss him.

    I is sorry if I upsets you by this, but this is goodbye.

    Your loving son

    John

I'd tell Max. One day, I'd tell him.

MORE FROM JANE LOVERING

We hope you enjoyed reading *The Forgotten House on the Moor*. If you did, please leave a review.

If you'd like to gift a copy, this book is also available as an ebook, digital audio download and audiobook CD.

Sign up to Jane Lovering's mailing list for news, competitions and updates on future books.

https://bit.ly/JaneLoveringNewsletter

Explore more funny and warm-hearted reads from Jane Lovering.

ABOUT THE AUTHOR

Jane Lovering is the bestselling and award-winning romantic comedy writer who won the RNA Novel of the Year Award in 2012 with *Please Don't Stop the Music*. She lives in Yorkshire and has a cat and a bonkers terrier, as well as five children who have now left home.

Visit Jane's website: www.janelovering.co.uk

Follow Jane on social media:

facebook.com/Jane-Lovering-Author-106404969412833

twitter.com/janelovering

bookbub.com/authors/jane-lovering

Printed in Great Britain
by Amazon

20823690R00142